ALL INCLUSIVE

Farzana Doctor

DUNDURN
TORONTO

Editor: Shannon Whibbs
Design: Laura Boyle
Cover Design: Laura Boyle
Image credits: Ocean Photography /veer.com
Printer: Webcom

Library and Archives Canada Cataloguing in Publication

Doctor, Farzana, author
       All inclusive / Farzana Doctor.
Issued in print and electronic formats.
ISBN 978-1-4597-3181-3 (pbk.).--ISBN 978-1-4597-3182-0 (pdf).-- ISBN 978-1-4597-3183-7 (epub)

I. Title.

PS8607.O35A65 2015   C813'.6   C2015-900897-2
                                             C2015-900898-0

1   2   3   4   5   19   18   17   16   15

 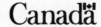 

We acknowledge the support of the **Canada Council for the Arts** and the **Ontario Arts Council** for our publishing program. We also acknowledge the financial support of the **Government of Canada** through the **Canada Book Fund** and **Livres Canada Books**, and the **Government of Ontario** through the **Ontario Book Publishing Tax Credit** and the **Ontario Media Development Corporation**.

Care has been taken to trace the ownership of copyright material used in this book. The author and the publisher welcome any information enabling them to rectify any references or credits in subsequent editions.

— *J. Kirk Howard, President*

The publisher is not responsible for websites or their content unless they are owned by the publisher.

Printed and bound in Canada.

VISIT US AT

Dundurn.com | @dundurnpress | Facebook.com/dundurnpress | Pinterest.com/dundurnpress

Dundurn
3 Church Street, Suite 500
Toronto, Ontario, Canada
M5E 1M2

For the ancestors who continue to guide me
long after they've left this world

Ameera

March 27, 2015, Huatulco, Mexico

Δ

A DC8 droned above.

"Here they come," I announced. Friday was our departure-arrival day. One sunburnt and grouchy group left for their northern homes, and another cohort, ecstatic and pale, touched down and took their place.

Roberto grabbed a plastic file box and gestured for me to sit beside him. I lowered myself onto the makeshift seat and wiped away a slick of perspiration from the creases behind my knees.

"Ameera, you hear about that tour rep getting fired over at Waves?" Roberto stroked his thin moustache.

"Nancy? Yeah, I'm still in shock." I hadn't known her well, but I'd gone clubbing with her and the other tour reps from our sister resorts a few times. She'd seemed all right to me.

The airplane circled closer, and, in unison, we clapped our hands over our ears and tilted our chins to the sky. After it had rolled across the tarmac and quieted its engines, we resumed our gossip.

"What I don't get is why someone in their late twenties would want to have sex with a fifteen-year-old." Roberto shook his head, as though trying to dislodge the idea.

"But didn't the kid lie about his age? He told her he was eighteen, right?" While I'd never in a million years sleep with a teenager, I could imagine how booze and loneliness could have led Nancy to her mistake.

"Who knows. There was no investigation." Roberto slouched, his lanky frame folding into itself.

"True. It's unfair." It *was* strange that there hadn't been an investigation. I couldn't imagine our cheerful manager, Anita, firing anyone.

"At least we're gonna get a local boss soon." Roberto was referring to our company's recent announcement that it would shift from an Ottawa-based management model to a Huatulco-based one. I was surprised he was raising the subject; we'd all been skirting it.

"It'll be strange though — one of us promoted over the others?" Not just strange. Awkward.

"Well, I think it should be Oscar. He's been working in the industry since he was a teenager."

"Maybe." Truthfully, I'd been fantasizing about the promotion since the memo's arrival. It would make staying in Huatulco for another three years worthwhile. So what if Oscar was way older than the rest of us? I had the best sales record.

I looked at our three co-workers: Manuela, Blythe, and Oscar, who stood listlessly in the glass-fronted airport terminal building. Did they all want the job as much as I did?

Luggage began to circle on the conveyer belt, nudging them out of their collective stupor. They sauntered our way.

"Still no tourists." Manuela fished an elastic from her pocket and gathered her long black hair into a messy ponytail.

"The customs guys take too long in there," Oscar said.

"It's getting bloody late," Blythe complained.

I checked my watch. We still had to welcome the incoming tourists, pack them onto Oceana's buses, and offer a perfunctory tour of the stretch of highway between the airport and hotel. When we arrived at Atlantis, our home resort, the vacationers would hold things up at the front desk, arguing for better rooms with king-size beds and oceanfront views. The whole tedious process would take about two and a half hours, provided that there weren't any lost suitcases, passengers, or other mishaps.

Manuela's giggling fit interrupted my thoughts. Roberto, a head taller, grinned down at the blush spreading across her face and neck. Oscar, too, looked amused, his mouth tight, his chin jutting out. Even though I'd missed their joke, I smiled along with them. I liked seeing my three Mexican coworkers like this, relaxed and natural, so different from their formal work demeanours.

Blythe prodded Manuela for a translation; neither she nor I were fluent enough in Spanish to understand jokes delivered in double-quick time.

"They're talking about that lady and her husband who left today. With the big muscles?" Manuela explained.

"Ameera, you know them. They spent a lot of time talking to you at the tour desk." Roberto flexed his biceps and sucked in his gut. The bodybuilders from Buffalo, Marina and Mike. I tensed, wondering what he'd seen.

"Oh, yeah?" I asked, trying to feign indifference. Roberto winked at me. Why do people wink? It's such a stupid gesture.

"A girl shouldn't get that big. Not natural. Women should have some fat on them," Oscar opined. Manuela adjusted her skirt, and stood a little taller in her black pumps. Blythe rolled her eyes.

I crossed my arms over my chest and squeezed my soft biceps, remembering how flabby I was in contrast to the bodybuilders' hard bodies. The previous night, when I'd straddled Marina, pinning her down on the bed, I'd felt foolish, like I couldn't convincingly carry off the move. But she'd played along, moaning and groaning while she pretended to struggle beneath my grip. I'd pushed my tongue into her mouth and my breasts against her flat chest. Meanwhile, Mike watched from the sofa, naked, except for a ridiculous lime-green sombrero upon his head.

"Bodybuilding is a very big trend these days," Blythe said authoritatively, tucking a stray lock of blond hair behind her ear. She had a habit of offering us insights about our Canadian and American tourists, even though she hailed from a small town in England.

"*Fea*. Ugly. There is your Word of the Week." Oscar peered over the top of his bifocals at me.

The others laughed — we'd long ago turned my weekly vocabulary-building exercise into a joke — but I was in no mood for it. I scanned the runway. The plane that had arrived earlier, belching a couple hundred men, women, and children onto the tarmac, was now the site of the departing group's mass exodus. I squinted to locate Marina's red coif and Mike's bright sombrero in the queue. There they were, at the front. I watched them climb the steps and disappear inside the dark of the airplane. When I turned back to my colleagues, Roberto was watching me with a bemused expression.

"Yes. *Fea*," Oscar repeated. He rubbed concentric circles into his back. And then, changing the subject as was his tendency, he said, "We need chairs out here."

"Chairs for us? Never gonna happen," Blythe sing-songed at him.

"We'll see," Oscar blurted. He raised the subject on a weekly basis even though management had told us chairs were not permitted because of some arbitrary airport regulation. "I will bring my own then. Yes, that is what I will do."

"Finally." I pointed to the tourists who were now trickling through the baggage area.

The five of us stepped into formation, and a middle-aged man approached our kiosk, his eyes skipping across our reception line of artificial smiles. He focused on Blythe.

"Welcome to Huatulco," she said blandly, reaching for their documents.

"You're on Ameera's bus. Bus Number Three, over that way folks," Oscar said with forced cheer.

A group of four young men wearing khakis and T-shirts bearing my alma mater's logo asked about welcome drinks and

Manuela promised them that they'd be sitting at an overflowing bar in an hour. I was about to ask them about campus life, but a beverage vendor yelled, "*Cerveza fría!* Cold beer here!" and the men followed his voice, like lemmings over a cliff.

A young couple with three children was among the last to approach the kiosk. The mother drooped under the weight of a sleepy toddler, while a young boy and a slightly older girl clung to her thighs. The father dragged a squeaky cart with three suitcases and four overstuffed — and threatening to topple — backpacks in various Disney motifs. Manuela directed the family to my bus, when suddenly their eldest girl ran off toward the tarmac, yelling, "I want to go home!" I dropped my clipboard and gave chase. I scooped her into my arms, and the girl sputtered a surprised laugh, her cheeks reddening. I giggled along with her as I ushered her dazed-looking parents onto my bus.

Before climbing aboard, I gazed at the afternoon sky to watch the outbound flight of vacationers, including the bodybuilders, fly away home.

Azeez

June 21, 1985, Hamilton, Ontario, Canada

∞

I'd been watching her for a full ten minutes. She sat at the table next to mine, reading a textbook entitled *Understanding World Religions*. It was the first day of summer and my second last in Canada.

She absent-mindedly played with her long auburn hair, her fingers moving like a magician's, conjuring it into a single braid. She didn't tie off the end, and her hair eventually resisted the arrangement and pulled itself free.

I nibbled my honey cruller, and waited for her to notice me. For another ten minutes, I scripted my words. I was a chatty fellow back then, but it took immense bravery to speak to a woman I didn't know. I chided myself: what did it matter if I sounded like a fool?

"That looks like interesting reading."

She glanced up, and her cheeks blushed crimson. I loved when white girls did that. It just isn't the same with brown girls; their pigment allows them to mute their embarrassment. The girl smiled and nodded and returned to her textbook, her lavender highlighter squeaking across the page. But I could tell she was no longer concentrating on the material.

My mother once told me that my best feature was my straight white teeth. So when the girl gazed in my direction again, I flashed a wide grin. I ran my fingers through my coarse black hair and patted it down, then feared that I might have salted my shoulders with dandruff.

"It's not bad. Dry, but okay." Her tone was friendly. She looked at me with large, round eyes. What colour were they? Hazel? Light brown? I sat up to stretch my five-foot-seven frame a little taller. I surmised we were about the same height.

"Have you reached the chapter on Islam yet? I'd be happy to explain anything you don't grasp. I'm Muslim, you know." Not exactly a worthy pickup line, but I was no Casanova.

"I'm reading it now, actually." She turned the book toward me and indeed, there was a photo of a gold-domed mosque on the page.

"I'm not a very strict Muslim, but there are many things about Islam that I appreciate." I rambled on about it being a religion of peace and equality. I spoke with uncharacteristic enthusiasm; I hadn't prayed or fasted since I'd come to Canada just over five years earlier to begin my PhD. The photo of the mosque made me think that I should visit the masjid when I went home. It would please my parents.

"I imagine all the world's religions share that. At their core, they're good. It's people who cause all the problems." The girl looked across the empty parking lot then, and I wondered what had suddenly made her pensive. I took the opportunity to study her freckles. They dotted their way down her neck to her chest. She wore an orange blouse that cut low across her large breasts. She was pleasantly plump around her midsection.

"True," I took another bite of my donut and its waxy coating flaked across my lap.

"I'm Nora." She reached out a hand and her scent of sandalwood wafted over. Her palm was cool, her grip firm.

"How is that spelled?" I can be idiotic when nervous. She spelled it slowly and then asked me my name.

"Spell it," she joked. With false bravado, I grabbed a pen from her table and wrote *A-Z-E-E-Z* on a paper napkin.

"I like names with double *e*'s. And look, two zeds." She studied my block lettering.

"So do my parents. They gave my brother and sister double *e* names, too." I wrote their names under my own and underlined the vowels. A well of sadness came over me then; I missed my siblings. I should have been excited for our reunion in two days. But perhaps a part of me knew something different.

I turned the conversation to her, asking her dozens of questions, which she seemed to like. I learned that she was an only child, had grown up in Hamilton, and had almost completed her B.A. She'd applied to do her Masters in Anthropology. Perhaps one day she'd do a PhD. She was an ambivalent Catholic (she pointed to chapter three of her textbook dismissively).

Eventually, I took a deep breath and asked if she had a boyfriend and she blushed again and shook her head.

I bought her a double-double and I had another tea and cruller. When she invited me to her apartment to listen to her cassette-tape collection, I gladly accepted.

Ameera

Δ

After my shift, I returned to my room, but Blythe and her boyfriend Rhion were arguing again, their voices ringing across our shared wall.

"I was daft to ever trust you, you bastard!"

Rhion murmured something back.

"How could you do this to me?"

Murmur, murmur, murmur.

Δ

I decamped to the staff cafeteria, and sat in the back corner where there was a Wi-Fi signal. I checked my e-mail on my phone, most of it junk. The last message to load was from Anita, my manager. The subject line read "Online Complaint." Curious, I clicked it open.

> Dear Ameera,
>   I'm writing to notify you that we received an anonymous complaint through our online comment form today. Although a record of it will be filed in your employee record, we will not follow up unless there are repeated complaints of a similar nature (it's nearly impossible to investigate when there is no contact information left by the complainant).

It said, *"Ameera is not professional. She's sexually inappropriate with Atlantis customers. She is
a bad example."*

I trust that you have been professional in your
conduct, but if there is anything you'd like to notify
me about that may have caused a complaint like
this, it would be best if you reported it.

Best,
Anita

My pulse quickened and I flushed shame. Gavin, my ex-
boyfriend, came to mind, an unwelcome intrusion. I pushed him
away, and refocused on Anita's message. I took a deep breath, hit
Reply and quickly composed:

Dear Anita,

Thank you very much for the heads-up about the
anonymous complaint. I can't imagine who would
write such a thing about me. There have been a
few tourists who have asked me on dates, and I've
declined (always politely). I wonder if this could be a
reaction to a rejection, or perhaps a prank of some
kind? Please do let me know if the issue escalates,
and be assured that I make every attempt to be
courteous and professional with our guests.

It must be freezing in Ottawa these days! I hope
you're weathering it well.

Best,
Ameera

I took another deep breath, reread my reply twice for typos,
and considered adding a happy face to the end of the last sentence. I decided against it and pressed Send.

My mind ticked through the meagre parade of tourists with whom I'd recently had sex. They were all nice enough folks. Who'd make a complaint like this? It didn't make any sense.

I closed my eyes and once again Gavin swaggered forward. This time I didn't resist him. His toothy smile flashed across my eyelids and then there was the heat and press of his lips on mine. His hands were warm and insistent. I drew my thighs together.

It was always unexpected, this wanton arousal. I could be walking along the street, and see a guy wearing a shirt that reminded me of Gavin. Or I could hear a song we'd listened to together. And then I'd be aching for him, the instinct Pavlovian. A stupid animal-like response.

We'd dated in six-month increments. When we were together we'd swear we were right for one another. We'd leave whomever we were dating and have an intense affair. Then we'd break up, parting with almost as much certainty as when we'd reunited. During our breaks we'd date other people, avoid texting, and remove one another from our Facebook news feeds. But soon enough we'd end up bumping into each other at Jackson Square Mall or out at a concert or gallery opening. And then, as though in some kind of evil carnival hypnotist's trance, we'd fall into one another's arms, dopey and happy and forgetting that we'd end up miserable.

A few months in we'd remember (or finally admit, again) that we weren't compatible. He was fairly sure he wanted marriage and kids and I was fairly sure I didn't. A deal-breaker for us both. My friends joked at the reversal of gender roles, called me a commitment-phobe. But that wasn't it. I *was* a romantic. I liked relationships, loyalty, commitment. I just didn't want to do it his way. I'd never pined for weddings or baby showers like most of my friends. I guess I hoped he'd change and he imagined that I would, too. Number one on the list of things not to do in a relationship.

Two months before I left Canada for Huatulco, we were broken up, the fourth time in four years. A mutual friend was having a birthday party at the Slainte bar. I knew he'd be there, too, but I thought I was over him. I wanted to be over him. I'd heard he was seeing someone else and was happy. They were engaged. I thought it would be safe.

I was the composed ex-girlfriend. I greeted Tamara, his fiancée, with an enthusiastic hello and graciously exclaimed over her sparkly cliché of an engagement ring. Gavin and I hugged hello, my right hip tingling where his hand had brushed over my jeans. We retreated to our separate corners. Later, we gazed at one another across the pool table and before I knew it, we were in the back alley, my tongue in his mouth, his hands up my blouse, me unzipping his pants. He came fast, with a howl and a laugh and a look of wonder. Pleasure was like that for Gavin, an unexpected, gleeful novelty. Without missing a beat, he slid his hand down my jeans, past the elastic of my underwear, and inside me. Every inch of me vibrated with his touch.

The back door slammed and Tamara and two of our friends wandered out for a cigarette. He pulled away from me, and one of my breasts flopped out of my bra. I stuffed it back in and his stickiness, still on my fingers, smeared across my blouse. He ran inside, following his girl, while my friends sighed and shook their heads. "Oh come on, Ameera. They're engaged," Robyn said with a sigh. She said *engaged* like it was something sacred.

"They're happy together. And it never works out between the two of you," Jennifer counselled.

I got the feeling that my friends blamed me for what happened, even though Gavin was equally responsible; they didn't invite me to two subsequent parties, but did include him. I heard that he and Tamara repaired things, and two months later, I left for Mexico, hoping for a fresh start. I'd meet someone new, or focus on my career for a change. Or something. I hadn't been home since. I wasn't ready to face everyone, especially Gavin.

Δ

I reread Anita's words, looking for meaning between their straight lines. She was a fan of emoticons and her writing style was typically informal, but this message was concise and cold. Perhaps Nancy's recent firing had got everyone at head office riled up. But Anita liked me, I knew that. I sat up tall, rolled the kinks out of my neck, and reassured myself that everything would be fine.

Azeez

∞

Nora's place was a small room just around the corner from the coffee shop. Like my own, a few blocks away, it had space for a desk, a dresser, and a single bed. She fiddled with her boom box, popped in a Duran Duran cassette, and then flopped onto the bed. She beckoned me over from where I stood awkwardly by the door. I sat gingerly beside her and she took my hand. I wasn't surprised by the gesture; she'd slipped her arm through mine on the walk over.

She leaned in close and I could tell she wanted me to kiss her. How unshrinking and unafraid Canadian girls were! I pushed my face into hers, and didn't breathe for a long time. I wrapped her in my arms and she let me hold her tightly.

We talked and kissed for hours. My fingers groped her soft waist, the downy peach-fuzz on her arms. When I gazed into her eyes I sensed a rare and special connection.

And then suddenly we were tearing away our clothes.

In my fantasies, it would have happened in cinematic slow motion. Unhurried, we'd have progressed to that point over several romantic dates. And when the disrobing finally happened it would be an alluring striptease. Perhaps in reality things always move more quickly.

∞

I left soon after the sex, lying to her about needing to get work done. I never did tell her that I would be on an airplane the following afternoon, but rather, I remained vague about my departure, speaking about the future as though it were more expansive than it was. Perhaps I didn't want to disappoint her.

I promised to call the next morning. Maybe we'd go for an early lunch. She gave me her number and, foolishly, I forgot to offer mine.

Ameera

Δ

After replying to Anita's e-mail, I headed to the bar. Enrique's long arms were all fluid motion as he served three customers at once. He glanced up, mid-pour, and puckered his lips into an air kiss. I held my breath until he released me from his gaze.

He'd been a big flirt from the beginning. When we first met, he complimented me on a sundress I was wearing, and since then, when I dressed in civilian clothes, I imagined his lustful eyes leering back at me through the mirror. *That colour is perfect for you against your brown skin, Ameera; you should show off your back more — have you been exercising?*

I hummed along with Katy Perry's "Firework," which blasted from the bar's sound system. Enrique tended to the next person in his line, a giggling brunette in her twenties, who was momentarily caught in a ray of his sunshine. I swivelled my stool so I didn't have to look at her.

I recognized a pair of men from my bus standing next to me. The two near-strangers were exchanging drunken holiday tales while they slurped cans of Tecate.

"Back in the DR, I stayed at a mega resort like this one. It was so big, me and my buddies stole one of them golf carts? But then we ended up smashing it into the kiddie playground. Yeah," he said, nodding, acknowledging his new friend's look of admiration, "I had a blast."

"I was jailed in Cuba!" the other man pronounced. He told a disjointed, barely believable story about driving without a licence and successfully bribing a police officer with Chiclets and a ten-dollar bill. "Ten dollars *Canadian*!" he boasted.

Playground Destroyer wobbled on his sandaled feet. His wife brought him a grilled-cheese-and-ham sandwich. He grabbed her left buttock, picked up a triangle, and shouted, "Ham and cheese! I read about these sandwiches on TripGuide! Ham and cheese! Now this is the money shot! The money shot!"

I guffawed loudly, but they didn't notice.

"Not so loud, hon," the wife shushed, tucking herself into his embrace.

Just then Enrique made it to my end of the bar. I passed him my travel mug, and he filled it from a jug from under the counter.

"It's my new drink. The Atlantis Mantis. Try it. I want your opinion." I was about to protest that I'd wanted a Cuba Libre, but the warmth of his hand on my shoulder pacified me.

"What's in it?" I peered into the dark liquid.

"Vodka, rum, mint leaves, cranberry juice, and ginger ale. Be careful. It's sweet but *fuerte*."

"Ham and cheese! The money shot!" The two men cheered, lifting their drinks above their heads. Enrique's eyes darted to them and then back to me, his eyebrows raised in weary superiority. I pursed my lips, nodded, and said goodbye just before he disappeared across the bar.

"Hey look! Tim Hortons!" Jailed-in-Cuba Guy regaled, referring to the logo on my travel mug.

"Yup," I replied.

"Hey, you're not from Canada, are you?" Playground Destroyer asked.

"Uh-huh. From Ontario. Hamilton. The Tim Hortons capital of the world." I took a swig of Enrique's sweet drink and swayed to "Single Ladies," mentally morphing into one of Beyonce's backup dancers.

"Cool. I'd never've guessed. You look Mexican," Jailed-in-Cuba Guy said.

"Yeah, I get that a lot."

"So what are you?" Playground Destroyer asked.

What am I? I inhaled and remembered that although off-shift, I was still an Oceana employee. "Half South Asian. Half white. Where are you folks from?"

"Winnipeg," The wife answered, raising her beer in a toast no one joined in on, "the friendliest city in Canada."

Δ

Back in my room, I flipped through the *Chatelaine* and *O* magazines that my mother had sent earlier that week. I wouldn't have bought them myself — I preferred *The New Yorker* or *Toronto Life* — but English-language magazines were scarce in Huatulco and I appreciated her hand-me-downs. Curiously, the envelope contained both February and March issues. She usually sent them one at a time, mid-month, and I'd missed her package the previous month.

Chatelaine featured a jumble of Valentine's Day crap. There was advice: "10 Ways to Spice Up Your Sex Life," "Drive Him Wild in Bed," and "5 Memorable Valentine's Day Dates." And of course there were quizzes: "What's your Romance IQ?"

As I turned the pages, I paid close attention to where Mom may have lingered, mulling over which articles might have captured her attention. I noticed the mysteries of a partially ripped page, a recipe or coupon clipped. I liked to study the pop psychology quizzes she completed, always in pencil, and later erased. I'd squint at the faint lines and indentations that remained, analyzing her financial, relationship, or communication-style scores.

I skimmed her faded answers to "What's Your Romance IQ?" Her score was thirty-two, a Timid Romantic. Not a shock; she hadn't gone beyond a third date in years.

I completed the survey myself, pushing hard against the somnolence of the drink. I scored fifty-five, which made me a Ready for Anything Romantic.

Perhaps it was the Atlantis Mantis, but the online complainant's judgment echoed: *Sexually inappropriate.*

I put down the magazine. Yes, I might have skated the line of appropriate. Sometimes I slept with Oceana tourists, which was technically not against the rules, but certainly would be frowned upon if word got to Anita. But I'd been discreet, and had learned to limit liaisons with guests to Thursdays, the night before their departures, in case anyone became too attached or uncomfortable. I avoided single male tourists, who had the tendency toward locker-room type bragging after the fact. Couples, on the other hand, were more reliable, their discretion guided by a respect for privacy or the taboo of their desires.

I knew my interests weren't exactly the norm, but come on, they weren't *sexually inappropriate.* I mean, there are plenty of weirder proclivities than an interest in threesomes. Still, I wondered who might have witnessed my dates with couples over the previous two and a half years. I'd have to try to be more careful.

I gulped back the rest of the Atlantis Mantis and switched off the light. A boozy heaviness took me over.

Azeez

∞

The evening sky was turning pink as I walked home from Nora's. I found my two roommates drinking on our porch.

"Azeez, you're moving out soon, eh?" Max flipped his blond dreadlocks off his face and a cloud of patchouli wafted my way.

"Yes. Tomorrow afternoon." While I had mixed feelings about ending my sojourn in Canada, I was thoroughly ready to leave Max and Jonathan. Our house was a filthy, rundown mess. Over the five years I'd resided there, the place had deteriorated as tidier guys had moved on and only these two remained. There was always some kind of unidentifiable grime I'd have to clean off the tub before I could take a shower. I'd taken to wearing my outside shoes everywhere in the house except in my own bedroom.

"Have a drink with us." Jonathan cleared a mouldy cardboard box off the folding chair next to him. Max passed me a beer.

They were smart fellows, PhD students entering their sixth year of studies and still a long way from completion. Canadian students were like that, never seeming to be in any hurry, not like us visa students with more limited budgets and under heavy expectation to finish. While my parents supervised me through weekly long-distance phone calls, inquiring about my health and research progress, these guys seemed rootless. Their families lived less than three hours away, but they made brief visits only once or twice a year. I pitied their frail familial connections.

Max and Jonathan toasted my dissertation, which I'd defended successfully two weeks earlier. Mummy had urged me to return home sooner, but I'd resisted. I'd wanted to prolong my independent Canadian life a touch longer. Soon, I'd be enveloped in the responsibilities and obligations of home. My job at the prestigious Indian Institute of Technology would begin two months hence. I'd be introduced to a number of prospective brides.

And so I booked my flight for June 22, telling Mummy that I needed time to pack and say goodbye to my Canadian friends. And anyway, I'd paid my rent to the end of June, I'd argued. Later she'd blame herself for not pushing the point more, believed that her anxiety about my return date was some sort of prescience.

I drank a second beer and we discussed Jonathan's research frustrations and Max's gripes regarding his supervisor. I accepted a third beer and boasted about my new academic post. And then my tongue loosened and I told them about my afternoon with Nora.

"Man, your life is golden!" Jonathan exclaimed.

"Fuck yeah. A PhD, a job lined up, and today you got some pussy!" Max added.

I didn't think it was nice for him to talk about Nora that way, but I grinned and burped. "It's quite golden, no?"

Ameera

Δ

My left eyebrow ached. Just the left one. I pinched it, the pain pooling red under my lids. I turned over and hid from the harsh light streaming through the window. No matter how I rigged the drapery panels, they refused to meet. My stomach gurgled a distress call and I lay still, vowing to never again drink a jumbo travel mug of Enrique's new concoction.

A dream fragment shifted behind my eyelids, and I willed it forward. There was a faint voice beckoning me, calling my name. I think it was a man's, but it was too hoarse to identify. It had stalked my nights for weeks and sometimes its residue of lonely dread lingered through the day. It was masochistic, maybe, but I closed my eyes tight to dwell within the dream's reach.

When Blythe flushed the toilet in our shared bathroom, the dream's vapours evaporated. I sprang awake; it was already 9:00 a.m. and I had to be ready for the new guest orientation in half an hour. Somehow, Blythe always managed to be in the shower when I needed it.

I hoisted myself out of bed and laid out my clothes. I sniffed yesterday's skirt and decided I could wear it another day. I chose new underwear and a fresh blouse. I left the mandatory navy-blue and aquamarine striped tie looped over the dresser mirror, dusty now from disuse. None of us wore the regulation accessory except during semi-annual inspections, except for

Oscar; he said it distinguished us from the gardeners and maintenance workers, who wore similar uniforms. Really though, I
think he enjoyed his conspicuous formality because it made him
appear as our superior.

Blythe belted out "Royals," out of tune, from the shower. The
water shut off and I waited for the lock on my side of the adjoining
bathroom to click open, then the door to Blythe's room to shut,
the signal that it was safe to go in. To distract from my overfull
bladder and complaining stomach, I switched on the TV and
found an American weather station. The newscaster was almost
pissing himself with excitement, reporting on a blizzard in New
Jersey. I turned it off and willed Blythe to finish in the washroom.

Since learning about the promotion, I'd been envisioning
my manager suite. It would come equipped with its own bathroom and sitting area. I'd mentally furnished it with local art
and tchotchkes, clay pots, and rugs. But that morning, self doubt
wormed its way into my daydreams. What if the complaint hin-
derd my promotion? Maybe I'd have to live in my drab quarters
and field tourist foibles for another three years.

I shook away the depressing thoughts; as the self-help gurus
in O magazine proclaimed in bold font, it wasn't productive! I
would remain positive!

I checked my phone to see if Anita had sent a reply to my
e-mail, but the cinder-block walls of the old building jammed
the wireless signal.

Amongst our crew, only Blythe and I took advantage of worker housing. Roberto used to live across the hall, but moved to
Santa Maria, forty-five minutes away, after he got married. Oscar
lived three blocks away from Roberto, with his wife and three
kids. Manuela stayed with her family in nearby La Crucecita,
but that made no sense to me; she was twenty-six and had to
share a bedroom with two sisters. I once tried to convince her to
move to Atlantis, but she lectured me about how Atlantis was a

make-believe town and she preferred to live in a real town with real stores and real people.

Even though I appreciated the simplicity of living on the resort — it kind of reminded me of a university campus — I understood what Manuela meant. I often ventured into La Crucecita's noisy streets on my days off for a dose of reality. I liked to watch people rush to work, do their banking, take their kids to the dentist. Each time, I'd wander into a grocery store and purchase a single mango, or a bag of Sabritas chips and bring them back to my rectangular room.

Minutes later, as I rinsed my hair in a lukewarm shower, "Royals" stalked my thoughts. I imagined the irksome tune hiding out in the faucet, escaping through the uneven spray, landing on my scalp, and colonizing my mind.

Δ

At 9:45, I joined Manuela and Oscar at the ampitheatre entrance. Together, we created a chorus of "good morning" and "welcome" as we handed out orientation leaflets. The tourists reciprocated with their own replies of "good morning" and "thank you," and the cheerful din brought back my headache. Blythe climbed onto the stage and adjusted a microphone stand.

"We've just been talking about Nancy at Waves," Manuela stage-whispered once the hall had filled. "Do you know her?"

"Yeah." My first year in Huatulco, I spent all my free time with foreign tour reps, including Nancy. We travelled in a pack, a dozen American, Canadian, and European women, nightclub-hopping and lying on the beach. We leaned on one another when homesick. We gossiped, had arguments, made up. It was like summer camp for grown-ups. Eventually, I grew bored with it and drifted from the group.

"It's a disgrace on our profession. I've worked in the industry over twenty-five years and nothing like that has ever happened," Oscar muttered.

"We don't know the full story, guys." I fumbled with my phone to check my e-mail. Still no reply from Anita.

"Good morning!" Blythe sang into the microphone. An electronic squeal ricocheted around the theatre, eliciting a collective startle response from the assembly.

Oscar hurried to the stage in a half-jog, his sciatica making his movements jerky. He adjusted the amplifier's dials and I covered my ears while Oscar and Blythe performed sound checks.

"Sorry! Let's try that again. Good morning!" Blythe yelled. This time, the audience droned a feeble reply.

"Okay, we're going to tell you all about the resort and the excursions in just a moment. But before we do that, we're going to play a little game!" The audience rustled its discomfort. I rubbed my temples, craving caffeine.

"All right, stand up if you are here in Huatulco for the first time!" Nearly everyone stood, except for a line of bored-looking people at the back.

"Stand if it is your first time travelling with Oceana! ... Stand if you are from Toronto! ... Edmonton! ... Montreal! ... Ottawa! ... Buffalo! ..." The flock, mostly persuadable, bobbed up and down as Blythe screamed out their hometowns.

"Who've I missed?" Blythe yelled.

The college-boy group I'd seen at the airport called out, "Hamilton!" The sound of my hometown caused a quiver in my belly. But maybe that was just Enrique's Atlantis Mantis.

At the conclusion of the "fun" portion of the presentation, Oscar joined Blythe onstage and together they performed a soft sell of the various crocodile, turtle, beach, city, and waterfall tours on offer. The harder sell would come later at the tour desk; we knew how to make each excursion sound both compelling and essential for a successful vacation. For example, the risk for dengue fever was very low in the region, but I referenced its dangers and sold bug spray for three dollars more than the gift shop did. Roberto said the waterfall

tour was a place where his "ancestors communed with the Gods."
Manuela flirted with men until they agreed to shopping trips.

I was no longer surprised that our tactics worked and wasn't
bothered by the manipulation; shilling for Oceana wasn't all that
different from the other jobs I'd held. I'd door-knocked for the local
children's hospital while in university, telling plaintive stories about
kids on ventilators and amazing leukemia remissions. After graduation, and not sure what to do next, I tagged along with a friend to
Birkenstock College, paying off my student loans by selling sens-
ible footwear. Later, I followed the advice of a travel agent friend,
got my tourism certificate, and sold vacation getaways. I'd learned
how to use my bright smile to talk people into buying things.

Manuela and I left the assembly to open our tour desk. We
joined Roberto, who was already there, unlocking and unfolding
doors, cupboards, and counters. We set up stools on both sides. I
unpacked our receipts and forms, Manuela warmed up the computer, and Roberto restocked the brochure racks. We performed
all of these functions quickly and wordlessly, and within five
minutes we were ready.

Δ

A couple in their thirties approached me an hour later. They were
deeply tanned, obviously not part of the recently arrived cohort. I
recalled seeing them around the resort in the previous days.

"Excuse me." The woman had an Italian accent, olive skin,
and coal-black eyes. "The Viva representative is supposed to be
here today, but I don't see her anywhere." She linked her long
fingers with those of the man, who was shirtless.

I looked over at the Viva kiosk, where a CLOSED sign hung.
The tour company served European vacationers. "I don't think
she'll be back until tomorrow," I lied, hoping to sell the couple an
excursion. Although I was already above quota, the extra sales
would look good to Anita.

"Oh, too bad." She pushed her lips into a pout.

"Can I help you with something? Are you interested in a tour?" I smiled first at the woman, and then at the man, holding each of their gazes a moment too long.

"Well, we leave here in two days. We haven't gone sightseeing yet," the man said hesitantly. He and the woman shared a look, and then she shrugged and nodded.

"Oh, I see. Well, you can go with Oceana to see the crocodiles tomorrow, if you'd like." The man's muscular chest swelled. A brush of thin curly hair ringed each of his nipples.

"Tell us more about that," the woman said, lowering to sit on the stool in front of me. She leaned forward, rested her elbows on the desk, her forearms framing her deep cleavage. "I'm Serena, and this is my husband Sebastiano."

"Ameera. What a beautiful name." Sebastiano's eyes locked on my nametag. "Do you lead the tours yourself?"

"Thanks. No, I only go when a French-speaking guide is needed," I explained. I hated tromping in the heat, while Roberto didn't like sitting at the tour desk. We switched shifts whenever possible.

While a long line formed behind them, I reviewed the tours at length, and the couple listened attentively. Eventually, they paid cash for the crocodile excursion, and I forgot to tell them about insect repellant. As they walked away, I exhaled, realizing the satisfaction I felt was not from exerting my sales muscle, but from the heat of their flirtation. I silently repeated their names three times before turning to the next person in line. *Serena Sebastiano Serena Sebastiano Serena Sebastiano.*

Azeez

∞

My goodbye-cum-congratulations drinks with my roommates left me with a sore head. I had sweat profusely during the night and awoke to damp sheets.

I never was terribly skilled at drinking, not having had much practice before Canada. At the end of my second year, I joined my students' celebrations and they taught me about rum, tequila, and vodka. I learned to choose bar rail drinks because they were usually on special before ten p.m. and my budget was tight and my bedtime early. My favourite drink was rum and coke; the cola's caffeine and sweetness perfectly counteracted the bitter alcohol's depressant effects.

I would be fine if I restricted myself to one or two, accompanied by peanuts or pretzels. Too few snacks or an extra drink would push me over the edge into nausea, headaches, and regrets. The previous night on the porch, I'd consumed four Budweisers and skipped my supper.

I covered my eyes with a pillow and sank in and out of a hungover sleep filled with thoughts of Nora. Over and over again, I dreamt that I was dialling her phone number and inviting her to lunch. Perhaps my unconscious mind was pushing me to make contact. When I awoke I told myself I'd wash up first, dress, and then speak with her.

I feared that not phoning would be unmannerly. What do you say to a woman with whom you've just had relations but will never see again? But I was waffling on that last point. I couldn't stop thinking about her russet curls. I'd never before run my fingers through such soft hair. And those pillowy breasts and bottom! Her silky white skin.

I was a scientist and didn't really believe in kismet or fate or karma, but that morning, in my hungover state, I engaged in the whimsy of *maybe we are meant to be!* I was entertaining delusional thoughts: I'd return for a visit or she could come see me in Bombay. She'd planned to study Eastern Religions and what better way for her to learn than to go to the source?

Perhaps it was because she was my first? Of course I didn't tell her that — I'd be mortified if she knew. Could she tell? I'd tried to be suave. I kissed her and moved my hands the way they did in the few pornographic movies I'd seen.

I'd never even crossed the threshold of a girl's bedroom before, let alone made love. I'd dated a couple of girls in Bombay and fooled around a little. Those experiences were memorable, but not even close to what I'd experienced with Nora. No, Nora was different.

Obviously she wasn't a virgin. I couldn't tell exactly how experienced she was, but besides a little nervous giggling, she appeared to know how to handle herself. Oh how warm and inviting she was! I'll never forget the sensation of losing myself inside her for those precious few minutes.

At midday, I dragged my luggage down the staircase. I dialled her number from the foyer phone. It rang and rang and my heart beat so quickly and my stomach churned so violently that I thought I might vomit. When she picked up, I shoved the receiver into its cradle.

Ameera

Δ

I caught Enrique's eye. His leer sent a wave of heat down my chest, past my stomach, and into my groin.

"How are you, beautiful?"

"Good. Tired. Always working."

"I know what you mean. We should go dancing again."

"Sure, let's do that." But I knew we wouldn't. I'd asked him out soon after arriving in Huatulco. *A first date*, I'd gushed to Manuela, who'd been skeptical but didn't say why. We drove to a club about forty minutes away, a hole in the wall in Santa Maria de Huatulco that boasted a Reggaeton DJ from Mexico City. I wasn't keen on the music, but I was thrilled to be with Enrique. We joined a small group of his friends, a mix of men and women, most in their early thirties, all stylishly dressed. On the dance floor, Enrique maintained a platonic distance, his body like a frowning chaperone.

Halfway into the evening, he swivelled me around and nudged me into the arms of his friend Antonio, who pulled me close for a sweaty slow dance. By the end of the song, I could feel Antonio's erection pressed against my stomach. When I realized that Enrique was at the bar, chatting with friends and oblivious to me, I pulled Antonio closer.

Enrique and I went clubbing a few times after that, but it was always the same. I'd long given up the idea of dating him, but I knew I still dressed for him. I told myself that unrequited crushes could be fun.

He returned to his bartending duties and I scanned the crowded lounge. As I'd expected, Serena and Sebastiano were perched near the front. I had a hunch they were waiting for me that evening.

For a moment, I wondered if they'd lied about their names; this was how some swinging couples played, seeking anonymity or trying on new personas. A few stumbled over their pseudonyms, letting their real names slip during moments of disinhibition and pleasure. Some chose alliterative fake monikers like June and Jeremy, Will and Winsome. The women often favoured aliases more exotic-sounding than their own names: Sophia, Andrina, Monique, Imani, Marina. When I'd later look them up in the Oceana database, I'd learn that they were really Susan, Tammy, Dianne, Joanne, or Jen. Serena and Sebastiano were not travelling with my company, so I had no way of double-checking.

"Ameera, *buona sera!*" Sebastiano held out a piña colada. I briefly hesitated in my reach for the glass, remembering Anita's letter. But Sebastiano's green eyes drew me in. I accepted the drink and Serena's smile widened.

We made polite small talk and I took care to maintain a professional posture. I was vigilant to onlookers and acknowledged other vacationers who passed by, because, even out of uniform, most viewed me as perpetually on duty. In fact, one lady interrupted our conversation to ask about her malfunctioning in-room safe.

I suggested that we move to a less busy part of the bar, a section with leather couches and dim lighting. Serena grabbed my wrist and playfully pulled me down next to her while Sebastiano settled onto an ottoman across from us, his knees brushing mine. The hair on his calves was thick and downy, and I stretched my legs to make full contact. I glanced Serena's way to see if she minded and she nudged closer, pushing her heavy breasts against my bare shoulder.

Our conversation remained polite during our second drink, even while our bodies spoke a language more intimate. They asked about my job: did I like being so far from home? Where did I live and eat? I'd grown accustomed to curiosity from tourists. Most worked nine-to-five jobs, had children and pets, and suffered long winters. They pictured my life as a year-round holiday. And perhaps I'd once imagined it would be that way, too.

Δ

Leave winter behind! Take on new challenges! Competitive salary!
The Oceana employment posting crossed my inbox in early May, a week after the incident with Gavin. I was about to delete it when my mother phoned.

"How's work?"

"Quiet. Dull. I think I need a change. Listen to this." I read the Oceana advertisement to her.

"Well, it would be a lateral move, but if they are a large company, there might be more opportunities. There's no room for movement where you are now." Her tone was neutral, which I appreciated.

"Yeah, I think I'll apply."

"It might not be a bad idea for you to get away, have some new experiences. It would give you a bit of space from Gavin, too."

"Well, that's over. For good. I saw him last week at a friend's birthday party and … well, I'm not gonna go there ever again." I knew I sounded defensive.

"I'm glad. Listen, have you thought about going back to school? These days everyone seems to need a graduate degree. I'd be happy to help with tuition." Her voice rose at the end of the sentence, her way of making a suggestion without imposing.

I changed the subject to an ongoing conflict with her neighbour who'd built a fence ten inches over her property line. The issue had consumed her for months. She'd sent two letters to her him and had met with her city councillor. I wondered why she hadn't just knocked on the guy's door and talked with him directly.

Two weeks later, I boarded an early train to Ottawa for a one o'clock interview, stumbled my way through the French oral exam, and then was interviewed by Anita McLeod. I was surprised that she was South Asian and wore a paisley-printed shalwaar kameez; her accent had sounded as Canadian as mine when we'd spoken over the phone. After the initial formal interview questions, she spoke more casually. She revealed that she had just returned from her honeymoon in Huatulco, where Oceana was developing its resorts. She gushed about her wedding, which included a combination of Hindu and Scottish traditions.

"I guess I'm a little old fashioned." She confessed that she'd taken her husband's surname.

"There's nothing wrong with that. It's all about making the choice that's good for you, right?" I said strategically, aware that I was still being interviewed. I didn't know anyone who followed the anachronistic marital convention anymore.

"Did you do the same? Is Gilbert your married name?"

"No, I'm single. My father is Indian, but my mother is Canadian. I took her surname because I didn't grow up with him." I fidgeted in my seat hoping I wasn't revealing too much about my unusual upbringing. But Anita didn't seem bothered by these details; she babbled on about immigrating to Canada when she was a preschooler and we bonded over our South Asian ancestries, with me doing my best to nod and smile knowingly at her first-generation anecdotes.

We went to Swiss Chalet for an early dinner and then she dropped me at the station in time for the evening train. A voice mail arrived the next day with an offer. Finally, after two dull years at the travel agency, I had some positive news to share with my friends: I'm moving to Mexico!

Over the next three weekends, I sold my furniture, winter clothing, and appliances on Craigslist. Everything else got crammed into eleven cardboard boxes that I lined up against my mother's townhouse basement wall. For Huatulco, I'd packed like a tourist, filling one large suitcase with summer dresses, toiletries, my laptop, and two boxes of condoms. At the last minute, I tucked in a hardcover book from my childhood, *Exploring India.*

∆

"Oh mio Dio! Your job is more boring than mine. And I'm an information technology manager at a hospital," Serena said after I'd told them all about my contract and routines. Usually, vacationers' responses to the mundane details of my life were bright-sided: "At least you get to be near the ocean, eh?" or "But the weather here, you can't beat that!"

"You must hate tourists by now, yes?" Sebastiano laughed.

"Well, sometimes. But some tourists I quite enjoy." I ogled him, and he matched my steady gaze.

By the time our third drink was delivered, I was aglow from alcohol and attention. I suspected that Sebastiano had been asking for doubles, because the cocktails tasted more rummy than usual. It was resort policy to water down liquor to counter our guests' over-indulgence and therefore reduce their accidental death liability.

"So, a pretty girl like you … you must have a boyfriend?" Serena stole the tiny cocktail spear from my glass and sucked on its pineapple chunk. The evening had progressed as I'd hoped.

"So?" Sebastiano persisted.

"No, no boyfriend … and no girlfriend, either." I filched Serena's cocktail spear, held it up in victory, laughed too loudly.

"Ah, so, you're, how you say it in English … flexible," Sebastiano quipped, waggling his eyebrows and taking a sip of his piña colada. White froth coated his upper lip. I wanted to lick it off.

"Yes, flexible is one way to put it," I replied.

"Just like my wife, *sí*, Serena?"

"*Sí*." Serena nodded.

Δ

I awoke in the dark, sandwiched between the Italians, damp from sex and sweat. The clock radio glared 3:07, shocking red numbers. I didn't normally do sleepovers; I couldn't sleep well with strangers. Just before I'd drifted into unconsciousness, a sheet was draped over me, a soothing palm stroked my lower back, and I'd succumbed.

I crawled my way down the centre of the bed. Without rousing, Sebastiano rolled into the empty space. He nudged his pelvis into Serena's lower back, and she reciprocated by shifting closer to him. Sensing that my absence barely mattered, I was tempted to sneak my way back into the heat between them.

In the darkness, I sorted through a pile of hastily discarded clothing and identified the cotton of my sundress. In the lit laneway, I inspected myself in a window's reflection, combed my hair with my fingers, and fastened a button I'd missed. Walking away from the Italians' villa, I sensed I was wearing the wrong underwear.

The resort was quiet at that hour, its inhabitants tucked neatly away into their beds, inhaling and exhaling the warm pre-dawn air. I slowed my gait. Without its daytime merriment, Atlantis almost resembled a sleepy rural village, like those on the Swiss tourism posters that hung in my old travel agency. I descended a staircase that led to the main restaurants and bar, pausing halfway to survey the landscape. To my left, the surf crashed against the shore and wind rustled the leaves of a tall palm tree. A small green lizard darted across my path. With my mind still hazy from the booze, I squinted and imagined the land before it was expropriated, before it was called Atlantis, when its inhabitants were Mexicans: verdant farms, thatched buildings, rolling hills.

I continued on, tripping over a poorly laid pavement stone. The path that intersected the main boulevard was under construction and a barely visible CUIDADO sign had been posted on a nearby fence. Beside it was a small hand-written note that read: CONSTRUCTION. I crouched and looked more closely at the jagged rock that had caused my stumble. Each flagstone was unique, differently shaped and sized, and fit together like a jigsaw puzzle. It looked to be slow, painstaking work.

A few minutes later, I passed the security station, and lowered my gaze. After almost three years, the officers could recognize me and the other foreign tour reps, even in the dark. They could tell stories about when this-one-or-that-one arrived home drunk in a taxi, or leaning on a guy she'd just met, or weaving, all alone, down the long driveway. Foreign tour reps were known for that sort of thing and in contrast, I lived a pretty quiet existence.

I looked up, met the security guard's eye. I considered Oceana's online complaint about me, and its mysterious sender. Worry rippled across my belly.

Azeez

∞

I pocketed Nora's phone number and deposited my keys on the cluttered dining table. No one was home to bid me farewell that afternoon.

On the way to the airport I jabbered non-stop about my new life in India. I told the driver about my academic job, and joked about how my mother, in that very moment, was searching for my wife. He was an older man, pink from the early summer sun, and a good listener. It was extravagant, but I left him a five-dollar tip.

At Toronto's Pearson International Airport, I took my place in the long queue and fiddled with my passport and tickets. There were large groups of Indian families, some in Western garb, most dressed semi-formally as though about to attend a fancy party. I wore jeans and a T-shirt, and I'd packed a kurta to change into before landing. After almost half an hour in the snaking lineup, I checked my bags and was lucky enough to get an aisle seat. I hoped there wouldn't be a bawling baby nearby or a seat-kicking child behind me.

At security, I watched tear-stained goodbyes. Relatives and friends clung to one another, gave good wishes, kissed cheeks. Family clusters split apart as passengers passed through security and their kin remained on the other side of the glass. Many of the travellers were teenagers, students who had likely just finished their term and were on their way to vacations with adoring grandparents. In one family, a father was the only one not travelling, in another, both parents. I wondered what it would be like to send one's children away, even if only for the summer holidays. Were my parents bereft when they dropped me off five years earlier?

I knew that in less than a day and half, after one stop in London and a connection in Delhi, they would be at the Bombay airport to greet me — my parents, sister, and brother. We'd have to squeeze into the car as we'd done since we were youngsters. How much had they changed since I'd left? My younger brother had joined my father's law firm. My little sister was already twenty-three, a young teacher, and recently engaged. I'd missed all the steps in between the days of their carefree youth and their solid adulthoods.

Thrice an announcer called out a delay and apologized for the inconvenience. The mood at the departure gate turned impatient, skittishness wrinkling the ladies' silk saris and the men's polyester suits. The children, oblivious to the adults' unspoken anxieties, skipped and ran and laughed, the airport an adequate playground. One little girl wore a Brownie uniform, with a dozen badges sewn to her sash. She whirled through the terminal like a dervish, her brown skirt flying up around her thighs.

Dull pain pooled across my forehead from the previous night's shenanigans, so I used the last of my Canadian currency to purchase aspirin and a cup of tea. I heard the words my mother used to soothe me: *fikhar nahi*. Don't worry. I smiled, buoyed by the notion that I'd soon be home, amongst my relations.

Ameera

Δ

Five hours later, I was dressed in a fresh uniform and ready to assist eighty-three crocodile-seekers onto their buses. I stood by the resort's driveway, inhaling the warming asphalt, checking off names and collecting excursion coupons. As I watched the buses drive down the road toward the Tonameca Lagoon, I realized that Serena and Sebastiano were not along for the ride. Interesting.

Δ

I hadn't expected Manuela to be at the tour desk when I arrived there later. She was a staunch believer in Sunday as a day of rest. For her, church was good for the soul, but more so a venue for meeting nice single men. She'd offered to take me to the Parroquia de Nuestra Señora de Guadalupe for both purposes, but I'd declined. I hadn't ventured into a Catholic church since my great-grandfather died over a decade earlier.

"I traded with Blythe. It's okay — I'm getting four days off in exchange. Plus, it means I don't have to go to Waves next week," Manuela explained. She'd been assigned Nancy's duties — orientation and excursion sales — at the five-star fifteen kilometres away. We all filled in when needed at our sister resorts, where smaller numbers of Oceana guests stayed. But we preferred Atlantis, where our shifts passed more quickly.

"Really? Is she with Rhion today?" Blythe had met the Iowan surfer five months earlier in the lineup at Chito's Juice Bar in La Crucecita. I didn't think much of him; the few times we'd met, he'd made eye contact with my breasts.

In the beginning, Blythe shared details about her love life on an almost daily basis, and prodded me to reciprocate with news about mine, *Come on, tell me everything!* But I'd stopped doing that. Once, over two years earlier, I'd told her about a tourist I'd slept with, only to find out that my confession had circulated to the other tour reps, who teased me about it the following day. She apologized, but I remained wary around her ever since, which probably wasn't fair. When I began to exclusively hook up with couples, I'd often confess a false crush on a resort worker to draw Blythe off my trail. I avoided bringing anyone back to my room. It wasn't practical, anyway — my dates tended to have their own king-size beds, which worked better when there were three bodies and six legs.

"They're going to a beach somewhere down the coast. She was excited. I guess things are getting serious between them?" Manuela asked.

"I wouldn't be so sure about that."

Blythe had been left at the altar just before Huatulco. She told me this over drinks early on in our contract, her blue eyes growing wet as they often did when she grappled with big emotions. Three hundred guests witnessed her humiliation from the church pews. Like a convert to a new religion, Blythe was almost evangelical about the wonders of casual relationships. She spoke of her ability to separate emotions from sex as though it were a badge of honour she'd pinned to her blouse. She lectured me about how to "turn off the girl-brain" and said she didn't care that Rhion planned to return to the U.S. in two months.

"¿*Verdad?*" Manuela asked. "Come on, tell me what you know!"

"Don't repeat this," I said with only a minor twinge of guilt, "I heard her yell, 'you cold-hearted asshole' last week. And then there was the sound of a door slamming and Rhion's flip-flops slapping down the corridor. And more yelling yesterday."

"Veeerrry interesting." Manuela stroked her chin.

"Yes. I asked her about it a few days ago, you know, to see if she was all right, but she denied anything was wrong." Blythe's eyes had been red, her skin pale and without its usual layer of foundation and blush. I'd felt like hugging her, but held back.

"Hmmm. And how are you today? You look tired." Manuela's eyes were wells of sympathy. She wore a new shade of eyeshadow, one that perfectly matched Oceana's turquoise logo.

"Yeah, I slept badly last night." I pushed back my shoulders and rubbed my eyes. "Where is everyone? It seems so quiet today."

"You sent off two busloads on the croc trip this morning. And well," she said, pointing to the recreation area, "Cardio Pump started a minute ago." The class was offered at 10:00 a.m. and new guests flocked to the Sunday class, full of good intentions. By Tuesday, Maria, the instructor, would be grumbling about her dwindling numbers. She trolled the beach distributing brochures that extolled: IT'S NOT EXERCISE, IT'S A PARTY!

"Right. And after that is the first Spanish class." I grinned at Manuela.

"They'll all be saying, '*olé Manuela, co-mo est-as*' afterward," she said, with a clenched jaw.

"And they'll feel so proud of themselves until you unceremoniously correct their errors. Like you do mine."

"*Escucha*, I need a little fun. Hey, but you could teach that class, if you were not so shy and practised more with us. Ameera. *Habla español*," Manuela teased.

"*Si. Si. Una cerveza, por favor.*" I rested my forehead against the desk.

"Aha, so it is a hangover then. *La cruda, en español.* Do we already have a Word of the Week?" Manuela poked my shoulder with a sharp purple fingernail. "So. Who did you go out with last night?"

"*Si, la cruda*. I stayed here, had a few drinks with *las turistas* at the bar." Inside their room, Serena had pulled me close, her kiss surprisingly hard, like a man's. But her skin was soft, her scent musky like sandalwood. Sebastiano closed in behind me, his arms encircling us, his belt buckle hard against the small of my back.

"Los *turistas*. *Turistas* is masculine," Manuela corrected.

"Right, *los turistas*." I knew that.

"I don't understand why you party with them! We spend the whole day dealing with their stupid problems. 'I ordered an ocean view room, but I can only see a partial ocean view!' Manuela drawled in her best Canadian accent, which sounded Bostonion to me.

"I know, I know. But it's easier than going all the way to town for a drink."

"'Why doesn't everyone here speak English!' 'I want a king-size bed!'" Manuela mock-whined.

"They're not so bad after they've had a couple of drinks. They become more human with booze." I laughed and Manuela snorted. "But I should have paced myself better."

The Cardio Pump ladies line-danced in the morning sunshine. Like flags on a windy day, their pale arms jerked to the rhythms of a salsa song. I considered how my usual vigilance seemed to be fraying. I'd gotten drunk with strangers and probably hadn't been careful enough about hiding my flirtation at the bar, even after receiving Anita's email the day before. And there had been other small, emotional accidents; I had a vague memory of disclosing too many personal details to Serena and Sebastiano and then I'd fallen asleep in their room.

Manuela sighed and shook her head, as though concurring with my silent thoughts. I turned my attention to the computer and saw that Anita had finally sent a reply.

Dear Ameera,
Thanks for your e-mail. I'll print our correspondence and file it along with the complaint.

Best,
Anita

I sighed, long and loud, troubling over the terse brevity of the
message. Was Anita truly bothered by the complaint, or had she
just been in a hurry? Maybe I was reading too much into it.

"*¿Qué pasó?* Are you okay?" Manuela asked.

"Oh, it's nothing. Just exhausted." I stood and tidied the information rack, making a show of looking industrious. I inhaled
deeply, arranging the brochures into symmetrical rows.

It will be fine.

"Did you say something?" I turned to Manuela.

"No, I was humming along to the music."

Once again the words rustled through my mind. *It will be fine.*

I briefly considered telling Manuela about the online complaint. She was my closest buddy in Huatulco, but there was so
much I didn't share with her. Like Blythe, I was trying on something new, experiencing sex as recreational, my own "girl-brain"
reconfiguring itself, perhaps. Except I was doing it through
threesomes. If I couldn't explain that to Manuela, how would I
talk about the complaint?

I stared out at the pool area. As usual, most of the chairs appeared to be occupied, but weren't; tourists were "saving" them
for when they returned later in the day. The resort had a rule
against this practice (it was Rule Number Seven on the painted
signboard near the pool) but it was mostly ignored by guests
and not enforced by staff. I thought about Malika then, and
wished she was nearby.

Δ

"It's scarcity thinking," Malika grumbled as she searched for a pool lounger. She was one of my old friends from Hamilton, the only one who'd come to visit the previous year. The others had maintained a stony silence.

"Oh come on, Malika. You're here to enjoy yourself. Don't take it so seriously," I scoffed.

"These people are jerks!"

By day three, Malika had frothed herself into an angry self-righteousness, and soon she was campaigning to sabotage the chair hoarders' efforts. She deliberately chose a "saved" chair, even when another was available, and swept the offending books and towels to the ground. She incited others to join her campaign, but no one seemed very interested.

But we had fun, too. Over the week we drank too many mojitos and lazed on the beach. She asked about my sex life and I shared in fragments, offering an anecdote here and there, while I watched her face for signs of criticism or judgment. The opposite happened; Malika was enthralled by my sexual encounters, and wanted details about swingers.

"Are couples more fun than one person at a time?" Malika's eyes were big with curiosity.

I pondered my preferences. I realized I hadn't articulated them much. Before Huatulco, I had zero knowledge of the swinger set. I'd believed non-monogamy was emotionally difficult and bad for long-term relationships. And the furthest I'd ever strayed from what I'd assumed to be my mostly heterosexual nature were a few late-night, drunken party kisses with female friends. I hadn't exactly been a prude, but I was comfortable with a pretty conventional sex life. Being far from home allowed me to travel outside the borders I'd once drawn for myself.

"It's kind of like if you have coffee with two people instead of one. The conversation is different, more dynamic. It's still intimate, but there are more ideas, more energy. " I frowned at my analogy, which was almost apt, but not quite.

"But are the men creepy? Maybe it's a stereotype about swingers, but that's what I'd worry about."

"I've had good luck. No creeps." I flipped through a mental photo album of my past lovers. One or two borderline creeps came to mind, but I didn't mention them.

"I'm impressed, girl! You seem happier now. Better than when you were with Gavin."

I nodded, grateful that she didn't mention that incident at the bar. Still, I flashed to the alleyway, the back door opening, Tamara's livid expression, Gavin's middle finger pulling out of me.

"I can't manage to get it on with even one person!" She laughed. "How do you hook up with these people, anyway?"

"There aren't a lot of them, but I kind of keep my eyes open. They seem to spot me as much as I do them. And then I find a way to make contact, flirt a little." I demonstrated cruising eye contact for Malika, which made her blush and giggle.

"So now you're biracial *and* bisexual," Malika teased, her grin taking over her round face. She, too, was of mixed ancestry, but with a white mother and Jamaican father. It was our lengthy debates about race and identity in undergrad that had cemented our friendship.

"You know I hate labels." And then, just to goad her I said, "You should try a threesome one day. You might like it."

"Oh me? I couldn't do that. I'm not as brave as you," Malika said, fanning herself.

I have to admit I was glad when it was time for her to go home, because her complaints about Atlantis grew to include food and water wastage, and her general displeasure with the resort's complete "walled-in-amusement park" experience. I was concerned that my friend might start an all-inclusive riot, given another week at the resort.

Δ

"Why don't you go take a nap and come back in an hour? Nothing's happening here. If it gets busy I'll text you," Manuela offered.

I went for coffee instead. When I passed near the pool, I glimpsed Sebastiano and Serena, sunning themselves, their bronzed skin slick with oil. Sebastiano lay on his stomach, a strip of orange spandex stretching across his almost flat backside. Serena's bikini top straps were pulled down low. I flashed to a moment from the night before when I'd lain on my side between them, Serena facing me, pressing a nipple into my mouth while Sebastiano entered me from behind. I'd rocked my pelvis back while pulling Serena's hips forward. With the memory, my body responded, my back arching, my face flushing, warmth spreading between my thighs.

I continued to ogle them from afar. Perhaps they hadn't planned to go on the crocodile trip in the first place and had spent ninety-five bucks to have me notice them. The thought made me even more aroused; the slightly sneaky and trans-actional nature of their strategy was kind of indecent.

With anyone else — like with the bodybuilders Marina and Mike — I might have felt manipulated by the fake excursion-buying. I blamed my poor judgment in bedding them on the three-week dry spell that had preceded them. I should've walked away when they asked me where I was from, and didn't accept "Hamilton" as a valid answer. Instead, I'd ordered another Cuba Libre and listened to their detailed account of the trip they'd taken to India four years earlier. *Oh, Ameera, you have to see the Taj Mahal. India is such a beautiful place, but oh my god, the poverty is astounding!* I swallowed my envy and irritation and let my libido take over. I mean, who wouldn't want to run their hands over biceps like theirs?

When they'd checked out of Atlantis on Friday morning, they'd left a note with the front desk clerk, thanking me for a "fantabulous" night and suggesting we hook up when I returned to Canada. The day after, a Facebook friend request and e-mail arrived. They'd look into a return trip to Atlantis at the end of April if they could get a sitter for their two bichon frise puppies. I'd discarded their note, deleted the message, and blocked them from my account.

Now at the far end of the pool, I considered stopping to say hello to Serena and Sebastiano, but hesitated. Couples were inconsistent with post-sex socializing. Some shied away from my glances the morning after, their flirtatious, sociable selves restricted to the night. Second dates were rare occurrences and a note like the bodybuilders' was a first. Of course, I could only guess about my one-night lovers' reactions and expectations; few made their feelings known directly. I assumed that things were different for swingers who had ongoing relationships. What might it be like to see Sebastiano and Serena again and again, I wondered. I'd read about long-term swinger relationships, or three lovers forming a kind of triad, and the idea appealed to me.

I ambled back from the staff cafeteria, carrying coffee and a plate of the butter cookies I knew Manuela favoured but rarely permitted herself. When I passed the pool again, the Italians had flipped onto their backs. Both wore sunglasses, so I couldn't tell if they could see me. I waved, but neither waved back.

Azeez

∞

My stomach grumbled. We'd taken off an hour and a half late and there wouldn't be a meal until after the stop in Montreal. When the little girl across the aisle offered me one of her candies, I accepted. I shook her hand, introduced myself formally, and learned that her name was Meena. She was the twirling Brownie from the airport.

"How old are you, Meena?"

"I just turned eight last month." When she smiled, her face creased into deep dimples.

"And is this your first trip to India?"

"No! We visited Nani and Nana three years ago," she said in a tone that suggested that I was most definitely a silly goose.

"Ah, so your second trip, then."

Meena's mother, who was seated beside her, smiled at me and said not to bother the nice man.

"On the contrary, I'm enjoying your daughter's company. And she was ever so kind to offer one of her Life Savers." I winked at Meena, who beamed proudly. Meena's mother nodded and shrugged as though to say "suit yourself" and resumed reading her novel.

∞

After Montreal, the head stewardess announced that it was the flight engineer's final trip and he would begin his retirement the following day. There was a round of hearty applause for him. Then she told us that a Hindi movie would be played after the meal was served. In an excited voice she added that there was a special bonus — a movie star from the film was on the flight with us. There was a collective gasp and passengers craned their necks to get a glimpse of the celebrity. I was completely out of the Bollywood loop by then and didn't recognize his name. The elderly woman sitting beside me opened *The Magic Carpet*, Air India's magazine, and showed me a picture of him posing beside a slender white woman.

Perhaps I should have allowed Meena's mother to rein in her chatty daughter. For the next two hours, she told me all about Miss Platt, her second-grade teacher, described each and every badge she'd earned in Brownies, and showed me the contents of her bag, which included three picture books, a change of clothing, and a Cabbage Patch doll. It was brown, fat-cheeked, and wore a sparkly crown. Meena asked me if I wanted to hold her for a minute and then thrust the doll into my arms. I stared into its painted-on gaze and laughed out loud.

Ameera

Δ

"We are going to go pack our bags now. We leave tomorrow morning," Serena said, with a wan smile. There was a purpling smudge on her neck, a mark I'd left behind.

"Have a good trip home, you two." I smiled politely and glanced at Manuela, who was flipping through a newspaper, likely eavesdropping.

Serena's long white tunic fell an inch below her knees, as ungainly as a paper bag. Sebastiano's Bermuda shorts and loose polo shirt cloaked his muscular frame, making him resemble any other middle-aged tourist. I realized, with a catch of disappointment in my stomach, that they weren't going to ask me out again. I imagined the late morning debrief that would have determined this. Had they evaluated my performance over coffee? Whose opinion would have held more sway? Never mind, I'd scope the bar again on Thursday.

"I wish we didn't have to leave this paradise." Sebastiano affected a sad-sack expression, his lower lip pushed out. I had an urge to taste the soft meat of it.

"Good luck with your search for your father." Serena said this with the kindness of a kindergarten teacher. I stiffened as the pair turned to walk away.

Frowning in concentration, I scrambled to recall the previous night's conversation. We'd all spoken casually about our families early in the evening, when we were making idle chatter about our lives. But what had I disclosed after the fourth drink? I wanted to jump up and follow them to find out what I'd forgotten, but my thighs were stuck to my stool's vinyl seat.

"You've never talked about your father before."

I looked off in the direction of the disappearing Italians, prickling under Manuela's curious stare. She apprised me of her family's news on a daily basis. Just that morning I'd learned that she'd mediated her sisters' bickering about the youngest's *quinceañera* party.

"Oh, yeah. I don't know anything about him." I shrugged, as though speaking about him didn't always cause a lump to form in my throat. I took a sip from my diet cola to push it down. Why would I have told Serena and Sebastiano about him?

"I always thought he'd died or something."

"My mother lost touch with him before I was born. I've been thinking about looking for him. Maybe. I dunno." These words, spoken aloud, sounded surreal. I had imagined a serious search for him numerous times over the years, but the idea hadn't progressed beyond an uneasy notion.

"Any idea where he might be?"

"India. Probably." I sucked down the last of my drink, aspirating through ice. "That's where he's from. But he could be anywhere."

"I wonder if you look like him. I don't think you look like your mother at all." Manuela said. She'd met her twice when Mom came to Huatulco on vacation.

"Mom says so, but she doesn't remember a lot of details. She only knew him for one day." I looked at my hand, the one part of me that matched my mother. We both had long, thin fingers, the middle one standing noticeably taller than the rest. A small birthmark squatted in the middle of each of our heart lines, a sign of good luck at midlife, according to a palm reader we'd once visited at the Ancaster Fair. As a child, I liked to press our matching hands together.

"One day?"

"Yeah."

"Wow," Manuela said. I doubted Manuela had ever had a one-night stand, or if she had, she'd never said so. She very much desired matrimony and motherhood. Three kids, preferably two girls and one boy, in that order, and she had chosen names. Although she'd accepted a promise ring from a previous suitor, none of the men she'd dated in recent years had turned out to be a potential husband. I'd long suspected that Manuela had a crush on Oscar, but when I once teased her about him, she vehemently denied it.

"Hey, we should go. It's quitting time." I looked at my watch.

We collected our things, and repacked and folded the tour desk until it once again resembled a locked rectangular box. We headed off in opposite directions, Manuela to the lobby, where a golf cart would shuttle her to the main road, and I toward the staff dining room.

I filled my dinner plate with rice, refried beans, and cooked vegetables. I avoided the mini-sausages, buns, and crudités, anything that might have been previously picked over by dirty hands. A large slice of angel food cake beckoned and I added it to my plate. It was just after six, early for most of the workers to eat dinner, and I easily found an empty table in a windowless corner. I stared at a painting across from me of a calm acrylic sea reflecting an orange sunset.

I shovelled in the bean and rice slop, its mushiness pleasant against the roof of my mouth. The lump in my throat made way and I swallowed it down with the food. I consumed the cake in three greedy swallows.

Δ

Having an unknown father marked me as different, even more different than I already felt as a light-brown-skinned daughter of a white single mother in a town where it seemed no one had a family like ours. Mom didn't like talking about him. I think it exposed her as someone she didn't want to be: the sort of girl who got pregnant with a visa student she'd known for only a single afternoon; the sort of girl who was sloppy about taking her birth-control pill; the sort of girl who had to turn her back on ambitious academic plans to raise a child.

When she did speak about him, her stories were designed to help me avoid the same choices she'd made. The more detailed the story, the more serious the warning. Some were told and re-told, with each recounting further embellished to properly high-light the specific lesson to be absorbed.

The night of my prom, Mom confessed that she'd met my biological father a few days after she'd been dumped by the boyfriend she'd been with all through university, a guy she'd expected to marry. Their ending was abrupt and humiliating and he'd begun dating someone else a few days later. So, when this exotic-looking guy showed interest in her, she impulsively asked him back to her place.

My heart was broken, and he seemed kind.

This was her lesson about rebounding.

She also admitted that she'd been too shy to talk about con-doms with him.

Prophylactics, she'd called them. I'd laughed nervously and Mom shushed me, urging me to pay attention.

I should have told him to wear one. I hadn't been consistent with the pill since the breakup..

She followed this admission with rushed reassurances about how glad she was that I had been born. About how if she could go back in time, she wouldn't change a thing, that life is a gift and other such clichés. And then she warned me to never trust a man with my body.

Don't believe it when they say they'll pull out.

I felt squirmy, like a dozen spiders crawling up my back. I didn't want to picture her under a panting man.

And you can never be too safe these days with AIDS and chlamydia and warts. Trust me.

Later, I stood at the school's bathroom mirrors, Usher's "You Make Me Wanna" wafting in from the gym. Rifling through my purse for lipgloss, my fingers brushed against a ticker-tape length of multi-coloured condoms. I showed my friends the rainbow rubber disks, and they laughed at Mom's stealth. They misinterpreted her deepest fear as her being a progressive mom. I distributed them, tucking a purple condom into my wallet, imagining it might taste like grape.

For years I wanted a better story. Perhaps if he was dead, even. A car accident, a tragic illness, a random shooting all would have been fine. I pined for a narrative that would provide closure and elicit sympathy, while leaving me intact, a child who was planned for, loved, even if I was still left. But Mom didn't know basic details like his exact height, what subject his PhD was in, or the name of his hometown. I wanted more. Needed more. What I had instead was an absence, a mystery, a relationship that never existed.

My ideas changed when I met Malika and other university friends who were brown girls with white mothers. Being different was no longer the same sort of problem as when I was a kid. Turned out, it was kind of cool. I finally had an identity that I could say in one sentence: I was the mixed-race daughter of a strong single mother. Period. I could almost forget that I didn't know my biological father's surname. Almost.

Mom caught me off guard when she raised the question of searching for him. I was in fourth year, nearing graduation. The same age she was when she met him.

"Have you ever wanted to know more about him?" She pulled out a tube of lip balm and ran it around and around until there was a thick, globby layer coating her mouth.

"I don't know. I don't need him. He's a stranger, right?" I gazed at her, gauging her reaction. She exhaled and applied another layer of lip balm.

"Well, you never know," she said hesitantly, as though she didn't want to believe her own words, "you might change your mind one day."

"I don't think so, Mom. You've done a great job being a mom and a dad." While my reassuring words were true, I just wasn't ready to risk my durable identity turning flimsy again.

Δ

I helped myself to a glass of milk. Then I cut myself a second slice of cake and carried both to my table. This time I ate slowly, wanting to extend my mealtime.

The murmurings of wait staff and employees arriving for their dinner felt like company. The cafeteria filled in around me, and a group of gardeners claimed the table next to mine. Ruben, the nice older man who mowed the grass in front of my building, beckoned me to join them. Did I look sad, sitting there all alone? I waved back, gesturing that I was finished eating, then left the cafeteria.

Azeez

∞

Satiated by chicken korma and a rum and Coke, I dozed after the movie. Meena had dropped off half an hour before me, her head in her mother's lap. There was little turbulence. I felt safe and lucky and on my way home.

A few hours later, I awoke to a breakfast tray sliding onto my table. My seatmate opened the blind to reveal a pink sunrise. I checked my watch, which I'd already corrected for London time, our next stop. It was just past 6:00 a.m. and I knew we were soaring above the Atlantic, though I couldn't see anything through the blanket of clouds. I rubbed my eyes, relished the fresh pour of steaming chai, and dug into my eggs.

Meena was awake but groggy and picking through her meal at her mother's insistence.

"We'll land in London soon," I told her.

"I know. I'm getting triangle chocolate at the airport." There was a dot of strawberry jam on her chin.

"Triangle chocolate?"

"Toblerone," Meena's mother clarified, and then wiped her daughter's face with a cloth napkin.

"Will you share some with me when we board again?"

"You can buy your own there, too, you know," she said earnestly.

Our trays were cleared and I opened A Passage to India, a novel my supervisor's wife had pulled off her shelf when, after my defence, I'd joked that I didn't want to think about chemistry for the rest of the summer. I laughed at the title and said it would make perfect airplane reading.

I was in the middle of page one when it happened. An enormous boom vibrated through my chest and skull. *A Passage to India* took flight and before I could catch it, I fell forward, my head knocking into the hard plastic of the seat in front of me. Everything turned sideways and I slid down into the aisle and against a man with terrified eyes. I lost control of my bladder, an embarrassing gush of urine soaking through my pants leg. There were yells and screams and prayers and curses. The smell of burning bananas and fear. I craned my neck to look for Meena, but couldn't see her. I hoped she was wearing her seatbelt. Frigid sunshine cracked open the airplane and there was a deafening buzz that killed all other sound.

And then there was a black silence.

I cannot explain it, but the next thing that happened was that there were two of me. Or perhaps I split into two halves. One part drifted upward into the clouds while another fell headlong from the sky. From above, I watched the other body strike the water. Miraculously, I was still breathing, although very broken and numb. There was no pain, no fear, only a peaceful submission. I sank and then the frigid ocean swallowed me, filling my nose and mouth and lungs.

There was a sudden jolt and I knew the end had come. Some part of me left my drowned body and joined the piece that shepherded from above. As we integrated, I felt a floaty euphoric sensation enveloping me. The two of us were one again.

Nothing in my science training could help me comprehend what was happening. I tried to make sense of it, but my brain was anesthetized. Probably for the best.

I watched the others fall to the sea. I recognized the pretty stewardess who had brought me my meals. She'd lost her sari and only her blouse and underskirt fluttered in the wind. There was a man with a bloody gash on his head and a piece of white plastic the size of a platter lodged in his thigh. A girl with arms twisted the wrong way. It was a sorrowful rain shower of bodies falling falling falling.

Dozens became hundreds. Most of us were brown, but some were white. I had a memory of that mattering five minutes earlier, and then the meaning faded. We were all the same in that moment, victims of a heinous calamity none of us yet understood.

Most of the others had left their bodies before they fell to the sea, and they congregated alongside me. We were a mostly subdued audience and together we observed the human wreckage before us. I was grateful for whatever it was that had paralyzed our minds.

I felt a hand in mine and turned to see Meena beside me. She frowned.

"I can't find my Cabbage Patch kid," she whispered.

"It's all right. She'll be fine." I squeezed her hand and we waited for her mother to join us.

Ameera

Δ

If there were a *Chatelaine* quiz on comfort with technology, Mom would have scored as a Paranoid Luddite. She didn't have Internet at home ("I'm on the computer all day long — why would I want to be in front of a screen at night?") and so our conversations were scheduled for Wednesday evenings, just before she left the bank. She closed her office door, wore headphones for additional privacy, and, not wanting any traceable personal correspondence on her work computer, used a laptop. She tapped into the neighbouring Crowne Plaza's free guest Wi-Fi. Our Skype calls had the feel of a covert operation.

Meanwhile, I sat on a couch in the Atlantis lobby where the Wi-Fi signal was reliable. I also used headphones, but only to hear her over the din around me.

"Honey, I only have ten minutes tonight. I'm sorry. I've got to leave soon." Mom adjusted the laptop so that her face was centred in the box on my screen.

"Oh yeah? Where are you going tonight?" Was she wearing blush and eyeshadow? The last time I'd seen her wear that kind of makeup was at my graduation.

"I have a date. Dinner. With a man. Well, of course it's a man," she laughed nervously. "Someone I met on *LifeLove.com*."

"That's great, Mom. How long have you been seeing him?" I'd been encouraging her to try online dating for years, and, back in the fall, I'd walked her through the registration process and helped her craft her profile. I'd nixed "I enjoy quiet evenings at home" and replaced it with "I enjoy films, cooking, and reading." I pressured her to post an attractive photo of herself. She hadn't mentioned the site in a long time and I'd assumed she'd deactivated her account.

"Since mid-January. Well, that's when we began talking online. It's been slow at work," she said sheepishly.

"Mom! Why didn't you say something before? What, that's three months already!"

"Two and half. Oh you know. I didn't want to make something out of nothing. We're only just getting to know one another."

"What's he like?"

"He's owns a plumbing company. He has a good sense of humour. Nice man." She paused, as though she was going to say something else. "But you're looking a little weary. Everything okay on your end?"

"Sure. Nothing new." I looked at my projection in the left hand corner of the screen. A new pimple had emerged on my cheek and my eyes had dark circles.

"Heard anything about the promotion yet?"

"Not yet. Our contracts are up at the end of May, so it'll have to be before then. I'm not too worried about it," I lied. Since the complaint, it was all I worried about. It was a relief to not have heard anything further from Anita.

I steered the conversation back to Mom's date. They'd corresponded by e-mail for two weeks and then spoken on the phone three times before meeting in person. Mom had Googled him to verify that he was indeed a plumber who had his own business. They'd had two coffee dates and this was going to be their second dinner. According to Mom, there hadn't been any "affection" yet.

After we hung up, I reflected on my mother's guardedness — even with me — and how different we were from one another.

Wasn't caution a learned behaviour rather than innate? And then I thought about Azeez. Mom had described my biological father as talkative, inquisitive, open. As I'd done many times before, I wondered if I was anything like him.

Azeez

∞

Three hundred and twenty-nine of us hovered over the ocean, watching the briny water swallow what remained of our bodies. We waited. I still had no physical sensations, but my mind glowed awake like a sunrise.

I think the others were also experiencing a growing awareness. Some of the adults distracted the children so they wouldn't view the gruesome drama below, but Meena told me it wasn't necessary.

"We're spirits. Children no more. Just like you're a man no more." She said this matter-of-factly, as though our demise was a simple and acceptable fact. Why wasn't she bawling her eyes out, having a fit, shaking in fear?

I looked down at my body, realizing that it was an illusion, a placeholder. I really was a man no more. But what else was I? Meena blinked and light glittered through her, a hundred stars filling her. We were still holding hands, but I was the one clinging to her now.

Time passed. Meena's mother made her way through the crowd, bewildered, and we huddled around her. Together we stared at the chunks of metal, bits of fabric, and floating bodies in the churning water below. There was less of it than before, the ocean slowly swallowing the evidence of our existence.

I wondered if my family knew of the crash yet. Would it be on the news? I hoped they'd learn of my death in the comfort of their sitting room rather than within the chaos of the airport's arrivals hall. I couldn't bear the thought of Mummy, Daddy, Nadeem, or Ameera facing that horror in public.

I wanted to go to them but was immobilized by invisible chains. Time and again, I willed myself to travel eastward, but I was rooted, weighed down, the substance of me like a marble statue. The others confirmed that it was happening to them, too. An older lady in our gathering said we were required to stay to the end, to witness everything. Which end? Witness what? I wanted to ask. But I remained quiet.

Helicopters and boats arrived. A fleeting and impossible notion cheered me: we were going to be rescued! Perhaps some of us were alive? But no. It was only our flesh and bone containers that were raised up, recovered. Carried away to safety, too late.

"Look," Meena said calmly, "There. They found me. I mean, the me that I was before."

A sobbing man in uniform dangled from a helicopter. He held Meena's corpse to his chest tightly yet gently, as though she were a living child, his own beloved daughter. He was lifted up and a pair of arms pulled him and his precious cargo inside the chopper. Meena's body was laid down beside others and covered in a blanket, as if being tucked in for the night. The uniformed man wiped his eyes, stepped toward the metal bird's open doors, and leapt out into thin air to continue his work.

I followed the drift of my own body down down down. It was faraway now, miles away, resting at the sandy bottom of the icy sea. I knew it would never be recovered. The deepest despair clutched at me then, and I knew that my family would suffer as a result of never seeing my corpse. It would be more difficult for them to say goodbye, to let go. Meena read my thoughts, and stretched her shape until she was six feet tall and broad like a quarterback. She held me in a long embrace, her form blending into mine, her light becoming my own.

Ameera

Δ

After Skyping with Mom, I collected my mail from the front office. There was an early birthday gift from Malika. The accompanying card read: *Hooray, your Saturn Return is over! (Or over soon!) When are you coming back to the armpit of Ontario? Love, Malika.*

I didn't believe in astrology but did sense a change coming as I neared the end of my twenties. I was ready for a more grown-up life, even if I didn't exactly know what that looked like. I pulled a mixed CD out of the envelope and smiled at Malika's choice of artists, ones she knew I liked from a few years ago: M.I.A., Lykke Li, Santigold, Erykah Badu. She'd written "Fierce Women" on the case. I laughed at the title, but loved that she remembered my birthday.

Also in my mailbox was a brown paper mailer envelope containing a DVD about suburban American swingers, which I'd ordered six weeks earlier.

Back in my room, I put on my headphones and popped the DVD into my laptop. A mostly naked and gleeful sixty-seven-year-old woman climbed into a sling and beckoned her lover over. She was chubby, veiny, wrinkled. In another segment, an eighty-two-year-old man gave a tour of his basement party room where he'd laid out wall-to-wall mattresses for a summer barbeque. There must have been twenty bed-nests.

At first I was shocked that most of the interviewees were senior citizens, but then I understood. They could speak candidly about the lifestyle, allowing the filmmaker into their homes and parties. They no longer harboured concerns about being seen as exemplary employees and parents. I envied them that freedom. I tried my best to watch without my hang-ups about old people having sex interfering. I didn't succeed.

I thought about Jan and Larry then, the couple who had introduced me to "the lifestyle."

It happened on a September evening, four months into my contract. Jan and Larry were in their late thirties, on a second honeymoon, their two kids at home with the grandparents in Edmonton. In hindsight I realized that they'd been courting me for days, lingering at the Oceana kiosk, trailing me on an excursion, offering gluten-free snacks they'd brought from home.

I could tell from their nervous small talk that they were about to ask me something important. Finally, Larry blurted, "Ameera, would you be open to a threesome with us?"

"A threesome?" I didn't know what to say. I studied their expectant expressions and realized that while a surprise, the invitation wasn't unwelcome. I looked into Larry's brown, sincere-looking eyes. I had noticed his developed quad muscles and pot-belly when he'd lazed by the pool and thought he was cute.

"Geez, I hope we haven't offended you," Jan said, laughing. I looked at her intelligent face and smiling green eyes. What would it be like to kiss her mouth? To be naked with her? With them both at the same time?

"No, I'm not … offended. You just caught me off guard," I rushed to explain. "I've never done anything like that before."

On the way to their room, I was so light-headed and awkward that it was all I could do to pay attention to placing one foot before the other. We passed other tourists and a few colleagues I recognized. I stumbled on a stone and fell and scraped my knee. Jan and Larry rushed to help me up and cast worried looks my way.

"Are you sure you want to do this?" Larry asked.

"You look a little pale, sweetie," Jan added.

"I'm fine." A stray idea, light and airy and cautious, drifted in, and I paused to listen to it. *Maybe this is a bad idea.* But then I was overpowered by a sense that what I was about to do, what we were about to do, was important. Pivotal. My body thrummed with a sudden feeling of being *sure*. Few of my decisions had felt like that. I couldn't turn back.

They choreographed the evening so that I could be passive, wide-eyed, a beginner. Jan offered instructions that sounded like suggestions: "Perhaps you'd like to lie between us on the bed? Can I kiss you? Would you like Larry to give you a massage?" Soon, she became more directive, telling me to take off my clothes, undress her husband, how to fellate him. Her take-charge approach was both reassuring and kind of hot.

Later, they told me there was something about me that hinted at open-mindedness, but they didn't reveal what that quality was. They joked about how it was rare to find a "unicorn" — a single woman on the scene. I scoffed at their lingo, insisting that I was neither a swinger nor a unicorn, that I'd just had my once-in-a-lifetime experience.

"Why only once in a lifetime?" Jan asked, eyebrows raised.

"I don't know." I really didn't.

"So ... how'd you end up in the ... scene?" I ventured, borrowing from their vocabulary. As I dressed, they told me that they were from conservative families. After marriage, they'd settled into a pleasant domestic routine filled with shared interests and activities. They had two children. By their tenth anniversary, something was missing. They tried salsa-dancing, rock-climbing, partner massage. Later, they visited adult stores and purchased sex toys. Then one day, Jan saw a newspaper article covering a controversy over a swingers club opening in Calgary.

"I showed him the article, sort of as a lark, but we were both curious. The first time, we went to watch. And then we went back a month later to try soft swings." Jan propped pillows behind her.

"Soft swings?" I pulled on my dress.

"No sex — just fooling around with another couple." Larry grabbed three diet colas from the mini-fridge, passed me one, and said, "You don't have to go so quick. Stay and chat if you're not in a hurry."

I perched awkwardly on the edge of the bed, uncomfortable to be fully clothed while they were still naked.

"Later, we moved on to full swings, which includes sex, mostly swapping, but sometimes the women get together. Once in a while we meet a single lady, but like we said, that's pretty rare," Jan continued, slurping her soda, "And we've also tried open swinging at sex parties, but we're not really into that."

"Orgies," Larry said, in response to my questioning look.

"Oh." I grew warm at the thought of a roomful of writhing bodies. "I bet that's kind of intimidating."

"You know, I'm surprised this is your first time. I hear it's pretty common for people to hook up at resorts. Besides, you're kind of a natural," Larry said, smiling.

"You think there are a lot of swingers at a place like this?" I asked, dodging the compliment. "Aren't they all at Hedonist or Crave?" A colleague had once shared bawdy anecdotes about working at one of those infamous hotels: a guest who'd used an inflatable sex doll as a pool toy, all night naked parties and an unusual number of broken beds.

"You're right, those places are set up for that," Larry said. "But it's so much nicer to meet someone in a low-key place like this."

"You know what I love most about swinging? It gives me a feeling of freedom, while also knowing that Larry is my guy." Jan looked wistfully at Larry.

"It's extracurricular without being extramarital," Larry concurred. They gazed at one another tenderly, Jan's eyes watering. I thought it might be time to say good night, to allow them their moment alone. While I was searching for my sandals, Jan steered me back into bed and Larry pulled down my dress.

When I walked back to my room, my body felt light, yet powerful, like a lioness. My pace slowed, my spine stretched, and my gait lengthened. I looked up at the starry sky and was at home in the humid night. The rush of being with Larry and Jan was akin to the heady chemistry I'd once experienced with Gavin. Since then, that surge of excitement, or a version of it, nearly always accompanied my threesomes.

Alone in my own bed, the high receded and other thoughts flooded in. What would it have been like if Gavin and I had had a ménage a trois? Not that he would have ever gone for such a thing. My mind substituted Enrique for Gavin. I climbed on top of him, my tongue running over sharp bottom teeth. Then Larry was there, his enthusiastic mouth on the back of my neck. Jan made an appearance too, her fingers grabbing my nipples. I pulled out my vibrator before easing into sleep.

Before Jan and Larry left Atlantis, I gave them my e-mail address and we kept in touch. At first, I didn't want to let them go; they were my only touchstones into an experience I knew I needed to repeat. I imagined visiting them in Edmonton, and encouraged them to return to Huatulco. Our e-mail exchanges grew less frequent over time.

I switched off the DVD, placed it in its case and hid it in my bottom dresser drawer along with my swinger books. Would Larry and Jan continue swinging into their retirement years. Would I?

Δ

Oscar bent forward, touched his calves and wobbled for a breath before flinging himself up with acrobatic flourish. Standing tall, he pulled his left thigh snug against his chest, his face contorting into a wince.

"Your back sore again today?" I asked. Oscar nodded grimly and I mumbled sympathy, which only seemed to cause him greater discomfort. I averted my gaze, picked at my cuticles. We were the first to arrive for our Friday shift and I'd already run out of small talk.

He continued his calisthenics and I stared off in the direction of the staff housing, hoping to spot Blythe making her way along the path. I'd been first into the shower that morning and when I knocked on her door, Blythe had told me to go on without her, her voice shrill from a fresh cry. Unsure what to do, I replied with a stupidly upbeat, "See you later, then."

"This damned sciatica," Oscar muttered, breaking the silence, "what kind of injury comes from sitting too much?"

I glanced at the chair he'd brought from home, still folded and awaiting the trip to the airport. I considered asking him about it but refrained; I'd learned long ago that Oscar had his own way of communicating — one that didn't always involve the participation of others.

"*Buenos días,*" Manuela said, striding up to the Oceana desk. "So you brought your chair after all." She made a show of inspecting it carefully.

"*¿Y tú? ¿Donde está tú silla?*" Oscar looked as though he was trying to maintain a straight face. The two of them often talked in a way that made me think they were sharing inside jokes.

"Ha! I don't need to sit." She dismissed him with a flirtatious laugh. Then, turning to me, she said, "Did you know that we burn thirty percent more calories if we work standing up? Sitting is also very bad for the back, right, Oscar?" He didn't answer her.

Manuela was unfailingly on one diet program or other. Sometimes I heeded Manuela's fitness facts; I'd put on a few pounds from eating at the staff buffet, or "the trough," as the English-speakers called it. Lately, I'd found the before and after shots of the dieting ladies in *Chatelaine* and *O* magazine interesting; their transformations, albeit superficial, were gratifying.

Roberto arrived and there was another round of greetings and observations about Oscar's new chair. Roberto unfolded it and tested its comfort while Manuela joked about its daisy and bluebird motif. Oscar pretended to ignore them, and made himself busy sorting through the printouts for the day, dividing them by tour representative. The rest of us joined him, stapling the lists and affixing them to clipboards. When we were finished, we climbed the steps to the lobby, where our vacationers would soon assemble for their departure buses.

"Where's Blythe?" Oscar asked. "She's late."

"I think she had a rough night," I said. Oscar strode ahead of us. Manuela gave me a sideways glance, and mouthed "Rhi-on?"

"I think they had another fight," I whispered to her. She pursed her lips.

In the lobby, a few dozen people milled about or stood in lines, having just checked out of Atlantis. Their luggage was in tidy rows, holding spots for owners who wanted to ensure a good seat on the bus. The guests were seamlessly re-entering the world of timetables and queues after a week without them. How long would it take me to return to my normal routines when I went home to Canada? I imagined my old self waiting for me at the Toronto airport, wearing a limo driver's uniform and holding a handwritten sign bearing my name. Would I wave and identify myself, or would I dodge her and disappear out the revolving doors?

My mind travelled to the Mumbai airport. I blended into the crowd, a chameleon amongst people who looked like me. I had my itinerary planned: Mumbai, Delhi, Agra, Jaipur, Kolkata,

Goa. Perhaps I'd search for Azeez, surprise him on his doorstep with a grand announcement. It would be like in a made-for-TV-movie: he'd be shocked at first, but then we'd stare into each other's eyes and recognize one another as family. He'd remember my mother. "Oh, yes, Nora. She made an impression. She was hard to forget," he'd say in a half-whisper.

A feeling of déjà vu crept over me and I realized that I'd dreamt that scene two nights before. Only in my dream, he'd invited me into his home and then vanished. I searched all through his empty apartment, each room opening up into another and another until I was too disoriented to find the exit.

My daydreaming was soon interrupted by tourists encircling like wild monkeys sniffing out a fresh picnic. Questions fluttered through the lobby, drifted up to the vaulted ceiling, creating a babble:

When does the airport bus arrive?

Where do we line up?

Is there food at the airport? Do we have to pay for it?

Can I still get a last-minute drink at the bar even though they've cut off my resort bracelet?

Hey, I tried to get a hot dog and they said I couldn't!

I'd learned to speak softly to vacationers in their final hour at Atlantis. Their resort bracelets, plastic umbilical cords, had been severed only moments earlier, and no longer provided security and sustenance. We soothed our guests then directed them to form new queues.

Blythe appeared ten minutes before the buses were scheduled to leave, announcing that "tummy troubles, nothing serious" had delayed her. She didn't meet my eyes, picked up a clipboard, and disappeared into the crowd.

We packed our charges onto the refrigerated buses. When we reached the airport, the guests were once again placated and directed to form new queues. Finally, the last tourist beeped through the security lines, and a DC-8 prepared to land, the rumble of its engine droning closer.

Blythe took my arm, her sweaty hand leaving a damp spot on my elbow. When we were inside the terminal and just out of the others' sight lines, she stopped. I was expecting her to disclose something about Rhion and her earlier upset.

"I spoke with Anita yesterday. She said that she wanted to discuss my interest in leadership positions within Oceana. Has she called you yet?"

"No," I admitted, disappointment welling in my stomach. Why hadn't Anita called *me*? A policeman with two guns on his belt walked by, leering at Blythe.

"I'm sure she will. Anyway, she asked me about you, in a sideways sort of way." Blythe's eyes roved over my face, her black mascara clumpy. "She asked if the women staff get harassed by the male tourists. I said I hadn't experienced anything unusual. Then she specifically asked if I was aware of that happening to you."

"What did you say?" My voice pitched higher than I wanted.

"That you hadn't mentioned anything, but sometimes in general, with all the drinking around here it wouldn't be all that unusual for a guy to go a little too far. And you're a pretty girl and all, so you get hit on. Then she asked if you're good at handling all that attention. I told her you seemed to be." I could smell peppermint, syrupy and strong, on her breath.

"That's weird." I raised my eyebrows in the direction of the cop who was still nearby. He was now staring at me. Blythe and I walked toward the washroom to avoid his gaze.

"Has something happened? Has someone been harassing you?" She rubbed my back in an efficient nurse sort of way.

"No. I have no idea why she's asking so many questions."

"Well, I thought I'd tell you, so you were aware." Blythe went into a cubicle and I listened to her pee.

My heart beat too fast. My brain fogged. I breathed deeply, then focused on my reflection in the mirror. *Don't worry. Don't worry*, whistled through my mind. Blythe flushed and I left the bathroom before her.

I pushed through the terminal doors, welcoming the hot outdoor air after the chill inside. I troubled over Blythe's words, knowing that Anita was investigating the complaint after all. Would Blythe's responses have calmed her misgivings?

Back at the kiosk, Oscar pulled out his new chair and dramatically unfolded it. He sat regally with a self-satisfied grunt. Although Roberto chuckled, and Manuela rolled her eyes, neither said anything. Oscar folded his arms behind his head and exhaled.

"Now this is the life," Oscar sighed, seeming to have paradoxically found relief from his back pain for the first time that day.

I hunkered down onto the plastic file box and brooded.

Azeez

∞

Soon after the crash, they told me I would reincarnate to "the next place" when I was ready.

"They" are difficult to describe; those who guided me didn't tell me their names or show me their physical form. They were wily that way. They came in a gyre of whispers and spoke in metaphors, riddles, lullabies.

In those early days, I didn't know who I was or how to behave. I was a meandering whoosh of energy, a confused swirl of light. I still had a sense of myself as Azeez — the son, brother, teacher, and student — but all of those identities soon became superfluous. I requested instructions, hoped for directives, but my guides left me alone to decipher their cryptic clues.

They told me they'd been accompanying me for two and a half centuries — in the last existence and the three previous ones. I asked them about those other lives; I believed that an enlightened view of the past would make clear the future. I'm a linear thinker, I suppose.

When I was alive, I would have said all this was nutty hogwash for hippies. I wouldn't have even expected Max and Jonathan to believe it.

The guides said the "in-between" place was a time to repay debts to loved ones.

Which specific love ones?

You'll know when you know.

But how many years will that take? I sputtered, growing impatient with their non-answers.

What, you have somewhere to be? They thought it was hilarious that I still had a sense of time.

I laughed at their ribbing and yet there was discomfort in my uncertainty. I watched for signs, tried to make sense of the guides' perplexing messages. I hoped I was on the right path.

Sticking close to my family seemed correct. And so I lingered in India. Perhaps it was my preparation, my training ground, for what I'd ultimately need to do.

Ameera

Δ

I was lost inside a maze of narrow hallways. Every wooden door I encountered was locked. Each was identical to the next and I grew confused about which doorknob I'd already twisted. The air grew musty and I longed for a breeze. Just when I began to lose hope of finding a way out of my father's house, the hallway widened into a large, airy living room. He sat on a green divan, a look of expectation on his face.

"I have so much to tell you," he said.

And then I awoke, sweaty and breathless. Blythe shower-sang, belting out the depressing lyrics to Adele's "Rolling in the Deep." I'd listened to her through two of my four breakups with Gavin and didn't want a miserable ear worm following me around all day.

I plugged my ears and the dream slipped back. I concentrated hard to recall my father's face, but it was faded like an old photograph. He'd said something just before I'd woken, but I couldn't conjure the words. This was the second time I'd had a dream like that about my biological father. I suppose it made sense; I'd recently talked about him with the Italians and then Manuela.

I hoisted myself out of bed and arranged my clothes for the day, glad to not be hung over that Saturday morning. Enrique had filled my travel mug with his version of sangria, but the mix had been too sweet and I'd dumped most of it down the sink. Sober, I'd fretted over Blythe's report on Anita's call and had managed to gain some perspective: Anita had sought reassurance from Blythe. Blythe had been decent enough to say the right things and to share the conversation with me. Things could be worse.

I needed a strategy to remind Anita that I was leadership material. I'd been mulling over a new excursion to Playa Escondido, a leftie community up the coast, after I'd gone there on my last vacation. I'd send her a proposal about it to show some initiative. The lock on my side of the bathroom clicked open and I entered the humid bathroom, humming Blythe's borrowed song.

I chose coffee and a danish over punctuality and arrived at orientation twenty minutes late. Blythe had just finished her opening games and she and Oscar were reviewing resort information. A guest near the back of the assembly turned, gazed at me, and raised her hand in a half-hearted wave. I donned my friendly tour rep expression and returned the gesture.

"Atlantis has three gourmet restaurants in addition to the main buffet," Oscar informed the group.

"Manuela, who's that woman over there? You know, the one in with the purple tank top? Third row from the back?" As though sensing she was being talked about, the woman glanced over her shoulder.

"Hmm, let me see. I think she was on my bus." Manuela sorted the pages on her clipboard.

"… each has a unique menu and is distinct from one another. Bring us your three green chits to make reservations." The microphone emitted a sonic squeal, as though protesting the lie; all the food was cooked in the same kitchen. Roberto rushed to the stage to adjust the amplifier.

"Oh, there she is," Manuela replied. "She's a repeat. Suzanne Elton. She told me she came here a year and a half ago."

"Hmm." A vague disquiet scratched at me.

"She's here with Todd Hewitt — the reservation is under his name."

I was still drawing a blank. Suzanne Elton put her arm around Todd Hewitt and whispered something in his ear. Manuela nudged me and we left with Roberto for the kiosk.

An hour later, I'd surpassed my sales quota, selling eight crocodile-and-turtle combos, five waterfalls, and four shopping excursions. Buoyed by my productivity and the knowledge that Anita would notice, I offered to close up the desk so my colleagues could go for lunch. I was locking the cash drawer when Suzanne approached.

"Hey there. Remember me? I was here last fall? My hair was brown and long back then," she said, cocking her head to the left and fluffing her short blond bob with her fingers. She rambled on nervously about how she'd been at Atlantis with her ex-husband, and they'd split up soon after. It wasn't unusual for Atlantis couples to tote marital discord with them on vacation. Many booked trips to rekindle romance and perhaps for some, the spark renewed. I suspected that for most of the unhappy pairs, a week together in a small hotel room was like being trapped in a burning building, smoke slowly wafting under the door.

Then I noticed the dolphin tattoo on her right bicep. *Doug and Suzanne McKay from Saskatoon.* I reflexively stepped away from her.

"Well, I wanted to tell you that I don't have any hard feelings about it all. We had that big fight at the airport — you probably heard — your colleague had to break it up. That guy over there," Suzanne said, pointing at Roberto's back. He was halfway down the hall, on his way to the cafeteria.

"Really? I didn't hear about that." Why hadn't anyone told me?

"We made kind of a scene. At the time I was pissed off, but it wasn't your fault — our relationship had been in a bad place for a long time already." I studied Suzanne's confusing appearance. She wore a plastic smile that barely disguised her anxiety.

"I see." Why was she telling me all of this? Why was she back at Atlantis?

As though sensing my questions, she continued on, "I never thought I'd be back at this resort after what happened, but then Todd — that's my new boyfriend — he bought this trip for me as a thirty-fifth-birthday present. Later he tried to change the booking for me, but it didn't work out. Well, I guess there's probably a reason the universe brought me here," Suzanne said. I nodded, my stomach lurching in alarm, despite her cordial tone.

Δ

I'd thought Suzanne was the more attractive of the pair, but it was Doug who'd unexpectedly charmed me. I liked his deep voice and the way his eyes widened with curiosity when I spoke to him. Suzanne was quiet. She just seemed shy to me.

Suzanne scrambled off the bed, and I paused from kissing Doug to see where she was going. She pulled on a T-shirt and pair of shorts. Doug shrugged and smiled apologetically, saying, "It's okay, that's how Suz is." I nodded, closed my eyes, hoping that everything was fine, ignoring the small voice in my head telling me otherwise.

His body was large, bear-like, covered in thick brown hair. I lay on my back, and allowed his furry weight to smother me and it was like my skin was disappearing into the heat of his. I inhaled; under his sweat was a hint of his cologne, a trace of bergamot. He rolled me on top of him and I allowed myself to be swept up in the motion, feeling secure in his arms. *You're extraordinary*, he'd said, and I'd wanted to believe it. I forgot all about his spouse who'd left in the middle of what was supposed to be a three-way.

Half an hour later, he wanted to spank me and I agreed. I'd never before been positioned so formally and I felt thrillingly off-balance on his lap. He smacked me, gently at first and then more forcefully. Heat spread across my bottom, the slaps stinging crimson and travelling deep inside me. I squirmed and he held me more tightly. When the heat turned to something that felt more like pain, I was unsure whether I liked it, but I allowed him to continue, feeling him stiffen under my thighs.

The next day I was inexplicably bereft. I'd had many one-night stands with couples by then and they'd tended to leave me uplifted, feeling desired, perhaps even a little smug. But that morning I moped and my thoughts roved in jealous loops: Doug would head home to Saskatoon with his wife. They'd carry on their wonderful life together. They'd pick up their two cats and border collie from the kennel on their way to the house. Maybe they'd order takeout from Ho Lee Chow. Meanwhile, I would be welcoming another planeload of guests who'd stay a week and then leave again. A senseless thought-chain materialized and linked to the first: why couldn't he stay here with me?

I avoided them at the airport by staying out of the terminal, offering instead to manage the queue outside. Roberto, happy to get out of the heat, took my post inside.

I spent the next few days consulting *Opening Up*, a book on non-monogamy that I'd ordered online but hadn't yet started reading. I focused on the chapters about jealousy, a murky emotion I didn't like. After a week, I felt better and could view the grief that had gripped me as odd sentimentality. My experience with Doug had been a rare moment of connection with a stranger. I wasn't sure how real it was or whether I wanted it to repeat. Like all the other guests I'd never see again, I resolved to let the McKays go, to winch up their anchor and set them adrift from my mind. I assumed they'd do they same with me.

Δ

And now Suzanne was back, albeit with a different man and a new hairdo.

I looked for Roberto in the staff cafeteria, questions crowding my mind. Normally, a spectacle like the one Suzanne and Doug had created at the airport would have been fodder for a good story. Roberto might have acted out each of Doug and Suzanne's parts, mimicking their voices and gestures while the others laughed, shaking their heads at the ridiculousness of vacationers. But Roberto hadn't shared the story, at least not with me, and possibly not with the others. Had he known they were arguing about me?

I found him scooping french fries from a metal platter. I lifted a plate from a tall warm stack that smelled like bleach. "There's pizza today," he pointed out.

I wasn't hungry but I helped myself to a slice and tailed him to the salad bar. I filled a bowl with lettuce, macaroni, and *nopales*. He drizzled Thousand Island dressing over his fries.

"Hey Roberto, funny story: there's a woman named Suzanne who was here over a year ago with her husband. She said they'd had a big fight at the airport and you had to break it up?" I tried to deliver the question like a joke.

"Really?" He chose a single cucumber slice from a platter and chewed it contemplatively.

"Yeah, she's short and used to have long brown hair and her husband was kind of a big guy? They made a scene, apparently," I chuckled but watched his face closely. He stroked his moustache and then his jaw tightened.

"Oh yeah. I think I remember them."

"Do you happen to remember what they were fighting about?" I held tightly to my plate.

"Well, it was hard to know exactly, with all the yelling ..." He walked toward the dining hall and I followed closely behind.

"Suzanne is back here. She said this weird thing ... that sounded like I might have been the cause of their argument. But I have no idea why." I chose a table far from the rest of our colleagues and motioned for him to sit. He hesitated, but took the chair across from me.

"Yeah. She was mad at you about something ... I think she was accusing him of cheating on her ... with you." He picked up his fork and fiddled with it.

"Why didn't you mention it to me? Did any of the other reps hear what she was saying?" I glanced over my shoulder. The cafeteria had filled and a wall of noise surrounded us.

"We were very busy that day. I think that was the same day that guy lost his passport? Blythe and Manuela had to go help him. Oscar was with me." He spiked five goopy fries with his fork.

"Did Oscar hear the argument?" Sweat prickled my armpits.

"Maybe, but he was occupied. When he asked, I told him it was a marital problem."

"The truth is ... there was sort of a miscommunication between them and well, Suzanne got upset. They ... they had an open relationship and ..." I blundered, realizing I was saying too much. "Anyway nothing happened, there was no cheating."

"Well, that's good. I didn't say anything because I didn't want to start rumours." He shoved another forkful of fries into his mouth, keeping his eyes on his food.

"Yeah, and it's so funny. Today, Suzanne sort of apologized for all the fuss." I forced a laugh, but it came out more like a gasp. "I hadn't even heard about it, so that's why I thought I'd ask you."

"Well, good. It all ended okay, then."

Just then, Joana, a clerk from the front desk, sat beside us and we nodded our greetings.

"Yes!" I said, forcing cheer into my voice. "Tourists are funny, eh?"

Azeez

∞

I sought comfort from dead relatives who came to claim me a few days after my death. They were a small delegation: my favourite grand-uncle and my paternal great-grandmother, who'd passed on before I was born. I had a hundred questions for this spectral pair, but they silenced me before I could ask a single one. *Wait. Fikhar nhai. Don't worry. You'll understand soon. Stay with your family for now,* they advised. And I complied because I didn't know what else to do.

Can I communicate with them?

You can try.

How?

There was no answer.

A colour television had replaced our old black-and-white. Mummy cried silent tears while the Canadian prime minister, Brian Mulroney, sombrely offered condolences to the Indian government and people. Ameera stroked Mummy's back and frowned. I leaned into my sister and squeezed her tightly, but she didn't register my touch. She turned in my direction and sighed loudly. Did she sense my presence? I inhaled the garlic on her breath, the oil in her hair. But something else happened, too. As I breathed her in, I detected her thoughts. The air she exhaled carried her words.

I heard her wondering about the politician's strange accent.

His sad eyes distracted her. She turned away from me, and I no longer could hear her. She held on to Mummy, and concentrated on the news.

I scrambled closer, pushed my face into hers. She bit her lip and exhaled into my face. There it was again! Her thoughts spilled out: *Why is this man offering us his condolences? Weren't most of the victims Canadians? And what good are his condolences anyway? They won't bring back Azeez.* I looked at Mummy to see if she'd heard, but she didn't react to Ameera's words.

I'm here! I'm still with you! I laughed with relief. I could talk to Ameera! But she stared blankly at the television. I yelled my words into her ear thrice more. Still nothing.

I fell back and sat on the opposite end of the room. The thought-listening had sapped my energy. How did it all work, anyway?

The newscaster reported the facts. *Worst airline tragedy in history. Three hundred and twenty-nine deaths. Two baggage handlers at Narita Airport killed in an incident thought to be a related event.* Gruesome images from the previous day flashed over the screen. Hunks of metal floated in the ocean. Rescue workers lifted corpses from the sea into helicopters. I didn't want to watch the instant replay, but couldn't stop myself. Mummy tilted forward, shaking Ameera off.

"He's going to make it. He knows swimming. They'll find him," she said, resolutely.

"No, Mummy. No one survived." Ameera's voice was deadpan, her eyes wide and vacant.

"He will make it. He has to," Mummy insisted. I went to her side and lingered near her mouth. Her anxiety was a thousand bees swarming in my head.

It's okay, Mummy! Don't worry! Everything is all right! I concentrated hard, imagining myself capable of telepathy. Once again I realized I was not.

"Why is this happening to us? Why have they taken my boy?" she wailed.

Δ

Daddy and Nadeem had left that morning on a flight to Cork, the city nearest to the crash site. Travel turned out to be simpler for me than communication. I could concentrate on their essence, will myself to their approximate destination and be there within moments. It took some sleuthing to find the hospital, which had transformed itself into a morgue. Cork had become a city of death.

I caught up with them outside. They were among a cluster of mourners who resembled them in their numb grief. Their coats were thin and the damp seeped through to their skin. Daddy's face was stern, Nadeem's desolate. When I drew close to Daddy to gather his exhalations I heard him think: *Walk only. One step at a time. No crying in front of Nadeem.*

A representative from the Indian Consulate, a middle-aged and efficient man, looked to be the only person who wasn't disoriented. He shuttled the few Indian families past kind-looking staff and bright white walls. Everything smelled of antiseptic and fear. He handed them a clipboard and pen and Nadeem and Daddy huddled to complete a form with my particulars — my age, height, weight, eye and hair colour. A memory of me leaving India puffed out of Nadeem. He recalled my nervous smile as I said goodbye. He wondered about my life in Canada: *Was Azeez happy? Did he get to have adventures there? Such a short life. No, don't cry in front of Daddy. He's barely keeping it together.*

I patted Nadeem's back and yelled into his ear: *I was happy. Oh! There are so many things I want to share with you about Canada! It was wonderful to be away and independent. I loved school, loved teaching. But it was also lonely. I missed you all so much.* As I rambled on, I realized my words were lost on him.

The consular staff collected the form and directed them to a waiting area. A woman in a sari demanded, "Where is the Canadian representative? Who is here to help us?" A number of people murmured and nodded. The Indian consulate man reassured them that help was on its way, but his bureaucratic voice crackled with uncertainty. Nothing in his fourteen-year career had prepared him for his tasks that day.

Later, Daddy and Nadeem were shown mug shots of the recovered bodies, wall after wall of them. Women, men, children. How did they bear the torture? More than a hundred ghostly faces stared back. The frozen expressions of shock and dread imprinted in their minds and it would take years for them to unremember them.

They found no trace of me. It was like I didn't exist, had never been on the flight. Daddy could almost imagine that if he phoned my house, my roommate Max might answer then pass the receiver over to me, as he'd done for years. Except that Nadeem had phoned earlier that day, and Max had told him I'd moved out.

"Was he on ... that plane?" Max only made the connection when he heard my brother's mournful voice. Although he'd heard about the crash in the news — there had been a great deal of coverage — a thin layer of detachment and denial had allowed him to imagine that I'd been on a different flight.

At first, Nadeem and Daddy watched with pity as other families found the bodies of their relations. They offered condolences and silent prayers to a God who'd betrayed them. As the day wore on, their pity turned to envy. But there were many others like them who wouldn't find tangible evidence of what they'd lost. The Indian consulate man informed them that almost two hundred bodies had not yet been retrieved.

"Perhaps it's for the best you didn't have to see him that way, no?" He was doing his best.

Daddy, a very polite and mild-mannered man in nearly every

situation sighed deeply and exhaled this silent thought: *Shut up you! Just shut up! Everyone shut up!* I pressed his shoulders, but they remained rigid.

They stayed on in Cork for another two days, visiting the hospital until they were told there was no point. On their last day, a little Irish girl stopped them in the drizzle. Her mother prodded her to give them the bouquet of flowers she clasped with both hands. Daddy dropped to his knees to accept the lilies and the wet of the pavement left behind two circles, like sloppily sewn patches, on his pants. He stared deeply into the girl's green eyes. She touched his elbow and he imagined he thought he saw light shining through her and into him. It was the first time since the bad news that he allowed himself to weep.

But who left him at the airport? How do we really know he was on the flight? Daddy's thoughts would befuddle him for months after. Like Mummy, he harboured a faint hope that I'd survived. Perhaps I'd booked in but never boarded. It was all some awful mistake and one day I'd turn up, having had an irresponsible jaunt through Europe or Thailand, my many postcards delayed in the post.

Ameera and Nadeem didn't hold such delusions. Both told their friends they'd felt a gnawing absence in their hearts when they'd first heard of the crash. They were patient with our parents, gently reasoning with them to accept my death. With their lives mostly ahead of them, they could manage these emotional gymnastics. They absorbed the lesson that life is short, fragile, and random, and continued living in a way my parents would never be able to do.

Hour after hour, day after day, I tried to offer my parents calming thoughts. But it was a futile exercise; I could listen to their misery, but couldn't transmit peace back.

Daddy found a measure of happiness after Ameera had her first child, two years later. Little Nafeesa became his singular focus, and he poured his energies into buying her small gifts, picking her up from preschool, and teaching her how to read. She became the life force he needed to go on.

Mummy, too, tried to move forward, but a part of her believed that a cosmic joke had been played on her, and life itself became an untrustworthy venture. She'd never been happy with my studying abroad and she'd anticipated our reunion with relief and joy. It had been so close. So close. For years she asked herself: *why didn't I push him to come home sooner? If only he'd returned a week earlier, a day earlier ...*

Ameera

Δ

I couldn't eat after talking with Roberto, so I returned, alone, to the tour desk. I wondered whether Suzanne was telling the truth about why she was back at Atlantis. Was her appearance as random as she said? Of course, I mentally linked her with the complaint, even though that made no sense.

And what about Roberto's uncharacteristic omission about Suzanne and Doug? How had he really interpreted the argument at the airport? I knew that I'd made a sketchy impression on him early on; he'd countless times heard me coming home at dawn, back when he'd lived across the hall from me in the staff residence. He'd witnessed a few bad brushes with single male tourists, a category of dates I'd learned to avoid after my first year at the resort.

Δ

The most memorable was Brandon, this pathetic dude from Niagara whose girlfriend had broken up with him five days before the trip, and rather than forfeit the romantic vacation, he'd travelled to Atlantis alone. My sympathy for him led to a night of dull sex and his weepy relationship revelations. I rejected his subsequent advances but he persisted for the next two days, following me around the resort like an abandoned puppy, moping and perpetually underfoot. On his fifth night, he declared his sad, drunken devotion to me at the bar, howling that I'd broken his heart. His vision was blurry with booze and love-sickness and I knew he was projecting his girlfriend's face onto mine, but wow, was he a pain. I pretended I didn't know Brandon and Roberto threw him out of the bar. Later, Roberto had to evict him from the staff residence when Brandon followed me back there.

I liked to think myself wary and wise, the sort of person who learned from my mistakes. After Brandon, I set a rule to never again sleep with a tourist unless he was nearing the end of the vacation, lest he turned stalker. It seemed a good solution, but then there was the Wednesday-night guy who went on a Thursday scuba trip, and told everyone on the boat ride how insatiable I was, even though I'd spent a total of thirty-four minutes in his room. I knew, because I'd watched the clock radio digitally turn time. The scuba instructor passed the word to Maria the Cardio Pump teacher, who told nearly everyone else.

The worst part was that the gossip reached Oscar's ears, and he berated me in front of my colleagues.

"Your behaviour gives us all a bad name. You are like the recreation staff!" Oscar's nose wrinkled and his lips receded to expose his yellowed front teeth. He was referring to the *male* recreation staff, resort playboys, who prowled the disco on arrivals night, choosing a woman with whom they'd spend the week, romancing them with moonlight walks on the beach, trips to local bars, and stolen kisses by the pool. On departure day, there were teary goodbyes, addresses exchanged and velvet declarations of *"te quiero, te amo."* Week after week, new women, new declarations.

"Oh come on, it's not Ameera's fault the tourists are such bastards," Blythe countered, in a show of solidarity. She was often the target of lechy attention.

"Oceana tour reps must not stoop to that level," Oscar continued, his finger wagging too close to my face.

"Oscar, that's enough," Manuela jumped in. Roberto didn't come to my defence, but his gaze was intense, as though seeing me for the first time.

An angry shame whirled through me, a tornado I hadn't felt since that night with Gavin in Hamilton. With my friends, I'd tried to explain and apologize and then escaped to Mexico, but with Oscar, I went mute, refusing to speak to him for two weeks. When communication was necessary, we relied on Roberto and Manuela as go-betweens. Eventually, Manuela interceded, conveying to me how hard-won Oscar's position was; he'd risen through the tourism ranks from wait staff, to bus driver, and now held the highly coveted and secure position of tour rep.

"But he was so condescending. Not to mention sexist!" I'd pouted.

"Maybe you don't understand, coming from Canada. I know you were only having fun. But we have to be careful. It's not as easy for us to get these jobs. Oscar feels protective of our status." I considered Manuela's words. Oceana was a filler between my previous job and the one that would come next. Although my ambitions had changed since news of the promotion, back then I hadn't been negotiating an industry hierarchy or building a career the way my Mexican colleagues were. I had just been enjoying myself with the tourist men, taking advantage of their seemingly complication-free and temporary affections.

"Okay." I sighed, uncertain about my role in the brewing conflict. My fury receded, the storm becoming a dusty wind.

Gradually, I made efforts to be polite with Oscar, and he, too, became easier to tolerate. I knew that Manuela had likely directed an intervention his way, too. *Ameera's a stranger here, all alone, no family*, she might have said to him.

I further revised my dating rules and gave up single tourist men altogether. I limited sex to swinger couples on Thursday nights. Nothing had gone wrong in the previous two years, not until Suzanne and Doug.

Δ

Back at the desk, Oscar set up his cash drawer. His expression was blank and I assumed that Roberto hadn't told him about Suzanne and Doug. A couple approached and I watched him outline the list of excursions we had on offer. He was trying too hard, his sales pitch too direct, almost bossy. The tourists listened politely and then wandered off without making a purchase. When Manuela, Blythe, and Roberto returned to the kiosk together, irrational thoughts swept over me. Had they been talking about Suzanne and Doug and me? I excused myself, telling them I was taking a washroom break.

Maybe I was weird. Was it normal to prefer sex with two people? Why didn't one person feel as satisfying? Would I ever find a partner who would tolerate the lifestyle? I trudged around the resort, noticing couples walking hand in hand, pairs splashing in the pool. I was single and lonely and a bit of a freak. Jan and Larry's words echoed in my mind: *free and secure*. Did I feel that way? Free, yes. But secure? Hardly. Sometimes I wished I could be part of a swinger couple, rather than the singleton walking home alone.

In the bathroom, I slammed the cubicle door behind me and sat on the toilet. I closed my eyes and slowed my breathing. Two women entered, their sandals flapping against the tile floor. There was flushing. Water running. Paper towels crumpling. My mind's rapid circling eased and I heard feather-light words stroking my brain: *You're going to be fine. It will be all right.* They repeated a few more times, took on a kind of slow melody, like a hymn. It lulled me to calm. I felt proud of myself; I'd never been very good at O magazine-style self-talk before.

As I turned on the tap to wash my hands, Suzanne startled me at a neighbouring sink. I smiled tersely at her reflection and she returned the fake smile. Once again, I flooded myself with the *It will be all right* song. I crossed the room to dry my hands, and glanced at Suzanne's back. Her curves filled out her lemon-sorbet bikini and her pale back was rosy from a fresh burn. A patch of sand clung resolutely to her left calf.

I flashed to an image of her lying on a bed. Doug and I were making out on a couch while Suzanne watched. Sensing her awkwardness, I went to her and unbuttoned her top. Her skin was goose pimpled despite the heat. I traced the lines of her dolphin tattoo.

"I was nineteen and stupid." She shivered when I ran my hand down her arm.

I kissed her lips, neck, and throat and she let me. Still, I sensed her hesitancy. Doug joined us on the bed, and it was shortly after that when Suzanne left the room.

What boundaries had we crossed that night?

When I turned around, she was gone.

I tossed my paper towel into the garbage and wondered: And what about Doug? Had he, too, moved on to another partner? Was he still in Saskatoon?

Did he ever think about me?

Azeez

∞

"Who called last night?" Daddy asked Mummy. I'd heard the phone ring once, right after everyone had retired to bed. I'd been listening to Nadeem's cerebral dreams about a complicated legal case he was working on that week.

"An administrator from Azeez's university. She asked if he was home. I said 'no.'"

"You didn't say he died?"

"No, I wasn't thinking. I was half asleep. It was midnight!" She looked flustered, and I realized that she'd woken in a panic, expecting bad news. Again.

"Do you think it was anything important?"

"His tuition is paid up. It's been over two months since he … they'll call again if there is a problem." Mummy shook her head. She didn't want to think about Canada anymore.

Another call came the following day. Jaya, our servant, didn't speak much English. She told Daddy that a girl had phoned.

A girl! I recalled the way I used to grow nervous when Anjali, one of the girls I'd briefly dated, had telephoned. To avoid parental censure, we maintained a flimsy facade of being classmates.

"Was it local, or long distance?" He asked her in Gujarati. She didn't know for sure, but she thought the call came from far away. "What did you tell her?"

"Azeez is gone. Not here anymore." I listened to Jaya's exhalations and heard her embarrassment, her desire to be less clumsy with her English words.

Assuming that it was a second call from the university, Daddy had his secretary draft a fax to the Office of Graduate Studies at McMaster University, notifying them of my death. He requested that they send any outstanding fees or notices to his work address. It was already well past the forty days of mourning and he didn't want his family to be bothered again.

Like my father, I guessed these calls were administrative in nature, but I wondered whether my university acquaintances knew of my death. While sociable with many, I was close to few in Hamilton, and my best friend, Abbas, a Pakistani biologist, had flown home a few weeks before me. I'd said my farewells to my professors, cohort, and students when we'd had celebratory drinks after my defence. They were aware I was leaving that summer, but only my roommates and family knew my exact departure date. I expected that most of my McMaster colleagues wouldn't draw a connection between the Air India bombing and me.

Ameera

Δ

My colleagues carried on with their casual banter and sales pitches. I relaxed into the afternoon routine, realizing that Roberto had remained mum about Suzanne. The lines thinned at the tour desk, and Blythe, Manuela, and Roberto, already over quota, took advantage of the early quit time and left mid-afternoon. Only Oscar remained, saying he could use more sales.

I checked e-mail, holding my breath while the messages loaded. Anita hadn't sent a follow-up about the complaint and I was tempted to check in. But what would I say? I didn't want to place Blythe in a difficult position by revealing our conversation. At the same time, I wanted confirmation that the issue was closed.

I spent an hour drafting a proposal about a new Playa Escondido excursion, suggesting that we offer it on Wednesday mornings as a full day trip with shopping and beach time. I provided two options for potential restaurant partners. Feeling pleased with myself, I did a final spell check.

As I hit Send, a message from Mom landed in my inbox.

Dear Ameera,
    I've sent you something for your birthday —
can you let me know if it's arrived? I was a little
late getting it in the mail — my apologies.

That was weird. It was not in my mother's character to be tardy for anything.

> I'd like to Skype Sunday (tomorrow) morning to say Happy Birthday "in person" — let me know what's a good time. I'll be having brunch at Victor's place and can use his computer (he's the man I told you about) so can you add his account — VictorManning?

So, Victor was his name! Mom wouldn't have offered the detail unless things were serious between them.

> I'm enjoying his company. He is a smoker, though — just a few a day — but still, and I'm not sure I like that, but otherwise it's going well.

Aha! She'd found something to fuss about. Smoking was a biggie. I smoked occasionally in Hamilton, and once she saw me bumming a cigarette while standing outside a bar. She lectured me for months about the dangers of tobacco addiction.

> Talk soon.
> Love, Mom.

I wrote back, "I miss you." I meant it.

Δ

"*¡Feliz cumpleaños!*" Manuela cheered when I arrived at her door the following evening, "How does it feel to be twenty-nine?"

How to answer this without being a downer? "Same as twenty-eight, I guess?" Every birthday, I couldn't help but assessing how close — really, how far — I was from achieving the things that marked one as a successful adult. I was certain I still had quite a distance to go.

Manuela's mother, Sara, and her father José, welcomed me. Manuela's sisters, Rosa and Giselle, ambled into the living room to wish me happy birthday. The Méndez daughters all closely resembled their mother. When I first met them, they were standing in a row, and I joked that they resembled a Ukrainian Matrushka doll set, each wearing a dress size slightly larger than the next in line. Their mother was now the smallest of the nesting dolls, having shrunken with age and a recent switch to a mostly vegetarian diet to counteract her high cholesterol.

Eating with the Méndez family was both comforting and unfamiliar. Family dinners growing up were just Mom and me, with the exception of infrequent visits by my grandparents. After I moved out on my own at twenty-four, we usually met once a week at a restaurant. At the Méndezes', I was a temporary fourth daughter. I listened to the girls' bickering, laughed at their jokes when they were translated, and was their consultant when they had a minor disagreement. Did I like Giselle's new hairstyle? Rosa wanted to quit her studies at the local business college. As a university graduate what did I think of that?

I wasn't much of a birthday person, but Manuela had insisted that I spend my previous two with her family. They set an extra place for me at Christmas and Easter as well, effortlessly including me at their crowded dining table. Sara always made *guisado de calabaza*, a squash stew, ever since she'd witnessed me almost licking my bowl the first time I was their guest. That night there was also rice and beans, barbequed steak, and chocolate cake baked by Manuela.

At home, I'd trained my mom and friends to be low key. When I told them, "No cake! No gifts," they mostly obeyed. But there was no resisting the blow-out-your-candles-thing at the Méndez house. I held my breath while they clapped their hands and sang *"Feliz Cumpleaños,"* grinning plastically. My face grew hot from the flames and their attention.

I closed my eyes and pondered the wish I'd make. The supervisor position? A fun swinger couple later that week? I settled on the first, opened my eyes and stared at the cake's white icing while I waited for them to finish the last verse.

The singing stopped, and Manuela said, "Come on, blow them out!" I took in a breath and I thought I heard someone behind me say: *Happy Birthday, Ameera.* I looked over my shoulder to see if someone had joined us, but no one was there.

"Come on, Ameera. They're dripping!"

I puffed out my cheeks, extinguished the flames, and the five Méndezes burst into applause. I'd forgotten to make my wish. I snuck another look behind me, but it was just the six of us at the table.

Manuela passed me an elaborately wrapped box with a silver bow. I concentrated on opening it without tearing the paper.

Inside was a cotton shirt. The label read MADE IN INDIA. It had purple and blue flowers and smelled of incense.

"Te gusta? I found it at that little import shop in town." Manuela's face beamed. My eyes welled with tears.

Azeez

∞

Like most discoveries, this one happened by accident.

I listened to my family's thoughts, breathing in their exhalations, for many years. My whispers went unheard and I despaired that our communication would forever be one-sided. I tried everything to make them notice me. I even practised moving furniture, dropping vases, turning lights on and off, but my psychokinetic talents were severely limited. I'd spend a few hours nudging a bouquet of flowers off a table, only to have the maid blame the wind.

One night, when the house was quiet and the family asleep, two-and-a-half-year-old Nafeesa awoke frightened after being chased by a lion. I'd been hovering by her side and so I curled myself around her. I sensed the little one could perceive my presence, even if she couldn't hear my words, because her demeanour often changed when I was near. Sometimes she followed my movements with her steady gaze, as though she could see my essence.

That night, in the gloaming half-light of her nursery, she sat up and reached for me. When she couldn't feel my substance, she backed up, and looked bewildered, her lids heavy with sleep. She whimpered and I said, *Baby, don't be scared, I'm here.* I repeated the statement, and she wobbled and fell forward, pressing her face into mine.

I sputtered my words directly into her mouth, instead of her ears: *I'm here!*

In her exhalations I heard, *I know.*

Mary had a little lamb? I sang directly into her mouth, coming up with the first song I could think of.

Little lamb, little lamb, she sang silently back to me.

Mary had a little lamb, I egged her on, my aura sparkling with delight.

Her fleece was white as snow.

We experimented for another ten minutes, until she fell asleep. How exciting it was! Of course! If I could read the thoughts of the living by listening to their breath, then maybe I could get them to breathe in mine! Why hadn't I thought of it before?

It worked best while she was asleep or groggy, less effectively when she was wide awake and distracted. I loved inserting thoughts at night. With each of her inhalations, I'd offer a simple idea such as *elephants are grey*. Then, to my amazement, she'd exhale *Babar*, her dreaming mind taking over my simple sentence, embellishing it into a story similar to the one her mother had read to her at bedtime. In the morning, she couldn't always remember what I'd told her, but later I heard her speak to her father at breakfast about dreaming of the elephant king.

After I'd rehearsed sufficiently with Nafeesa, I worked my breath-telepathy on other children, then teenagers, and later on adults. A pattern emerged; the younger the listener, the more adept they were at "hearing" me. I learned that some were more naturally psychic than others, more attuned to voices from the other side.

Adults' sleep states tended to be too light and easily disturbed. My insertions were forgotten more often than not. An alarm could disrupt "dreams." Other things, too: a snoring spouse, a worry, song lyrics. And yet, I could get through a tad if the listener was sufficiently open and I was doggedly persistent.

In time I became more adroit at assessing Nafeesa's openness to me, and I realized I could make myself heard during waking hours only when she was relaxed and deep in thought. The first time it happened, she was concentrating hard on a problem, her face screwed up over "what sound does the duck make?"

Ruff ruff? I teased.

No, not ruff ruff! Quack quack!

I began offering more useful ideas, like, *You're good at that* or *You can figure it out*, when she was uncertain, upset, or scared. I could soothe her with my *uncleji* voice, as long as she was quiet enough to listen.

The same theory applied to adults, but their concentration had to be strong and their emotional guards low. I often exhausted myself yelling and puffing much hot wind into their mouths. Sometimes my siblings heard me, but disregarded my guidance as their own errant, insignificant or wise thoughts.

After years of "chatting" with Nafeesa, she began calling me by name, even though I hadn't ever introduced myself. We'd been playing a math game when she exclaimed, "No, *Mamaji Azeez*, you're giving me the wrong answer!"

I never figured out how she intuited that it was I. While I was in awe of her psychic brilliance, I made sure to instruct her never to utter my name aloud in front of others. They wouldn't have understood.

Every time I entered little Nafeesa's awake mind it was like I was turning on a lamp in a dark room. With her as my new playmate I was no longer so lonely.

Ameera

Δ

On Tuesday night, just after I'd finished my shift, there was a knock at my door.

"Can I help you?" Suzanne and Todd stood at my threshold. I was confused; tourists rarely ventured to our shabby wing, which, next to the renovated buildings and cottages, resembled a maintenance hangar. Not since Brandon, two years earlier, had I been followed home.

"We were on our way to the bar and wanted to invite you along. Oh, Ameera, this is Todd. Todd, this is Ameera." Suzanne giggled. She teetered in her silver high heels and slanted into Todd's bulky frame.

"Want to join us?" Something green was snagged between Todd's front teeth. A thick mat of curly brown hair covered his arms, and poked out of his collar.

"Uh, thanks, but no." I sensed they were both already tanked.

"Oh come on, Ameera. Todd has a big lezzie threesome fantasy, just like Doug did." Suzanne brushed past me and bounced on my bed like a child. I flinched and crossed my arms over my chest.

"What do you say? Come out for a little bit?" Todd asked, taking my hand into his damp palm.

"No!" I grabbed my hand away.

"C'mon, it'll be fun." He leaned close and smiled, but it was more like a sneer.

"I'm tired and I am going to have an early night." My heart thumped in my throat. Would they leave? Todd stared at me for a beat, rage widening his eyes.

"All right," he finally said, his words crackling with irritation. "Suzanne, let's get out of here."

"Why? Are you chickening out, Todd?" Suzanne stood, then slumped into me. She was heavier than she looked and I staggered with her. She planted a wet kiss on my mouth that tasted like mint gum and gin. I pried her off me and shoved her into Todd's arms.

"Please leave now." I pointed to the door.

"Oh, now *she's* not into it. You wanted it last year, didn't you? Or maybe you just wanted my husband," Suzanne said with a jaundiced laugh.

"Let's go, Suzanne!" Todd growled and took her by the arm into the hallway. I shoved the door closed behind them.

Shaken by their intrusion, I listened, ear to door, as they stumbled down the hallway. I held my breath until I heard them exit the building. Just as the outer door slammed, the lock on my side of the bathroom clicked closed, and a toilet flushed shortly after. Blythe was awake! Well, maybe that would have been a good thing if they'd refused to go. I laid flat on my back, the mattress sagging beneath me, mentally replaying Suzanne and Todd's entrance, trying to recall which words had been loud enough to traverse eight feet of tiles and porcelain.

I slept poorly, curling and stretching throughout the night, a nightmare repeating. Suzanne at the bathroom sink, then lying on my bed, cackling. Todd onstage at the orientation session, announcing to the audience, "For those of you who prefer swinger excursions and entertainment, please see Ameera, the Atlantis orgy specialist." The tourist assembly turned, en masse, to stare at me.

I snapped awake, frightened in the darkness, believing that Suzanne and Todd had broken into my room. I turned on the light to reassure myself that I was alone. The dream's creepy presence lingered, and I waited until it dissipated and my breathing calmed before turning off the light.

And then I heard, *You are fine. You are all right.* I switched the light on again. I wasn't sure where those reassuring words were coming from, but I repeated them to myself until I was sleepy. It took what felt like an hour, but I eventually fell asleep.

I steered clear of Suzanne and Todd for the next three days. At the airport, we avoided eye contact, but I remained vigilant, monitoring their progress in the flight check-in line. I was nervous that Suzanne would repeat the scene she'd enacted a year and a half earlier.

Blythe noticed me squinting in their direction. "Is there a problem?"

Suzanne and Todd were three back in the security lineup. Todd looked over his shoulder, in my direction.

"Did you hear that kerfuffle a few nights back? Some people yelling at my door?" I asked.

"Yeah, I meant to ask you about that. Sounded like some drunk tourists." Blythe followed my gaze to the couple.

"It was those two." I pointed at Suzanne and Todd's backs. Suzanne paused to stare at me. They were now two back from the front of the line. "And yes, drunk."

"We need a lock on the outside door." Blythe shook her head.

"You didn't hear what they said? It was pretty insane. I would've thought you and half the building would have heard them."

"No, not really." Blythe shook her head. I frowned and studied her neutral expression. When I glanced their way again, Suzanne and Todd had passed through the security gates.

Δ

Waiting in the mailroom that evening was a large yellow parcel from Mom. I tore it open and inhaled sugar, perfume swatches, and printer's ink. It contained April's magazines, my favourite candy, and a long sundress in a floral print. Not really my style, but that was all right. There was also a birthday card that read, HAPPY BIRTHDAY MY GIRL! WISHING YOU ALL THE BEST FOR THIS COMING YEAR. XO MOM. Back in my room, I taped the card to my mirror and discarded last year's version.

O magazine's cover promised test-yourself quizzes on money and advice on avoiding toxic relationships. When I peered at the quizzes under bright light, there were very few rubbed-out pencil marks. Even the dog-eared pages suggested little about Mom's exigencies but rather appeared to be placeholders, forgotten and no longer needed. Someone had used *O* as a coaster, leaving a watermark over Oprah's face. I traced the circle with my index finger and flipped open the cover.

I sucked on a sour ju jube and stopped at an article about relationship patterns. It blathered on about how people unconsciously seek out a particular psychological "type" when choosing a mate, one that reinforces skewed childhood notions about love. I then pondered Gavin, troubling over my childhood love notions and what he might have had to do with them.

I stuffed six ju jubes into my cheeks, wincing at the sour taking over my mouth. The article suggested that awareness was key to changing my negative relationship patterns. But what were they? Magazines always contained pat sound bites, written in large font, inside grayscale boxes.

A questionnaire titled "What's Your Psychological Type?" accompanied the column. I was about to complete it, but stopped myself. I didn't feel like being slotted into a category that day.

But then I reconsidered the pop psychology column's wisdom when I reflected on Doug. Why had I been so attracted to him in the first place? Why had I pined over him after he'd left? It dawned on me that Todd was a version of Doug, probably charismatic, generous, and a good listener at first, and inattentive and rude to Suzanne later. Very likely this self-centredness would have extended to me too, once I was no longer Doug's fresh meat.

A leftover longing for a man I'd barely known alighted from my chest like a butterfly into the wind.

Gavin, on the other hand, remained stuck to my brain like a garden slug to a tomato plant.

Azeez

∞

Kanishka was the name of an ancient emperor known for his violence and faithlessness. He controlled much of Central Asia for almost a quarter century. It was supernatural forces that made the powerful man repent his life's grave errors and submit to a more just life. That's the lore, anyway.

Kanishka was the name of the aircraft that plummeted into the ocean.

For over two decades, my family followed the seemingly unending Canadian inquiry into Kanishka's bombing. It uncovered a cascading series of blunders beginning with the RCMP's investigations prior to the attack, and ending with mistakes by airport check-in and security staff, any of which, had they not occurred, might have prevented the tragedy.

Ameera and Nadeem were watching the news that delivered the final analyses. Two cups of cold tea sat before them. Neither spoke. They didn't know what to make of these grave errors. And who would repent for their violence, they wondered, as the faithless killers walked free.

My guides said that, in the end, those guilty men would have to face themselves. There was a plan for them, just as there was a plan for me. My previous life's early demise was part of a larger, longer, more complicated blueprint. Like Kanishka, the terrorists would be forced to fall to their knees before the divine.

Kanishka was a part of all of our destinies, perhaps.

I whispered messages about fate and acceptance into my family's nostrils and open mouths, but I feared my arguments were unconvincing, perhaps because I only halfway believed them myself.

Well, I tried.

Perhaps for my family, hate was like an old blanket they could wrap around themselves. It was no longer soft, but they could be sure it would keep the wind out. They hunkered down inside it and hid themselves from neighbours and colleagues and old friends who looked like the men who blew up my airplane. Their children inherited their parents' self-protective postures.

It wasn't just that they developed an irrational fear and hatred of Sikhs. They learned to hate Canada, too, for Canada had stolen their child.

Ameera

Δ

Weak sunlight peeked through the space between my drapes.
I rolled over, squeezed my eyelids shut, and willed myself back
into the slumber I so badly needed; I'd slept fitfully most of the
night. But at 6:03, all I could think of was Anita.

I showered and made my way to the cafeteria. I reread the
e-mail I'd already read three times the previous evening. I didn't
usually check e-mail before bed, but something, a dread or a
foreboding, had prodded me to do so.

At 5:05 p.m. on Friday, she'd written:

> Ameera,
>
> A second complaint, somewhat similar to the
> first, arrived yesterday afternoon. It, too, is an-
> onymous, but is more specific than the first. Can
> you make yourself available on Saturday at 4:00
> p.m. CDT for a teleconference so we can discuss
> the matter further?
>
> Best,
> Anita

The fourth reading didn't help. My stomach churned with
fear as I puzzled over the vague words: "somewhat similar" and
"more specific." Who was the complainant this time, and was he

or she the same person as before? And what was I accused of?
I wished Anita had provided more information so that I could
prepare for the meeting.

My earlier paranoia that Suzanne was behind the first complaint now seemed credible. Conflicted about her trip, she'd
sent it before her arrival. And then, embarrassed and livid,
she'd typed the second complaint two days after she and Todd
burst into my room. She had to be the one responsible for this
crap. But how would I explain to Anita that an angry woman
was holding a grudge about a ménage a trois gone wrong? It
sounded sketchy to me, even.

I sipped a cup of coffee, perseverating on Suzanne and Todd,
then Suzanne and Doug, then back again to Suzanne and Todd.
Manuela strolled over with her breakfast plate and planted herself across from me.

"Good morning! How are you today?" She sliced a hard-
boiled egg into two with gusto. Then, looking more closely at
me, she asked, "What's wrong?"

"I'm fine." Would Anita now want to speak with the rest of my
colleagues about my professionalism? Roberto had witnessed first-
hand something of the Suzanne-Doug debacle a year ago. Blythe
had likely overheard the recent interaction with Suzanne and Todd,
even if she was downplaying it. And Oscar — well, I'd never forget
his look of disgust when he scolded me about dating tourists.

"You look terrible." Manuela popped the egg into her mouth.
"Sorry to say it."

"I couldn't sleep last night." I peered at her. I had to talk to
someone. "Actually, it's because of an e-mail that Anita sent me."

"What about?" She set down her cutlery.

"Someone has been making anonymous complaints about
me. On the online comment form. All lies." A worker wiped
down the table next to us, someone I didn't recognize. We paused
our conversation until she finished.

"Really? What kind of lies?" Manuela whispered, her perfectly tweezed eyebrows raised in alarm. I carefully considered my words. "The first one was about not being professional and dating tourists ... the second complaint I'm not sure about ... I'll know more later. I have a teleconference this afternoon with Anita."

"Unprofessional? I can't imagine anyone saying that about *you*." Manuela pointed a sparkly purple nail at me. "I mean, it's been a long time since you've had trouble with tourist guys, right?"

"Yeah. It may be nothing. I mean, they were online complaints. Could just be someone's idea of a prank. But, just in case ... would you vouch for me if Anita asks you about it?"

"Of course! And I would only be telling Anita the truth. You do a good job. You're a top seller of the excursions." She opened a packet of strawberry jam and smeared it on a slice of whole wheat toast.

"Thanks. Don't say anything about that stuff from two years ago? It'll just make Anita suspicious."

"That's in the past, Ameera. I won't mention it," Manuela said, nodding earnestly. "Our Word of the Week will be *solidaridad*!"

"*Solidaridad!*" I echoed, clinking my coffee cup with hers. I hadn't ever heard Manuela use political language like that. I looked at her gratefully, knowing that her solidarity involved unknowingly lying on my behalf.

Δ

The work of greeting happy vacationers killed an hour. We'd officially entered low season at the beginning of April, filling three chartered buses instead of five, and so the assembly hall was only half full.

Blythe's games appeared to be less provocative that day, and many of our guests simply ignored her cheery questions. However, a large group of South Asians stood at her urging, indicating they were from Toronto. They looked to be in their sixties, although it was hard to tell. They took up an entire row in the middle of the hall, with a few stragglers in chairs behind the rest. The women mostly paired off with other women and the men with men.

"They really are a big group," I said to Manuela.

"Sixteen — eight couples. Their kids bought them the packages." Manuela's lips turned down, which meant that she approved.

"Aren't they the same culture as you?" Manuela asked, and then corrected herself, "I mean, where your father is from?"

"I don't know. Maybe. I can't see them that well from here."

Of course, I'd noticed them at the airport. One woman had carried a clipboard and collected her group's all-inclusive envelopes while her companions caroused like moderately well-behaved adolescents on a school trip. Surrounding the group were an impossible number of black, wheeled suitcases with multi-hued stripes of masking tape adhered to their tops and sides: luggage Morse Code.

One of the men had said something that caused the guy beside him to laugh raucously. The other men craned their necks to see what was so funny. There was a huddle and the joke was discreetly shared. The ladies rolled their eyes at their men, dug deep into their purses, and extracted juice boxes for everyone. A momentary hush fell over the group as sharp straws punctured foil and fruit cocktail was sucked up. I had an urge to chat with Clipboard Lady, but a weird shyness overtook me.

Δ

Halfway through the morning, the South Asian group leader herded her fifteen charges down the hallway toward our tour desk.

"Come on, everyone! Line up! Let's choose our excursions," she instructed. The group un-clumped from its previous gendered dyads and triads, husbands and wives finding one another and linking arms as though in preparation for a square dance. The pairs fanned out across our five lineups.

A man with a salt-and-pepper comb-over and a woman with a stylish, blunt-cut bob sat before me. I reviewed their options and attempted Roberto's spiritual fib.

"Who else is going to the waterfall on Monday?" The man hollered to the others. Two other couples yelled affirmative replies.

"Shall we also do the shopping trip? We need to get gifts for the children," his wife considered.

"Or maybe you ladies can go together and we gents can sit on the beach?" Once again, there was a conference across the counter, with all eight couples chiming their preferences. After some back and forth, and muttering from two men that "there was no way they were going to waste their holiday shopping," and rebuttals from three women about "not wanting to spend every minute with you men anyway," it was decided that everyone would see the waterfalls on Monday morning and the women would shop in the afternoon.

"No, no, that's too much in one day," protested a woman from Blythe's station. "Let's not create a hectic pace." This began another round of fussing about activities and dates. The five of us tour reps exchanged weary glances, unsure how to reign in the chaos.

"How about Wednesday afternoon instead?" I stood to get everyone's attention. "We have a half-day trip that leaves at 1:00 p.m." There were hums of agreement from the delegation.

My couple finalized their choices and the husband pulled out cash from a brown leather wallet that bulged with photographs, bits of paper, and three different monetary currencies. While I wrote receipts for Mr. and Mrs. Kheriwala, the man leaned forward to read my nametag. "Ameera. You must be Muslim?" He nodded before I could answer.

"Well, sort of. My father was from India." It was a familiar, well-worn statement, factual and concise.

"What part of India? We're from Mumbai, originally."

"Actually, I'm not sure. I've never met him," I mumbled, the conversation now off-course.

"Oh. Sorry, sorry," he said, his forehead wrinkling.

"He didn't mean to be nosy," Mrs. Kheriwala cooed apologetically.

"It's okay. He died before I was born." The lie, a brand-new one, spat itself out with an ease that startled me. It was as though I'd had this conversation before. I frowned and concentrated, picking up the frayed threads in my mind.

"Oh," Mr. Kheriwala repeated, "that's terrible."

"It's all right." My body went cold and I wondered if my fiction could be true. I brushed aside the idea.

"Doesn't she look like Muneera's daughter, what's her name?" Mr. Kheriwala turned to his wife.

"Miriam. Yes, the spitting image," she nodded, appraising me.

"Is Muneera in your group?" My words fluttered forward before I could catch them. I scanned the cohort.

"No, she couldn't join us," Mrs. Kheriwala said.

"Your mother must be missing you, with you living and working here," Mr. Kheriwala said, "our Sherebanu and Ali live far away, too." He flipped open his wallet, and displayed plastic-sheathed photos of his children. He proudly told me that Ali was an immigration lawyer in Vancouver and Sherebanu a biology professor in Philadelphia.

"Yeah, I miss my mom a lot. We're close, but we keep in touch." The last two times we'd spoken, she'd called from Victor's kitchen. I'd checked out the stainless-steel appliances, red cupboards, and industrial espresso machine behind her. From the way she'd described him, I hadn't expected that sort of modern style. I'd kept my eye on the edges of the frame, hoping he'd step in front of the webcam.

"Very nice," Mr. Kheriwala said approvingly.

They joined the rest of their group, who were debating the merits of swimming in the pool versus the ocean. New vacationers took their places in front of us. I overheard one of them gripe to Blythe, "Those East Indians sure did hold the line up."

I bristled at the impatient tourist's words. When I was twelve, my mother informed me that "South Asian" was the new correct term to use. Mom's workplace had just held a lunchtime educational event. Before that, she used to say East Indian, as in "you're half East Indian. Your biological father was from India." She always said "biological" to emphasize that my connection to him was not parental.

Mom bought us tickets to the Hamilton South Asian Society's Dance Ensemble that year and we put on dresses and attended a Bharatanatyum performance. When the Society offered classical dance classes in the summer, she registered me for a children's weekend. I stayed home, faking a stomachache. I developed an interest in my ancestry much later, when I was in university.

It wasn't that I wasn't curious about my father as a child. Ever since Mom explained who he was, I began studying South Asians on the street, at the library, behind the McDonald's counter. I examined their features, speech, gestures, and wondered if I might possess any of their same characteristics.

The men's faces were most intriguing. I pondered lips, cheekbones, nostrils, imagining genetic matches. Intellectually, I knew that it was impossible for me to meet him on the street. Still, when I saw a South Asian man who might be the right age, the possibility of kinship crossed my mind.

Azeez

∞

Fifteen years after my death, I travelled west, visiting my old haunts, so to speak: the McMaster Burke Sciences Building, the basement of the Mills Library and the Phoenix Campus Pub. With the optimism of the turn of the century, so much had changed and been updated, but the parcel of land on which McMaster University sat was still the same, bordered by the gritty city and lush ravines. I'd expected everything to look smaller so many years later, but the chemistry laboratories were spiffy and spacious, and the canopy of trees in the courtyards loomed like giants veiled with snow. The student population appeared to have grown in size, too, although individually, the youngsters were very much the same as before, hunched over in their parkas, their backpacks and deadlines weighing them down.

I looked for the old house I'd shared with Max and Jonathan, half expecting to see them loafing on the porch with their Budweisers. The three-storey Victorian stood where it had, but the old flaking grey paint had been stripped away to reveal its original russet brick. Four teal Adirondack chairs sat on the widened front verandah. A man in his forties shovelled the walk. I looked more closely at his features. It was Max! The house had once belonged to his grandmother, so perhaps it had been bequeathed to him.

The snow was heavy and so was his breathing. He brooded over an argument he'd had with his wife earlier in the day.

His two children, a ten-year-old girl and twelve-year-old boy, wouldn't be home for a few hours and he was glad for the rare peace. The odious task of marking awaited him on his desk. Despite his full house, loneliness coated him like a thin layer of frost.

I left him outdoors and found the room I'd occupied for five years. A large oak desk and an easy chair filled the space. How tidy it was! I looked closely at a pile of half-graded physics tests and saw his name on the header: Professor M. Cohen. I bet he was tenured by then. I lingered over the papers a minute, enjoying the simplicity of undergraduate calculations. I once was very good at physics, top of my class. But chemistry had been my true love.

I supposed I might have had a life much like his, but set in a Mumbai suburb near the Indian Institute of Technology. Like Max, I would have earned tenure, and published many books related to my research into sterols. Perhaps I might have just argued with my wife or puzzled over my prepubescent children's interests or willingly engaged in a mid-life crisis.

I returned to Max and trumpeted into his inhalations:

You're alive! Thank your lucky stars. Man, you're alive!

I flew to Westdale, three blocks away, and ventured into the coffee shop where I'd met Nora. Just as before, students filled the seats, drinking double-doubles and cramming for exams. I chose the same table where I'd chatted with her and concentrated hard to sleuth her whereabouts. Did she still reside in Hamilton? If she'd pursued an academic life, she might be at a university in Canada or anywhere in the world! I grumped to my guides.

Have faith. You'll find her.

When?

Oh come now. Sit still, a minute, won't you?

It took all day and night for me to perceive her; the connection between us was barely discernable. The staff worked around

me, cleaned, closed up, and new patrons replaced the old. Of
course, no one noticed me, but at the same time, no one sat atop
me. The few occasions someone occupied the seat across from
me, it was always for very short periods of time. I'd experienced
it over and over, and yet it still gave me pause when a living person unconsciously sensed and avoided me.

My meditations drew me downtown to Jackson Square Mall.
I flitted in and out of a dozen women's clothing stores before my
intuition drew me into a bank. I examined the clients waiting by
the banking machines and those in the short lineup for the tellers.
Finally, I saw Nora behind the counter. I loitered beside her for a
good half hour, watching her work. She appeared to have some
kind of authority over the other tellers — from time to time they
approached her counter and proffered a supervisory signature.
She counted out three hundred dollars for a customer, smiled, and
then placed a CLOSED sign in front of her.

I admired her pretty hair, freckles, and curvy body. But she was
different now, her youthful vivacity contained within a buttoned-
up blouse, blazer, and dress skirt. Why wasn't she at a university
podium or meeting with a student about an essay?

She gathered her purse and lunch bag and we rode the bus
together. I leaned my face against hers and took in her stale breath:
she was looking forward to seeing a man, but she questioned
whether he truly loved her; she wondered why she hadn't been invited to her co-worker's engagement party; she travelled through
the fridge to see what she'd cook for dinner; she tried to remember what time her daughter's band practice was over.

I wanted so badly to wrap my arms around her, to feel her flesh
again, but I'd long understood the futility of attempting touch.

The bus laboured up the mountain. She counted her steps as
we walked the two blocks to her building. The elevator climbed
to the ninth floor and before she could fish her keys out of her
purse, a man in his late thirties greeted her at the door; he'd been

anticipating the sound of her feet in the hallway. There was a palpable warmth between them, a curiosity, an excitement, similar to how I'd felt when I first met her.

"I've unpacked my stuff, baby." He scooped her into his arms and smiled wide and she squealed with delight. He had terrible acne, but Nora didn't seem to mind at all. Was that a pang of jealousy that rippled through me? He drew her into the bedroom.

I remained on the other side of the door; it's voyeuristic for spirits to eavesdrop on carnal pleasures. However, I did listen to their yelps and grunts, recalling my afternoon in bed with her. It was a distant memory. Yes, a lifetime ago.

∞

I scrambled on top of her and she pulled my hips to her.

"Do you have protection?" she whispered in my ear. I thought about the unopened box of condoms in my dresser drawer, supplies I'd purchased years earlier, but hadn't touched.

"No. Are you on the pill?" A stupid to thing to say in hindsight, but I'd heard that all Canadian university girls were on it.

She nodded, but looked uneasy.

"Don't worry, I'm clean. But I'll pull out if you want me to." Because I couldn't imagine not being inside her.

And she'd said, "Okay. Good." Perhaps she thought I knew what I was doing.

I'd left her that afternoon, full of youthful pride. I could have skipped all the way home. My future was a banquet of promise. And no longer sexually inexperienced, I'd have plenty of sexual adventures ahead of me!

Well, then.

Their sex noises stopped and I left Nora's building, despondent. Sure, I'd found her, but there was nothing there for me. Whatever had pulled me west was not about Nora.

On my way around the circular driveway, I noticed a teenaged girl. She wore a short coat and a determined expression. She had beautiful eyes and reminded me of my sister. For a moment, I considered breathing her in and finding out more about her, but I'd learned to avoid this sort of distraction. There were just too many people, too many hearts, too many stories. A spirit couldn't get involved with them all.

Besides, the strong ropes that connected me to my family were tugging me home.

Ameera

Δ

"Is it, like, safe to go to town? I heard news reports about muggings and stuff and last year someone was killed." I peered at the young woman in front of me and relaxed my jaw to force a smile.

"That was in Cancun, if I recall. That kind of thing doesn't happen in La Crucecita." I gave her instructions on how to take a taxi to town. I checked my watch, as I had been doing all afternoon. My meeting with Anita was in half an hour.

"Is there anything worthwhile to see there?" She flipped her hair and looked at me skeptically. I glanced at Manuela and sensed derisive darts shooting our way.

"Yes, it's a pretty town. There's an old church, a zócalo, shops, restaurants." And then, to get her to go away I said, "It's a truly authentic Mexican town."

She took my brochure and wandered in the direction of the swim-up bar.

Δ

Manuela offered to forward Anita's call to a private office off the lobby. I headed there ten minutes early, checked twice that the ringer was on, then paced the office's six square feet like a caged animal. When it rang, I pounced before the second ring.

"I have to say that I'm perplexed," Anita delved into the issue after half a minute of small talk. "We've never received complaints of this kind and never two in a row." Anita read the anonymous missive out loud and I copied it onto Atlantis stationary: *Ameera at Atlantis is a swinger and has sex with tourists. She should be fired.*

I asked her to repeat the sentence; I needed a few seconds to gather my thoughts. The office was suddenly hot and I pushed the door open for air and then shut it again.

"I'm perplexed, too." I tried to channel my panic into a tone that conveyed innocence. "I have no idea why someone would say something like that. I'm not a swinger!" My stomach sank, not so much from the fear of being found out, but from denying something true about myself. It sounded wrong. Felt wrong.

"Look, employees' social lives are none of my business, unless they interfere with the job. But I need to know, did something happen? Is there a tiny kernel of truth that would have a customer all riled up about you?"

My pulse accelerated as Suzanne and Todd's angry faces shoved their way into my mind. Then thoughts of the bodybuilders crept forward, likely irrelevant and adding to my confusion. They'd continued to send e-mails once a week, all of which I'd ignored. The last one had an offended tone. I held my head in my hands, silently chastising myself for so badly managing my sex life.

"No … nothing. Like I said before, I get hit on a lot. I decline a lot. People don't always deal with rejection well …". I knew I sounded defensive.

"All right. I believe you. But I'm in a difficult position. I've been instructed by my manager to conduct an investigation." I heard keyboard tapping on her end of the phone. What was she writing about me? "We recently had a similar type of situation at another resort, so, we have to be more vigilant about these issues."

"Are you referring to Nancy?" I squeaked. Surely she couldn't be equating our situations? I was hot all over, my back wet with sweat.

"You heard about that? It was supposed to be confidential." How clueless was she to not know that we tour reps functioned like a small village with gossip spreading faster than she could send e-mails on her BlackBerry.

"That's a totally different sort of situation!" I sputtered.

"Of course it's a different situation, but Oceana is sensitive to issues … of a sexual nature."

"But … how will you investigate an anonymous complaint?" I tried to slow my breathing. I readied my pen so I could jot down Anita's words. I needed a record of the conversation, didn't I?

"I'll interview your colleagues. And I suspect that will be it. Don't worry about this too much. I'm sure everything will turn out fine." The typing continued. Wait, was she on her speakerphone? Who else was listening?

"Will you tell my colleagues the nature of the complaints? That I was accused of being a swinger? I mean, that's just embarrassing. And it won't stay confidential. I can guarantee you that. There will be rumours, and even though they're not true, everyone will assume they are." I rubbed my temples.

"Okay, calm down. I won't get into the swinger stuff. I'll ask only about professional conduct, specifically sexual conduct with tourists," Anita said. I wanted to ask her why she'd already questioned Blythe, but I held my tongue.

"Okay." I sighed. At least she wouldn't get the gossip mill running. Or at least not running wild.

"I'd like to confirm your statements about turning down tourists so that I can put this to bed, so to speak." She laughed nervously. "It's a procedural step before I can deal with contract renewals and promotions." A small well of hope rose in me; maybe I was still in the running for the promotion?

"Thanks for filling me in," I said, uncertainly. We said our goodbyes, worries troubling my belly. *It will be fine*, I heard thrumming through my mind, but I didn't believe it. What would my colleagues say about my "sexual conduct with tourists"? I was sure Manuela would deny any issues, but what about the others?

I rushed back to the desk to find Blythe alone. "Where'd everyone go?"

"It was quiet, and so I offered to stay and close up. Where've you been?" Blythe said.

"Teleconference with Anita. Listen I need to speak with all of you about that. I wish the others hadn't left early." I rifled through a drawer and found the week's shift schedule. Roberto wasn't due back until Monday, and Oscar not until Tuesday. I was especially disappointed that Manuela had gone home early; I really needed to debrief the call with her. I checked my phone. There was a missed call from her.

"What's up? Is there a problem?" Blythe asked, leaning in. Her eyes were deep blue pools framed by mascaraed lashes.

"There have been two anonymous complaints about me. Both insinuate that I've been unprofessional by dating tourists. Anita is going to investigate by interviewing you all." My head felt foggy, like I had sunstroke.

"Really? Is this connected to what she asked me about last week?" Blythe scratched her chin and looked pensive.

"Probably." I explained that Anita had spoken with her between the two complaints and might phone her again.

"Huh. That's odd. Well you can count on me to give you a good reference." Blythe said. The tight screw in my head loosened. It was nice of Blythe to offer before I asked.

"Could you mention that I get hit on by tourists and that I politely decline their invitations? Something like that? That's what I told Anita, and that's been the truth for a long time anyway."

"Absolutely. Sorry you've got this stress," Blythe cooed and shook her head.

"Anita says it's just procedure. That they're cracking down because of Nancy. But this is my reputation on the line." I was aware that my voice was growing shrill. I coughed and added, "Ah well, I guess the person who complained has bigger problems."

"A nutter for sure," Blythe agreed. "Don't worry. This will all soon blow over."

As I lay in bed that night, I bargained with myself: if I could get through Anita's investigation without it affecting my employment, I'd stop seeing swingers, at least while working for Oceana. I wouldn't date tourists at all. Perhaps I'd find a lover in La Crucecita, or just be celibate for a spell. After all, I'd enjoyed a couple of years of sexual thrills — it would be all right to take a break. I repeated to myself: *it will be fine.*

Azeez

∞

Mummy and Daddy were on their way home from a distant relative's wedding, stuffed full of biryani, kebabs, mutton stew, and haalwa. The journey was jerky, full of abrupt stops and starts and a cacophony of honks as their driver navigated Mumbai's chaos. Mummy was used to this and closed her eyes. Daddy, perhaps inspired by the romance of the nuptials they'd witnessed, put his arm around her.

Out of nowhere, a brightly painted lorry ploughed into their car. The truck driver was untouched, but both Mummy and Daddy were rushed to hospital, where they remained unconscious for several days. Their driver died on impact.

I was leaving Hamilton when the accident happened, but my guides offered me a vision of their final moments before the impact: satiety, affection, Mummy's head on Daddy's shoulder. Then: shock, fear, momentary piercing pain, unconsciousness.

They rested in a private room and my siblings and other relatives surrounded them in shifts, saying prayers, squeezing hands, ensuring round-the-clock care for their bruised bodies. I camped out, too, doing most of my listening at night, after everyone went home.

They were confused about their imprisonment and wanted their bodies to release them. Mummy listened to her children's chatter, hearing sounds, but not understanding the meaning of words. She couldn't make out Daddy's voice and believed he'd already passed. Daddy, too, listened for her and was at peace imagining that she was someplace better. For almost a week, they anticipated greeting the other.

The veil between our worlds was gossamer-thin and I didn't have to holler to be heard. I could soothe them like babies:

Be patient. I'll be there to welcome you at the door. We three will be together soon. I didn't correct their assumptions about the other's deaths in order to prevent further upset.

In the middle of the eighth night, after everyone had gone home, Mummy relinquished her body and drifted across the hospital room to sit beside me. I made my form as recognizable to her as I could. Reunions like these are not as one might expect, with violins and heavenly light and bliss. She surveyed the hospital room, bewildered, exhausted. The machine over her bed beeped shrilly.

"He's still here?" She frowned. I held her tightly.

"Yes, but he's almost done, too." We smiled at my choice of words, ones too ordinary for the transition that was about to occur. Staff rushed in and handled her death as the routine it was.

I'm dead?

Yes. You've passed on.

Auto accident, no? I could tell from her quick blinking that she was remembering.

Yes, over a week ago. I drew myself closer to her. She kept her gaze on Daddy's still form.

You're here with me, she said, perhaps only then realizing who I was. *I'm very glad to see you.*

Me, too, I whispered.

You've been … all right?

Just fine. I knew not to say too much. There would be time to explain things more thoroughly, and both she and Daddy would receive their orientation briefing soon. Her guides had already arrived and were standing by silently, awaiting her notice. I hadn't recognized mine until a day after my death.

Half an hour later, Daddy let go. His soul lifted away from his body, and he became a shaft of light tilting in our direction. Wordlessly, I beckoned him and then grew in form so that I could cradle them both, one parent on each arm.

My sister and brother arrived an hour later, shaken from their sleep by the news. They stayed with my parents' vacated bodies, as though protecting them from further harm. I hovered near my sister and realized that she was mentally travelling back fifteen years, my death and our parents' a collision in her mind. She looked to Nadeem and felt alone in her grief while he busied himself with the hospital staff, made phone calls, took care of things, as was his way.

"Come, we can go now," I told the spirits who were once my parents. They were reticent to leave their children, but I assured them that they'd be able to look in on them again. I wasn't certain about this, though. Perhaps they would reincarnate quickly, if they didn't have unfinished business. They took one last glance at the aged people they once were, and I nudged them away.

Months later, they did reincarnate, validation that they'd accomplished what was required of them in their lifetimes. I was proud of them, but envious, too. I anticipated the novelty that would come with a brand-new body, family, and circumstance. I was ready to engage with the world as a person again, to communicate freely, to touch and be touched, to taste food. To even struggle and sweat and be frightened. While there was truth and beauty and peace in my detached liminal form, it was often lonely.

But the hows and whens of the transition weren't up to me. My guides whispered that it wasn't time, that there was one relative I still had to watch over.

But it's been over fifteen years! Haven't I been a good son? A good brother? A good uncle?

Yes. Yes you have. Their calming energy wafted over me like a tranquilizer.

Is it Nadeem? I asked. There was only silence in response.

Or Ameera? I felt their nod.

But it's not your sister, Azeez. It's another Ameera.

Ameera

Δ

I intercepted Roberto before he left for the waterfalls Monday morning.

"You know I had an online complaint two years ago. Some guy thought I was rude to him," he told me, after I'd explained the problem. "People can be stupid. Don't worry so much."

"Why didn't you say anything about it back then?"

"I was still new. Embarrassed." He shrugged, as though the feeling wasn't important. "I didn't tell anyone except Oscar. Anyway, nothing came of it. It will be the same for you." He patted me between my tight shoulder blades and his palm's heat was a balm.

"I feel embarrassed, too. I don't want rumours to spread like they did a couple of years ago. Or like they did with Nancy," I whispered. Guests were beginning to mill around the desk, early for the tour.

"That didn't last long." It was true that no one was gossiping about Nancy anymore, but that was because she'd been shipped home three weeks earlier. Roberto grabbed his lunch bag and clipboard.

"Wait. Do you mind passing this on to Oscar when you see him tomorrow?" I wasn't keen to approach Oscar on this subject after the way he'd reacted to my dating fiasco a couple of years earlier. That old conflict was healed-over skin, a faint scar. I hoped Roberto would be able to find a way to make him understand without reopening old wounds.

"No problem." Roberto headed off, waving reassurance. His sun hat flopped with each of his bouncy steps. Guests followed him like acolytes up the stairs to the lobby.

Now that I'd spoken to everyone, I wasn't sure what else to do. The previous two days had been hell, the complainant's words creeping into my thoughts whenever I wasn't occupied. *Ameera at Atlantis is a swinger.* I'd flung the thoughts away, but then they'd return, whipping back at me with fuller force.

Now, as they flew back in my direction, I didn't duck, but allowed them to land:

Ameera at Atlantis is a swinger.

The label fit, I supposed. But wasn't I just myself? Wasn't I just Ameera at Atlantis? Hadn't I done a good job for three years? Hadn't I sold a ton of excursions and bug spray? I pictured Jan and Larry in an imaginary conversation with me. Wouldn't they nod and ask, "What does it matter that your sex life is unconventional?"

But I knew most people didn't view the world like Jan and Larry. I'd brought all of this drama onto myself by being careless.

Ameera at Atlantis is a swinger.

What if people found out? A slideshow of old friends flashed expressions of disgust. Then Gavin and Tamara. Next my mother. I inhaled sharply, uneasy that she'd joined the queue. Of course, I wouldn't tell her anything about this.

I had to calm down. The issue would go away, like Roberto said. There was no proof. Or was there? I could deny everything.

Tears welled up. I willed my body to move, to shake free of the repetitive, fearful thoughts. I wandered to the beach at the far edge of the resort. The tide was especially strong there, the grass long, the bushes unruly, and the sand unraked. Large CAUTION signs dissuaded tourists from venturing farther. When I'd first arrived in Huatulco, I'd wander to Wild Beach most evenings after my shift, dipping my toes, listening to the sea roar furiously as it crashed against the rocky shore. At some point, I stopped going as often, the ocean becoming a backdrop.

I descended a cliff, taking care to not snag my shorts in the prickly brush. My calves and hamstrings pumped and stretched, my breathing slowed, and I imagined my troubles washing away in the waves.

Unfortunately, I wasn't alone. Near the shore, I spotted the South Asian group, all sixteen of them, spread out across the sand. China-white plates dotted their picnic blankets like orbiting moons. Each was piled high with pizza, hamburgers, rice, and chicken. I wondered how they'd managed to smuggle it all out of the buffet, past the restaurant staff who stood, sentry-like at the doors.

"Pass the Tabasco sauce!" someone yelled.

"Altaf! It's right beside you!"

"What?"

"The Tabasco! Pass it to Shabnam!"

Altaf handed the red bottle to someone beside him, who gave it to the next person and the next, until it reached Shabnam's waiting hand.

"They call this fancy four-star food? It's so bland," someone carped.

I was about to turn back when Mrs. Kheriwala noticed me and waved me down the hill.

I was like a bashful pre-teen attending her first school dance. The eager expressions of sixteen middle-aged vacationers beckoned.

"Are you having a good time?" I slipped into tour rep mode.

"It's very nice here. Very peaceful and beautiful," said Mr. Kheriwala. There were multiple murmurs of agreement. *Very good. Very nice. Just lovely. Such good weather.*

"Come, sit down and join us." Before I could say no, Mrs. Kheriwala passed me a slice of pizza dotted with red hot sauce.

"Is today your day off?" asked Clipboard Lady.

"Yes, you're not wearing your usual outfit," Clipboard Lady's husband observed. Thirty-two eyes appraised my thin tank top, skull-and-crossbones-patterned shorts, and yellow canvas sneakers.

"It is," I confirmed. Mr. and Mrs. Clipboard offered more food while the other fourteen returned to their plates and chatter. "I'm Mustafa Presswala, and this my wife, Zahabia," he said, shaking my hand.

"I see you're organizing the group," I said to Zahabia.

"Yes, they require quite a lot of coordination," she replied, flashing me a knowing look. "I feel like Julie McCoy on *The Love Boat*." I vaguely recognized the television show, but couldn't recall which character was Julie.

"It's like herding cats," Mustafa whispered, smiling conspiratorially at me.

"I heard your children bought the trip for all of you." Hot sauce burned my tongue.

"Yes, it was actually our daughter, Shirin. She owns a travel agency, and she and our son, Hunaid — he's an accountant — wanted to give this to us for our thirtieth wedding anniversary. And then she sent out e-mails to all our friends' children," explained Zahabia.

"She got thirty percent off for everyone," Mustafa added.

"That's pretty good. We get a forty percent discount for our families."

"And where is your family living?" Asked Zahabia.

"In Hamilton. Which is where I grew up, too. It's just my mom and me." Was I rambling?

"Hey, don't go in too far. Read the sign! It is dangerous!" Zahabia jumped up and hurried over to a couple who were dipping their toes in the water. They played at dragging her into the surf, and she shrieked in protest.

"We heard your father is from India, just like us," Mustafa said. "You ever been to India?"

"No, never. But I'd love to go someday." I stuffed the pizza in my mouth.

"Yes, you should. It's good to reconnect with your roots. What part of India is your father's family from?" His face was animated.

Mumbai.

"Mumbai, I think." My answer felt like a certainty. Then I remembered that I'd given the Kheriwalas, the couple I'd sold the excursions to, a different answer a few days earlier. "But we're not really sure, because he died before I was born, and my mother hasn't had much contact with his family." The words rushed from my mouth.

"Oh, yes, right. I heard. It's a pity they haven't kept in contact," Mustafa said.

"Maybe one day I'll meet them." I'd imagined this family many times before, had sketched out my namesake aunt and uncle. I'd gone further to draw half-siblings, cousins, grandparents. Now, I visualized them welcoming me at the Mumbai airport.

Δ

My mother told me that she'd met Azeez while studying for the last of her exams, Sociology 3SS3, Eastern Religions. A month later, she graduated with an anthropology degree, with a minor in Asian Studies.

"He was friendly, smart. Chatty," Mom told me, when I was seven years old.

"What'd he look like?" I'd heard the story many times before, but liked to hear her retell it.

"Have you forgotten already?" She tapped my nose teasingly and studied my face, "He had really white teeth. As white as the mug he was drinking from. Black hair. Skinny like you. His skin just a shade darker than yours. Brown eyes. He was so different from anyone I'd ever met."

"And his sister's name was Ameera, right?" I didn't know anyone else with the same name as me. I wanted so badly to meet another Ameera.

"Said I reminded him of her. Quite a line, eh?" She chuckled, caught in the memory, "Then he spelled his name and the names of his brother and sister for me on a paper napkin."

"Aunt Ameera. Uncle Nadeem," I whispered under my breath.

"Yes."

"He's a professor, right?" I didn't really know what that meant, but I imagined someone like my grade two teacher, Mr. Niblett, only more important, somehow.

"Yes, in India. A science professor. Probably. He was going home, later that summer, to start a new job." She bit her lip and frowned and then told me to brush my teeth and get ready for bed.

Δ

"India is a wonderful place. They have luxury hotels, nicer even than this one," Mustafa Presswala said.

"Please, please, have some more food! Samina brought a whole chocolate cake from the dining hall." Samina, hearing her name mentioned, pointed at the cake enthusiastically with a silver spatula. I held out my plate, and three hands passed it to her and formed a human conveyor belt to return it.

I crossed my legs and dug into the sun-warmed cake with my fingers, wondering what it might be like to be one of the eight couples' good children. I imagined these young professionals joining their parents in a couple of months, everyone cramming into someone's suburban rec room to listen to vacation stories. Perhaps the Presswalas might create a PowerPoint presentation of their time at Atlantis, complete with photos of picnics of smuggled-out hamburgers and sweating chocolate cake. In one of the group shots, they might see a younger woman in shorts and a tank top smiling amongst the sixteen. One of the kids might point and ask about me, and Zahabia Presswala would explain that I was one of the staff. Her husband might add that I was a nice girl, half Indian, but didn't know where she was from. The other parents might murmur about my father's early, tragic death.

Perhaps the Presswalas' daughter would take a long look at the photo and comment on how the stranger blended in with the group, as though I were one of them.

Azeez

∞

I visited every Ameera I'd ever known: a classmate from primary school; a cousin who'd moved to New Zealand; and a neighbour from down the block. I paid them each numerous visits, over many years. None of them thought about me, none of them needed me. None of them was she.

I was growing impatient with the guides' riddles, but I chose to occupy myself with getting acquainted with my siblings and their families. It was a consolation that if I couldn't know them in life, at least I could be with them as a spirit.

Nadeem was a lawyer, who for years remained a bachelor, focusing on his work and a series of short-lived affairs with married women. When I'd first learned of his lifestyle, I'd been shocked by his capacity to sneak around, sometimes with the wives of his colleagues. His duplicity troubled me and I attempted to counsel him on morality at night, even though my guides suggested Nadeem had to learn his own lessons in his own way. It was frustrating to witness his emotional bungling but be ineffective in helping him to evolve. Eventually I left him alone because despite his monkey business, I saw he was a kind and sensitive fellow who treated his lovers with a tenderness I recognized from his boyhood.

It wasn't until seven years after Mummy and Daddy died, in 2007, that he wedded a secretary from his office, a woman named

Usha, twenty years his junior. I think it was the first time he'd fallen in love because his gait noticeably slowed, his walk demonstrating his heart's more peaceful rhythm. At night I put my ear to his chest, and listened to its joyous thrum. After marriage, he continued to be drawn to other women, and had occasional secret dalliances with them, but he'd return to Usha with increased devotion.

Three years into the marriage, when he was almost fifty years old, he became a father. They named their son after me. I argued against the idea, not that anyone was listening. I worried my name would forever link Nadeem to his memory of shivering in the Cork rain, bereft and wishing he was home. Why submit a child to titanic grief? But it didn't work out that way; whenever Nadeem held his newborn and thought of me, it was reminiscences of our youth that stepped forward: me teaching him how to swing a cricket bat, walking him to school, us talking about his first adolescent crush on a girl. He referred back to my big-brotherliness as he grew into his paternal role.

Ameera was a third-standard teacher and married to a good man she had never truly loved. Her deep sighs told me she was happy enough with her husband's companionship, but that she longed for the whirlwind romance in the sappy Bollywood films she watched each weekend. As with Nadeem, I had little wisdom to counteract her malaise. Just like him, she wanted things she couldn't have, wasn't satisfied with the richness before her.

You have love! You have a good life! Be happy! I yelled futilely into her lungs.

I'd forged a deep connection with her daughter Nafeesa. We'd been communicating since her babyhood and my Nafu continued to "hear" me even as a young adult. It was our psychic communion that piqued her interest in spiritual matters and she became a Buddhist as well as a Muslim. She invited me in during her meditation sessions, her easy breathing and open mind facilitating our silent conversations.

Mamaji, are you there? She called out telepathically to me when she was twenty-three.

I'm always here. Whenever you want.

I have something on my mind.

Go ahead, tell me, Nafu.

I think … I want to transition. Be a man. Her idea, only recently acknowledged and still a secret, puffed out boldly. My niece had been a tomboy, the fastest runner in her preschool. As a teenager, she'd cut her hair short and refused her mother's pushy feminine fashion sense. Now as a young adult, her spirit was genderless, but her terrestrial body and mind was certainly leaning toward the masculine. Her parents did not approve.

Follow your heart. You can be a man if you want. Why not? Simple and unconventional advice, I know, but death allowed me to be that sort of uncle.

I want to be Nafees, not Nafeesa.

Am I still allowed to call you Nafu? In both genders, the name meant "precious." It was all the same to me.

∞

Over the next three years, scolding, cajoling, and educating Nafu's parents became my mission. But Nafu did quite well on his own, approaching their resistance with consideration and love, which was his way.

Without a deeply felt sense of time, months passed in what seemed like days. I'd turn my attention from Ameera to Nafees, and realize that another school term was over. Then to Nadeem, who was already celebrating his boy's third birthday. At the same time, a growing restlessness was building within my core. I had to admit that I'd grown too comfortable in the in-between world. I was hindering my own passage to my next life.

I once again turned to my spirit guides for assistance. *Where is she? Where do I find Ameera?*

Do you think you've already met her? They liked to answer my questions with questions.

How should I know? I've gone through all the Ameeras I know.

Are you still pulled to the West? They asked, all exasperation.

Yes, I had continued to be drawn that way. It was an insistent tug that I'd ignored. I'd wracked my brain for the Ameeras I might have known in Canada. Certainly there was no one in my educational cohort. No professors or students by that name; I was sure I would have remembered.

You saw her when you last went back. But you didn't meet her.

Oh come on! I saw plenty of women I never met in Hamilton. This is impossible!

She was a girl back then.

Fifteen years ago? She was there fifteen years ago? Perhaps a university student at the coffee shop or university? Someone at Nora's bank? And then I remembered the teenager outside Nora's apartment. Her expression was sullen, her features familiar. She'd reminded me of my sister.

Ameera

Δ

"But what're you concerned about? What's been said about me?"
My voice rose in fear.

Ameera at Atlantis is a swinger. These were the words that
caused Anita to "investigate" me. And now new words were
joining them: *There are concerns regarding your professional conduct.* She'd intimated that her investigation had confirmed these
concerns. She'd put me on probation until the end of my contract. Probation!

"I'm not at liberty to say. This was a confidential investigation."
I imagined Anita's thin, tight lips enunciating into the phone. I
hoped she was squirming in her ergonomic office chair, like I
was, my armpits dampening with each uncomfortable word.

"Did you hear from the complainer again?" *Complainant?
Complainee?* I tapped my pen against the desk blotter and tried
to regain my focus.

"No. There hasn't been another complaint. I'm sorry, I can't
divulge anything else." Her tone was like a door closing. I put my
shoulder to it.

"But how can I defend myself if I don't know what's been
said?" A mix of self-righteousness and fear and humiliation
cloyed at me. It was happening again. It wasn't fair and no one
would take my side. I was back in a bar's dark alley, my integrity
scraped away. It was Gavin and Tamara all over again.

"My hands are tied. I've got my own pressures coming down from my boss. I'd be happy to ignore this but I'm *forced* to take the complaint seriously and probation is the lightest and least disruptive measure." Then she informed me that I would need to complete a two-hour training module administered by the Human Resources department. Was I supposed to feel grateful?

"My contract won't be renewed, will it?" I tried not to sound like a small, whining child. I curled into a tight ball, and my chair rolled itself away from the desk, the phone cord unwinding and stretching itself taut.

"We've got a lot of restructuring going on around here. I suggest that you continue to do the great job you're doing. But," Anita said gaily, her tone incongruous with her words, "I'd like you to be more formal with guests in general."

I pulled myself back to the desk and took a deep breath. *It will be fine.*

"Did you get my proposal about the Playa Escondido excursion?"

"Yes, but we're putting a hold on new excursions for now. Perhaps we'll think about that when we add a second resort in the area next year," Anita said, noncommittally.

The conversation left me in a paranoid funk. I spent interminable hours alone in my room analyzing my defamation. Roberto, Manuela, and Blythe wouldn't have mentioned anything that suggested I hadn't been professional, would they? No. There was only person who would have intentionally said anything negative about me. Oscar.

I imagined his arrogant tone as he detailed a list of indiscretions to Anita. *She acts like the recreation staff!*

But why would Anita take him seriously? Surely with three other positive references, Oscar would sound like a grumpy outlier, perhaps even a prude. Three against one. Unless he had some specific information that connected me undeniably to the complaints. But what?

And why? I could see him doing it just to unload his old grudge. Or maybe he had a misguided strategy to raise his own profile; his sales stats were the lowest and mine the highest. He probably thought he could out-compete me for the supervisor job by badmouthing me. The jerk.

Δ

Nightly trips to the bar offered respite from my brooding, and forced me to shower, put on a sundress, and a brave face for Enrique. I sat for hours, sipping and casting glances at his deft hands and toned biceps. I returned his flirtatious smiles and could almost lose myself in the fantasy of his warm lips on my neck. By the third Atlantis Mantis, my fears were so dulled I could imagine that I was having fun. I allowed a single man to ask me the half-dozen inane questions that would lead him to imagine me sharing his bed, and then slurred good night. I tottered down the path to my room.

Azeez

∞

It didn't take long to find Nora. She worked at the same bank, but had her own office with a sign on the door that indicated she was a manager. She spent long hours there in front of her computer. I eavesdropped on her for a day, observing screen after screen of confidential numbers that defined and governed the lives of humans. It was horribly boring.

Nora's new townhouse was a few blocks from her old apartment building. She lived alone now. She had a home gym, with a treadmill and dumbbells that she used three times a week. There was also a guest bedroom with a single bed, dresser, and desk. Its walls were painted a soft yellow and the closet and drawers were empty.

On my second day with her, I read a magazine over her shoulder. It was dated February 2015 but I could tell from the darkness outside that it was still mid-January.

She skimmed articles about love and romance and sighed a breeze of hopelessness. Errant thoughts of previous boyfriends flashed across her consciousness, yet I found it difficult to know her true feelings from her exhalations; she was rather guarded, even with herself. I put my head to her breast and her heartbeat was slow and steady. She was so different from the girl with whom I'd once shared an afternoon.

While I wasn't sure, I had a strong suspicion who Ameera was and why I'd had to wait for her. I snooped around Nora's home,

and observed a number of framed photographs of her: as a young
girl with pigtails: in fancy dress at a high school dance; enrobed
in a university graduation portrait. In the middle of the night,
I spent an hour pulling open an armoire (telekinesis was still a
chore) and found a drawer full of albums. One of them read:

AMEERA'S 6TH BIRTHDAY PARTY, APRIL 1992

A younger version of Nora held a cake in front of a little girl,
the candles brightening her face.

I did the math. Ameera was born in April 1986. The first and
only time I'd ever had sex was summer solstice, 1985. I hadn't
thought to bring a condom, hadn't imagined I'd be so lucky that day.

It was 1985. Thirty years had passed and I'd been a spirit for
longer than I'd lived on earth. Was it really possible that I had a
daughter the same age as I had been when I died?

Nora had remembered my sister's name. I'm so glad I'd been
been silly enough to write my siblings' names on a paper napkin
that day at the coffee shop.

Ameera, the one I was supposed to watch over, was Nora's
daughter. Our daughter. My daughter.

What was she like? Was she anything like me? Was she studying or did she have a job? Did she like science?

I spent many long days hovering near Nora's lips. Her mind
was like a concrete fortress and most of the time I couldn't cross
the moat. While she slept, I repeated her daughter's name, and
every so often she took the bait. She had inane, robotic conversations with her daughter about food, the weather, clothing. Often,
sadness drifted in and out of these dreams.

Is Ameera dead? I asked my spirit guides.

No, Nora just misses her.

Where is she?

Are you pulled south?

A clue!

South? Where south? How far south?

South. You know we're not very good at giving directions.

I focused on my imagined version of Ameera, but there were no beacons drawing me anywhere specific. While I could picture her face from Nora's collection of photos, I couldn't perceive her energy, her essence, her mind. Many more days passed and I grew listless. Is that what humans call depression? I found myself so close to finding Ameera, yet also so far. I couldn't comprehend why her mother wouldn't breathe me Ameera's whereabouts.

Just as my energy was depleting, Nora's perked up. I watched her shop for new clothes. In the mornings, she put on lipstick and eyeliner. One night she brought home a bottle of perfume and removed it from the box, looking lovingly at it. When she twisted the cap I leaned in to sniff it. Sandlewood. Ah, there it was, a little of the old Nora back! She dabbed a drop on her neck and I burrowed my neck into her, her scent taking me back in time, back to her bed in Westdale.

∞

"Don't you think you should pull out now?" She asked. I opened my eyes briefly to see a note of alarm in hers. I nodded and raised myself onto my forearms. But I didn't pull out, not then.

No, I kept going. My flesh was singing warm and free. Oh, how lovely was her embrace!

And then, in the millisecond when I ought to have paused, I let go, depositing two hundred million sperm into her.

The wiry hair on my neck stood in alarm and I panicked. What if one of my sperm hit its egg target? That's how I imagined her eggs: microscopic dartboards with impatient bulls-eyes. After all, she was twenty-one, her body yearning and likely fertile. I scurried to the bathroom to wash, as though she was the one who'd polluted me.

I'd behaved badly.

∞

Nora went out that night and didn't come home until very late. A middle-aged man dropped her off at her house. He kissed her good night and blew impulsivity and kindness. In a vulnerable moment, Nora exhaled: *smittensmittensmitten!* Her pale cheeks flushed pink.

Yet something was bothering her. Almost nightly, soon after starting to date that man, Nora awoke from nightmares. Free-floating anxiety coated her dreams like acid rain. Late for work. Missing an exam. Searching for bathrooms with a full bladder. Her daughter's plane crashing. While she fretted in her dreams, I whispered *shhhh, shhhh, shhhh. It's okay, you are fine.* I'm not sure if I got through to her.

Meanwhile, I worried that I was somehow responsible for her disquiet.

Ameera

Δ

In the midday heat, Oscar lounged in his chair, while the rest of us perched on file boxes or leaned uncomfortably against the airport kiosk.

"How are things regarding that complaint? I spoke with Anita on Monday," Blythe asked. Despite her hushed tone, the others paused their conversations to hear my answer. I'd been avoiding them and this topic for days. I'd eaten meals in my room, hadn't returned Manuela's calls, and tried not to cross paths with Blythe in the residence.

"She called me on Tuesday," Manuela added.

"You got a good reference from me," said Roberto. I nodded to them and then turned to Oscar.

"*Yo tambien*. Me, too," Oscar concurred.

"I don't want to talk about it," I said stonily. I continued to stare at Oscar. Manuela looked at us curiously, her eyes darting between my cranky expression and Oscar's clueless one. I should have told Manuela what was happening, but I couldn't talk about the probation. I was like a volcano ready to erupt, bilious lava threatening to spew from my mouth.

"Oh, I'm sure they'll sort it all out soon," Blythe said, sympathetically.

"Online complaints are stupid." Roberto nodded.

"They are." I stood and released Oscar from my gaze just as the tourists trickled out of the terminal.

Δ

Nearly everyone had been checked in and was on their assigned buses, waiting to be delivered to Atlantis. There was one glitch, though — a family of four from Windsor, the Doiges, was not on Oceana's list. Mr. Doige had grown increasingly frustrated discussing the situation with Oscar, and was now flapping a sheet with his confirmation number in my face. I waved my colleagues into the kiosk to confer about the irregularity.

"This has never happened before, right?" I asked Manuela.

"Not that I can recall," Blythe answered.

"Never. Something's wrong," Oscar agreed. "Let's put them on Manuela's bus. We can deal with this at Atlantis. We're late."

"I'll go talk to them," Blythe volunteered. We watched her explain the situation to the Doiges.

"Finally. Such incompetents," muttered Mr. Doige. I had earlier caught a whiff of beer on his breath. He dabbed his forehead and neck with a handkerchief, and spoke and moved with an authoritative air. I stifled a nervous laugh. I wanted to think him ridiculous, but couldn't help feeling a tang of danger beneath his entitlement.

"Come on, Martin, they're doing their best," his wife said. Their two daughters trailed behind her. "I don't like to book things online."

"Jeanie, it's the twenty-first century. Everyone books online." He snatched up the handles to their rolling suitcases and strode ahead of her.

"Sorry," she said to us when her husband was out of range, "it's just been a very long day. Jessica! Marianna! Follow your father."

"¿Y para nosotros? Our day is long, too! And now that they're on my bus, they're my problem." Manuela's lipliner was smudged and her shoulders slumped with exhaustion.

"Manuela, I'll deal with them. After all, I don't have a commute home," I offered.

"*Bueno,*" Oscar said.

"I'm doing it for Manuela, not you," I shot back. His dark eyes flashed confusion.

"Thanks," Manuela said, frowning at my outburst.

Δ

When we reached the resort, I instructed a waiter to bring the Doiges welcome drinks. I was tempted to grab one, too.

"I don't have a copy." Mr. Doige handed me his confirmation papers. "You'd better make a photocopy."

"Of course." *Ass*, I added silently.

"Fine then," said Mr. Doige. I felt his gaze rove across my chest, left to right, as though reading an invisible slogan emblazoned upon my shirt.

I slipped behind the main desk and entered the confirmation numbers into an Atlantis computer. I deleted, then re-entered them twice more. Each time, they matched the correct day and month — April 17 — but from 2014, the year before. The customer names were wrong, too — assigned instead to John and Margo Thompson, for a deluxe suite. I waved to Elias, the front desk manager.

"It could be a computer error," Elias speculated, squinting at the monitor. He touched the knot of his striped tie, and pulled it tight, although it was already snug.

"But it's odd that it matches a previous reservation, isn't it?" I looked at the Doiges, who sat on the couches drinking their cocktails. Mrs. Doige laughed and whispered something to Mr. Doige. He grinned and then kissed his wife on the lips, almost tenderly. When he glanced up and noticed my gaze, his smile became a scowl. He finished his drink in a single gulp. Jessica, the younger daughter, slumped against her mother. Marianna, the elder, stared glassy-eyed at the lineup of tourists awaiting their room assignments.

"It might be fraud." Elias re-entered the numbers only to get the same results. "If it is, it will be up to Oceana to deal with it. Atlantis has already received payment from you guys."

"Fraud, really? What happens if it's fraud?" One of the front desk clerks paused and looked our way, probably because I'd said "fraud" way too excitedly. We didn't get routine-breaking moments like this very often.

"Well, resort policy is to call the police. I think the tour operators tend to be more lenient. You'll have to find out from Oceana what position they prefer to take." He stood and fastened the middle button of his suit jacket.

"Huh. Have you ever called the police on guests? Do they go to jail?" It was a complete reversal of the customer-is-always-right approach normally required of us.

"It's rare. Two times in the last five years. It's a very strict policy." His expression was grim, yet his sparse eyebrows danced as he spoke.

"Wow, I'll have to phone my supervisor tomorrow morning. But what should we do with them in the meantime?" The situation's novelty was losing its lustre. I glanced at Marianna, who had shifted to a wicker chair a few feet away from the rest of her family. Then she wandered over to the terrace and looked over its edge.

"We have space." Elias made a series of taps to his keyboard, each followed by a shake of his head. "But the best I can offer is pool view with two doubles."

"Really? Their receipt is for a double-king suite. And an ocean view." I had a feeling this was not going to go well. During low season, Oceana offered inexpensive upgrades for luxury rooms and they were the first to go.

"Sorry, we only have the cheaper rooms left." Elias smiled sympathetically and passed me the plastic key cards.

As I approached them, Mr. Doige pumped his knee in an agitated manner and Mrs. Doige bit her lip. The children matched their parents' looks of worry. Their stress was like an infectious illness that crept under my skin.

"Well, I have some bad news for you, I'm afraid. Your confirmation numbers don't match up with our reservation system and so we —" I began.

"This is appalling. This is unacceptable," fumed Mr. Doige.

I attempted again. "But we can accommodate you anyway, sir."

"You're damned right you're going to accommodate us. It's not our problem that you have some sort of flawed reservation system." Two crimson spots appeared on his cheeks like clown makeup.

"Let her finish, Martin. So you can give us the room we reserved?" Mrs. Doige asked, smiling hopefully.

"No. The deluxe suites are taken, but we can put you in a double room for now and in the morning we'll call our head office and see if we can make some other arrangements."

"A double room? What does that have?" Mrs. Doige asked. I shifted into an aggressive sales mode, pitching their assignation as an ideal option for families. *So close to the pool!*

"I can't believe this. We made our booking in September! September! That was months ago!" He ranted on for another minute, and the red spots on his cheeks spread south, dispersing and pimpling his neck.

"I'll phone our main office first thing in the morning. If we can't adequately accommodate you here, we'll find another suitable room at a partner resort if the issue is Oceana's mistake."

"If it is Oceana's mistake? Who else's mistake would this be?" Mr. Doige snarled, standing to face me. He blew sour, alcoholic breath into my face. I balled my fists, willing myself to remain still. *Calm down*, I thought. *You have to calm down.* But I didn't want to. I wanted Mr. Doige to step closer, stamp on my toes, poke an accusing finger into my chest so that I could finally vomit magma all over someone.

"Let's take the double room, and then see what she can work out tomorrow," Mrs. Doige said and her husband slowly backed away from me. I handed her the key cards, feeling both relieved and ripped off that she'd interrupted the conflict. Mr. Doige redirected his ire at the bellboy. I glanced at Marianna. Although she still faced away, I could tell that the girl's back was rigid, her arms crossed tightly across her chest.

When no one was looking, I downed a plastic cup of the welcome drink, savouring the warmth of the booze as it licked its way down my throat.

Δ

I phoned Anita during the orientation session the next day. While I dreaded speaking to her so soon after the probation conversation, I was glad to have a different reason for phoning. I left a voice mail and spent the morning waiting for her return call while remaining vigilant for the Doiges. Uncertainty troubled my stomach. At 11:00 a.m., I again tried Anita, who picked up on the fourth ring.

"Sorry, I just got in. We've got a major freak snowstorm here and traffic was horrific — I passed three accidents and it took me almost two hours to get here. And in mid-April! Bet you're glad you're there and not here, eh?" I was pleased to receive Anita's weather report; the small talk suggested that things might be normalizing between us. When Anita paused midway into the Ottawa weekend forecast, I updated her about the Doiges.

"I don't understand how this could have happened. I'll look into it. It may take until tomorrow."

"The sooner the better. He's kind of a dick," I said, and then wished I'd said something more neutral and professional-sounding. "I'd expected him to be hounding me all morning after his hostile reaction yesterday evening."

"Maybe he's chilling out now that he's on vacation." She suggested that I ask the resort manager to throw in a spa freebie until we had an answer.

"Okay," I said, doubting a massage or manicure would make a difference.

"Oh, and Ameera, I hope there're no hard feelings about the probation."

"Well, I still have questions." *No hard feelings? Really?* I pushed aside my irritation. "I wish I could respond to whoever has been defaming me. It just feels really unfair."

I still hadn't told my coworkers about the probation. Overnight, my rage had cooled, leaving behind an ashy layer of annoyance. And, well, embarrassment.

"I know. But I have to keep confidentiality. I had to make the best decision with the information I had. I'm sorry."

I sighed loudly into the phone. Maybe she really did have proof. Maybe I was getting off easy.

"But I'm happy you're handling this situation with the Doiges. You're good with people," Anita consoled.

"Thanks." We hung up. I puzzled over Anita's words: how was it that I could be both unprofessional and good with people? "The Word of the Week should be *contradicción*," I grumbled to myself, as I headed to the lobby to speak with Elias.

Δ

At 3:00 p.m., Mr. and Mrs. Doige turned up at the tour desk. His expression was stern as he rocked back and forth on his heels, while Mrs. Doige had the stance of his dutiful secretary, anxiously awaiting a memo to type. They both were in bathing suits and a fresh sunburn streaked his nose. He probably wasn't feeling it yet; it would roast overnight and smart by morning. Still, I had an urge to poke my fingernail into his burnt skin, leaving behind a crescent-moon-shaped welt.

"Have you been enjoying the day? I see you've been swimming," I said, attempting a congenial tone.

"Oh yes, very much," Mrs. Doige answered, voice pitched high, "the beach is lovely. And the kids are having a great time at the Kids Club. It's so nice to have some time on our own for a —"

"So what's the situation with our reservation?" Mr. Doige barked. A fly circled his head, and he swatted at it. His wife joined in the effort. I waited for them to finish. I'd read somewhere that flies feed mostly on fecal matter and rotting food, and deposit leftovers wherever they landed. The thought calmed me. The couple shifted a few feet to the left, which seemed to confuse the invader.

"I'm still waiting on an answer from my supervisor. We'll know more by the end of the weekend." I almost laughed as the insect continued its flight path over Mr. Doige's scalp. He, in turn, resumed his irritated swatting. Palm and pest met, the fly's wings whirring to a stop momentarily.

"I find this unacceptable. What an inconvenience. It's three o'clock! I gave you all day to sort this out and you clearly haven't." Mr. Doige's sunburnt nose glowed.

"There was a snowstorm in Ottawa, so everyone got in late today." I shrugged. "Strange for April. But you know Ottawa."

"Well, we'll just wait to hear what comes next." Mrs. Doige raised her eyebrows high on her face and looked meaningfully at Mr. Doige. He frowned in response, and Mrs. Doige took his arm and patted it maternally.

"I cannot believe it!" Mr. Doige slammed his hand against the counter.

"Well, how about I offer the two of you complimentary massages to help you relax while we wait for my supervisor to get back to me?" Earlier that afternoon, Elias had grudgingly relinquished the coupons. I hoped I wasn't prematurely using up my only tourist-calming strategy. Mrs. Doige gasped with delight.

"Are they even licensed therapists?" Mr. Doige griped.

"Let's go make an appointment while the children are in their program!" Mrs. Doige beamed. The pair walked toward the lobby, Mrs. Doige whispering something in her husband's ear. He laughed, put his arm around her shoulders, pulling her close. His arm swept down to her bottom. I frowned as they ambled around a corner and disappeared from sight.

Near the end of our shift, Manuela passed me a message she'd taken while I'd been on a break. She'd written it on the company's lavender telephone form.

From: Jerome Lewis (Online Supervisor).

She'd checked off the box indicating that I should call back.

Urgent.
Manuela's initials and a :-)

"The phone number isn't Oceana's one-eight-hundred line. It looks like a private line."

"Maybe he's calling from home?" Manuela guessed.

I dialled the number. Jerome Lewis's outgoing voicemail recording was a Lykke Li song, "Jerome". Malika had included in on my birthday CD, which I'd been listening to almost daily since its arrival. I sang along until the beep and left a message.

Azeez

∞

I became an invisible tenant in Nora's house, settling into her life as much as I had my Mumbai home. I eavesdropped on her conversations, ruminations, and aspirations, many of which centred on Victor, her suitor.

They'd met in January, and within two months were spending most evenings and weekends together. I whispered cautionary messages to slow down, take her time, but she wouldn't hear me. On the outside, she was the bold girl I'd met thirty years earlier. At night, she tossed and turned with a torment I couldn't calm.

I ate dinner with them, watched their favourite show, *Parks and Recreation*, listened to their snores. It was confounding that I couldn't sense Ameera's location. In fact, I couldn't pick up on her at all. I whinged to my guides: *If she's my daughter, shouldn't I be able to feel her?* I'd been able to find other humans without much difficulty.

She doesn't know you. And you don't know her. Yet.

But how is she going to know me if I can't go to her? And vice versa?

You must go to her first. Then she will begin to know you.

But how will I find her?

Around and around we went. And then, my answer arrived.

∞

Nora's magazine was dated March 2015, which matched the late-winter sunshine slanting through the window. She called out to Victor, attempting to draw him into her reading.

"C'mon, do this quiz with me. It'll be fun! It's about your romance IQ." She laughed nervously and I leaned in. Her breath smelled of coffee and anxiety. She and Victor hadn't shared intimacy that week. She worried their ardour was already fizzling out.

"Babe, I've gotta get ready for work," he yelled back.

Nora sighed, deciding his answer was confirmation of her fears. She completed the quiz in pencil, then calculated her score: thirty-two. The box in the sidebar indicated that she was a Timid Romantic. She hastily erased her answers until the page was pristine.

She opened the second magazine to a spread of women's lingerie, pausing at a display of crimson satin teddies. I wondered if Victor was the type to purchase something like that for her. On Valentine's Day all he managed was a grocery-store bouquet and a box of chocolates.

Leave the page open on the table for him to notice, I coached her.

She frowned, put the magazine on the coffee table, splayed open. Had she heard me? Then she seemed to change her mind and stacked the magazines one atop the other. Once again she frowned and then exclaimed, "I forgot to mail them! February and March! Where's my head at?"

"What did you say, babe?" Victor strolled into the living room with toothpaste frothing from the corners of his mouth.

"Oh, nothing. I just forgot to send Ameera these magazines last month. And her birthday is in three weeks. I better get on that, too — sometimes the mail is really slow. I still need to buy her a present."

At her tidy desk in the corner of her kitchen, she reached for a large yellow envelope and stuffed the magazines inside. She fumbled in her drawer for a slip of paper, and then, with a green marker, addressed the package to her daughter in neat, deliberate block letters. I'd poked through that drawer, sifted through her address book, but hadn't seen that scrap with Ameera's address. How had I missed it?

It wasn't time yet, my guides chimed in unison.

I sighed weariness into the cosmos. But, finally, I had a destination.

Ameera

Δ

"A dedicated bunch." I wiped sweat from my brow. Blythe and I were sipping coffee and gazing out at the Sunday morning exercise class. Although the morning had been especially hot, half the dance floor was covered by sneakered, dancing feet.

"Bonkers to do it in this heat."

As the class progressed, the participants withered, their swings and swoops shifting into near slow motion. The phone rang and Blythe answered.

"Anita, hullo! Oppressively hot ... oh yes, I signed it last week and e-mailed it back. Don't worry, of course I haven't. Yes, and neither the other matter," Blythe spoke in a hushed tone and then glanced at me nervously. She said her goodbyes and passed me the phone. She ignored my curious look.

"Hi, Ameera. Well I have news. Your Mr. and Mrs. Doige are nowhere to be found in our system. There's no record of payment. We suspect that they hacked into our system and created fraudulent confirmation numbers."

"Really? How?"

"We're still sorting that out. The online department has to answer for the lack of security that allowed this to happen," she said with annoyance.

"Is Oceana going to take legal action?" I hoped I wouldn't have to call the police on them.

"I doubt our legal department will want to spend money on this. Also, there's a small chance the Doiges are victims of a third party, perhaps a travel agent, looking to make some extra money on the side. If that's the case, they will have to take it up with their credit card company."

"What happens next?" I pulled up a stool in preparation for her reply.

"Oceana can't afford to give away free rooms." She explained that the Doiges would have to pay for the hotel cost for the days they'd stayed and any additional time they wanted.

"Okay." I remembered a recent company newsletter that boasted our highest profits in five years. "So who tells them all this?" My stomach sank, predicting the answer.

"You've been the main contact. And hey," she said, sounding as though she was stage-whispering, "this will give me an opportunity to write a commendation in your file, you know, to balance things out a bit? I'll make sure to tell our director about your handling of the situation." Anita's conspiratorial tone gave me pause. Perhaps things would turn out all right. Maybe this probation thing wasn't as career-damaging as I'd feared.

"Use a soft but firm touch. Get Roberto or Oscar to help. It might be good to have a man on hand." I wondered what Marianna, the elder daughter with the long braid down her back, would feel about all of this.

Anita requested a follow-up report the next day and then we said goodbye. I vented to Blythe and she offered to assist, but I declined; Roberto would be back with the turtle sight-seers in two hours and I agreed with Anita's advice to recruit a man. Mr. Doige seemed the sort who wouldn't accept a woman's authority.

"So what were you talking to Anita about? What's the secret thing you signed?" I eyed Blythe. The mysterious comments had stayed with me, even with the greater distraction of the Doiges.

"Oh, nothing. Everyone's going to get their contracts and there are some changes, but Anita wants to deal with everyone individually," Blythe said.

"Oh come on, Blythe. Spill."

"Sorry. I really can't. But don't worry. I'm sure you'll hear something soon about your contract offer." She smiled earnestly at me.

"Yeah, if Oscar didn't completely ruin my chances. I'm fairly certain he said something awful to Anita when she was conducting her so-called investigation."

"Well … that wouldn't surprise me," Blythe said, nodding sagely. "Are you going to talk to him about it?"

"I don't know. Probably not. What's the point?"

"Yeah. You know how he is," she said, looking out toward the cardio class, her forehead wrinkled in concentration.

Δ

A few minutes later, the phone rang again.

"Is this Ameera?" The man asked. His voice was scratchy like Gavin's and for a moment I was awash in expectation, my heart fluttering, my stomach dropping. But then he cleared his throat and his voice grew clearer and deeper. "This is Jerome, I'm Supervisor of Oceana Online Sales."

"Oh. Hello. Yes, this is Ameera."

"Good. I need to chat with you about the fraud. It's urgent." He spoke quickly and sounded stressed.

"Sure, but listen, Anita just called and gave me the lowdown. She gave me instructions on what to do."

"She did? That's weird. Um …" He seemed to be thinking aloud. "Sorry, we must have our wires crossed. For some reason I thought I was supposed to phone you. Well…I'm glad things are taken care of."

"Thanks for phoning on your day off. And that's a great song on your outgoing message, by the way."

"Yeah I just heard it yesterday and changed my message as a lark."

We said goodbye and I turned my mind back to the Doiges.

How exactly would I deliver their eviction notice with a "soft but firm" touch?

Azeez

∞

She resembled my sister, with intense, dark eyes, a perfect oval face, light brown skin, shoulder-length brown hair. But this description was too mundane for my Ameera. Her eyes shone like a sky full of stars. Her smile was a thousand joys. She carried herself with a royal air. But you had to look closely. If you didn't, she'd be any other pretty young woman.

I was overcome by her. My spirit's aura turned indigo with the elation of new love.

I was certain it was my fate to meet her before transitioning to the next world, but I was less clear on what to do next. What influence was I supposed to have on this wondrous being? What would I need to learn from her? What was our unfinished business?

I stuck close, gathered information, and gradually introduced myself while she slept. She allowed me to enter her dreams, although my messages often transmitted in patchy sound bites. And nothing passed through when she was intoxicated. Alcohol is the ghost's kryptonite.

While she slept, I offered her lush dreams, and told her whatever I could about myself. But when she was awake, I endeavoured to make my words sound like her own internal voice, like intuition, gut feelings. I got overexcited and switched to Gujarati once. Sometimes I forgot to be neutral and conversed with her as myself, which I'm sure was odd-sounding at best, and creepy at worst. I didn't want to scare her. Humans don't like to feel haunted. But I was encouraged! Through short transmissions, my girl could hear me, even if she didn't know it!

I followed her around her strange paradise. I'd seen similar resorts when I'd surveilled my brother on his extramarital trips to Goa or Thailand. I suspected that Ameera had enjoyed Atlantis once, but by the time I found her she was indifferent to its earthly miracles. She was itchy for new experiences and pleasures, the nature of which she only partly understood.

She had unconventional relations. I did not focus on the physical details of them; I didn't want to snoop. TMI, Nafees would have said. Besides, we spirits are far afield from flesh. For us, human sex is a neutral thing, like playing a game of cards, negotiating a business transaction, or having a conversation. None of these activities are better or worse than the other, healthier or more moral. All can inspire truth and beauty or treachery and ugliness.

I knew from my single experience that humans don't see it this way. Sex is loaded with judgments and fears and hopes and desires. It can even be magical. And I suppose for me it was because look! It created her.

While I didn't watch her corporeal explorations, I did listen to her thoughts about her liaisons, what it all meant to her. I was keen to understand her reflections on the bodybuilders, or that couple from Italy. I could tell she was open to sensation and delight. But she'd also get herself into trouble when she didn't listen to her intuition, and, like her mother, she made poor choices when she was too full of the yearning she couldn't name.

What was that yearning? Not to be narcissistic, but I think Ameera was longing for me. To know me, my story, to know who she was in relation to me. I'd seen and heard it each time she'd struggled to speak our murky story — with her drunken lovers, with the Indians on the beach. We all need family, to know our ancestry.

And so I whispered to her in her sleep:

Ameera! Death is like a strange, long-distance relationship. Except there are no telephones. I know it sometimes feels one-way, but it isn't. You must trust that I am here, at the other end of the connection. Listen carefully. I'm here. Ameera!

Ameera

Δ

"Well good morning! Do you have news for us?" Mrs. Doige asked. I detected a note of trepidation just below her pleasantness.

"Yes. Please come down to the main lobby." I held the phone tightly in my hand. "It's better that we go through all the details. In person." Roberto had suggested this strategy. Mrs. Doige said nothing and then there was a sound like a breeze blowing through the phone.

"Yes, what is it?" Mr. Doige came on the line. I bet he'd snatched the receiver from his wife's hand.

"I'll meet you in the lobby. See you soon!" My excessively cheery tone, followed by my abrupt hang-up, probably made me sound foolish, but it was all I could manage. I looked at Roberto, who nodded his approval. I was glad that Anita wasn't there to observe my nervous bumbling.

The phone rang at the lobby's front counter. A clerk answered and gestured that it was the Doiges calling back. Roberto took the call and restated my instructions twice more.

"He didn't want to come down. But he's getting dressed and will be here in fifteen minutes," he reported.

"Thanks. You called security, right?"

"Yes. And I'll tell the rest of staff." Roberto's tone was formal and serious, but as he turned to go, he patted my shoulder and smiled.

"I wish we could just call the cops on them," I grumbled. I stepped into the cool of the air-conditioned main office and waited for the wet around my armpits to dry.

Δ

The Doiges arrived half an hour later, dressed for a day at the beach, in bathing suits, flip-flops, and with towels slung over their shoulders. Jessica, the younger girl, wore an inflated ring around her waist. Marianna carried a red flutter board and a look of unease. The family was guided to one end of the lobby's main counter, a barrier behind which Roberto and I positioned ourselves.

"Thanks for meeting us here." I breathlessly delivered their options. I handed them their bill and an itemized list of what they'd owe if they remained at Atlantis or transferred to a sister resort. I told them that Oceana suspected fraud without directly accusing them of the crime. I tried to sound firm, but Mr. Doige interrupted multiple times and Roberto, like a backup singer, had to jump in and echo some of my lines.

Mrs. Doige's mouth formed a surprised and innocent O. Then her eyes welled with tears, and fear paled her face. Jessica pinched her inflatable ring, as though testing its strength, and Marianna smacked her fingers and took her by the hand, guiding her to a nearby wicker sofa. She'd abandoned her flutter board, leaning it against her father's knee. He didn't notice because he was occupied with his yelling, his voice flinging itself high above us and up to the lobby's ceiling fans. Their blades turned slowly, half-heartedly combining his words and humid air before nudging them back down.

A small crowd of vacationers and staff collected in the lobby, drawn by the drama. I counted nine sets of demanding eyes — they were looking at me, as though I were to blame for the commotion — and I felt my face flush hot.

I wished I could take the girls down to the beach. We'd pull off our shoes and feel cool sand squishing between our toes. Then we'd wade into the sea, the ocean frothing around our shins, raising goose bumps up our thighs. We'd stay there until the surf's spray had misted cool on our faces and its roar had quieted the memory of their father's noise.

But Mr. Doige's voice wasn't quieting. Rather, it had grown from indignation into something that sounded like the inside of a wasps' nest. I glanced at Roberto. His mouth moved and his arms gestured, but I couldn't hear him over the buzzing in my head.

Breathe. The noise dimmed and I could hear: *It will be fine. Look at Roberto. Breathe.*

Roberto laid his hand on my forearm, and, like in a game of freeze tag, I thawed. My head cleared and his voice became audible. He said, "Please calm down. Mr. Doige. This is not constructive. If you don't calm down now, we will have to ask security to escort you out."

You can do this. You're stronger than him. Than all of them.

I scanned the blaming crowd and narrowed my eyes at them, daring them to look away. I forced my attention back to Mr. Doige, who was now yelling at me, alternating his gaze between my face and cleavage. I crossed my arms over my chest, but then, after a moment, let them drop. There was a pain in my back ribs, a slow burning ache, so I stretched a little taller, uncurling my spine. I filled my lungs with warm Huatulco air and bellowed, "Stop! That's enough."

My words filled the lobby, gathered strength, and boomeranged louder. They forced Mr. Doige to shut his trap. "Listen, we've presented your options, and that's all we have to say." I held up my hand to stop Mr. Doige from resuming his argument. He and I locked eyes into a stare-down until he faltered. His glare was like an injured cockroach, landing on the lobby's tile floor and skittering away into a dusty corner to hide and recover.

"That's all we have to say," Roberto chimed in.

"Our concierge can help you find other accommodations and will assist you to contact your credit card company," I said, looking first at Mr. Doige, and then at Mrs. Doige.

"Well!" Mr. Doige fumed. "You haven't heard the end of this!" He took Mrs. Doige by the arm, and they hurried from the lobby. Their daughters remained on the couch, facing away from the counter, apparently oblivious to their parents' departure. How did they manage to space out? I was about to go to them when Mrs. Doige rushed back a minute later. She collected her children, explaining to them that they had to pack up and go to another hotel. Jessica whined, "But I want to go to the beach!"

"Don't worry about him. He knows we've caught him. I think we *have* heard the end of this," Roberto said, quietly.

"God, I hope so. What an asshole."

"There's your Word of the Week: *Pendejo. El es un pendejo.*" I managed a feeble smile.

We returned to the tour desk and awaited further news about the Doiges. I stressed about whether they'd trash their room, or write a complaint about me. What if a third letter ended up in my employee file? At least there would be witnesses this time.

I later learned that the family had left, managing to slip past the security guard who swore he never strayed from their hallway. When the housekeeping staff entered their room, they found the room empty and clean, almost as though the Doiges had never been there in the first place. A red foam flutter board, abandoned in the lobby, was the only concrete evidence of the family's stay.

Δ

Their strange disappearance made me think about Raymond. Mom dated him for a couple of months when I was in high school, her first serious guy in over a decade. His presence was weird for me. It had always just been the two of us, and then she permitted this stranger into our private world.

He smiled a perfect straight line of white, like an actor in a toothpaste commercial. His good teeth must have distracted Mom from his shaggy hair and stinky breath. They'd met at a work holiday party and she told me they danced to Dan Hill's "Sometimes When We Touch." Anyway, a few weeks later, he lost his job and revised his resumé, typing our address as his own.

In the end he only lived with us for a month and a half, and moved out just when I was getting used to him being there.

The night before he left, I'd listened to them argue from my bedroom and wasn't sure what to do. As her voice became inaudible, his grew louder, his angry sentences bouncing off the wallpaper. After a few minutes the yelling stopped and he slammed the door behind him.

I went out to her. I'd only seen Mom cry a half-dozen times before that. Her skin was blotchy, her nose ran, and her eyes stayed red for hours after. But she told me there was nothing to be concerned about. She let me hug her for a minute, her body stiff as cardboard. Then we went to bed.

After school the next day, I could tell he was gone for good. It was more than that his shoes and coat were missing from the hall closet; he'd left behind something that felt like a void. I realized then that even though I barely knew the guy, and didn't love the idea of him living with us, I'd hoped that things would work out between them.

She arrived two hours later and I followed her on her tour of the apartment. She opened her bedroom closet and stared at the empty space on his side of the rack. Then she rearranged her pantsuits and dresses, spacing the hangers evenly across the bar. I stood stock-still in the doorway, not knowing how to console her.

Mom opened and closed each of Raymond's three dress-er drawers, open-shut, open-shut, open-shut, so quickly that I couldn't tell if they'd been emptied, too. When I checked the following day after school, they were full of her socks and underwear.

She never explained what happened, saying that it was a "personal adult matter." But, bitter from the breakup, Mom had muttered, "Ameera, men are like that. All they want is sex. Everyone I've dated. Even your biological father. They're all the same."

I received her hypothesis with resistance. I was young and completely inexperienced with things that had to do with sex and relationships, so I could have believed her. But I didn't want to believe her.

After Raymond disappeared, I had strange thoughts about Azeez, and they took over my brain for a couple of weeks. I puzzled over why Azeez didn't call her. Why he didn't want to know my mother better. A further impossible question: even though he didn't know of my existence, why didn't he stay for me?

Azeez

∞

There was so much I wanted Ameera to know. I offered her glimpses of her aunt and uncle, her cousins. I told her the story of how her great-grandfather moved from Gujarat to Bombay with little more than a suitcase and a dozen rupees. I showed her pictures of Mummy and Daddy. I called the spirits of my ancestors to watch over her.

I hadn't yet disclosed the details of my demise. Although it was far in the past, I still preferred to avoid my memories of explosions and drowning. I didn't want to burden her with such images. Not yet.

I advised her that she needn't worry so much. My guides had shown me flashes of her future, probably to convey to me that I needn't worry so much. I'm not allowed to share the particulars, but the girl had a good life ahead of her. She'd find love. She'd find contentment.

Now that I'd finally found her, I wondered how long we had together. It was an utterly human sort of question and yet I was asking it.

You'll have as long as you both need.

How long is that?

Time is but a construct. You'll know.

But I've just begun to know my daughter!

My guides remained quiet.

∞

That night I said to her:

I'm sorry I didn't come sooner. I truly apologize for the delay. Blame the guides — they were no help. Just kidding.

Ameera

Δ

I slept fitfully that week. Twitchy conversations between Anita and my colleagues filled my dreamscape. I begged Oscar, Manuela, Roberto, and Blythe to keep my secrets and to give my work a positive review. Instead, they conspired to have me fired, all four reporting to Anita that I was unfit for the job.

Thankfully, my lucid mind interrupted some of these nightmares. It flew me to India and I strolled a Mumbai suburb in the middle of the night. The air was warm and still, the moon full, its luminosity shining down on a place that felt like home. But then the quiet streets gradually transformed into Atlantis's stone pathways and I'd bump into my duplicitous co-workers again.

When distraction came on Thursday night, I reached for it. It had been almost a month since Serena and Sebastiano, and although I'd been tempted by one potential attractive couple the previous week, I'd steered clear of swingers since the complaint. It was hard for me; I'd become accustomed to getting laid on a fairly regular basis. The more I had sex, the more I wanted it.

I renegotiated my bargain with myself: once in a while would be fine. Besides, after dealing with the Doiges, I deserved a treat. I showered, put on good underwear and chose a strapless bra. I'd never before been asked out by a lesbian couple. At least I assumed that's what was happening. I expected it might be something like my usual swinger dates, only with two women.

But then again, Wanda and Jessie didn't follow the usual script of swinger women. Those invitations tended to be flirtatious, yet indirect. Wives usually employed coy looks and smiles and pretend passivity. Their men normally took the lead and were in a hurry to make things happen.

Not so with Wanda and Jessie. They'd found me earlier that day and asked me to join them for drinks, both of them looking me in the eye. When I said yes, Wanda blurted that they'd wanted to ask me out for days, blushing coral with her admission.

I fussed over what to wear; would my usual strappy sundress and flip-flops do? I'd observed Wanda and Jessie around the resort all week, noticed that Jessie had a masculine style and Wanda a more feminine one. I knew the stereotypes about "who wore the pants" were mostly nonsense, but still, I saw that Jessie opened doors, pulled out chairs, and carried the drinks for Wanda. I thought it was sweet. I abandoned my bra and chose a dress with deep cleavage and an empire waist.

When I arrived at the bar five minutes early, they were already there waiting for me.

"How was dinner?" They'd gone to one of Atlantis's à la carte restaurants, China Lily.

"Fake Chinese food. Normally I can't stand the stuff, but we needed a break from the buffet," Jessie said.

"Nothing like your mother cooks," Wanda agreed, explaining that Jessie's family had emigrated from Hong Kong.

"And what was with the decor? There were a bunch of Chinese lanterns, but the tapestries looked Middle Eastern or something," asked Jessie, running her hand through her short black hair.

"Oh, right. That's because until a year and a half ago it was The Sultan, a Moroccan restaurant. Wasn't as popular. I guess the management thought it was a waste to get rid of the wall hangings and pillows and stuff." I hadn't before given any thought to the ridiculous ethnic mishmash.

Like the beginnings of most dates, the conversation loped along clumsily at first. Wanda asked, "Did you know *Pope Joan* was shot in Morocco?" Then Jessie discussed two other films they'd recently seen, both of which I hadn't heard of; since coming to Huatulco the only movies I'd watched were documentaries about swingers.

Wanda told me they were winter sports enthusiasts, and normally took skiing holidays in Vail each winter. This was their first sun vacation because Wanda was recovering from a sprained ankle caused by ice dancing at the Toronto Harbourfront rink on New Year's Eve.

"She was doing a lot of fancy Lady Gaga moves," Jessie teased, posing with her hand on her hip and popping her shoulder forward.

"And then down I went, crash! Since I turned thirty-five, everything takes longer to heal." Wanda's smile revealed deep dimples. I wondered who was going to have to make the first move — one of them? Me?

"Yeah, yeah, old lady!" Jessie laughed. At this, the three of us took a moment to disclose our ages: Wanda, thirty-six; Jessie thirty-two; me, twenty-nine. Then there was a round of sharing of astrological signs: Sagittarius, Taurus, Aries. I suppressed a laugh when Wanda nodded pensively at our answers and Jessie rolled her eyes.

"But anyway, New Year's Eve was a gorgeous night, even with the fall," Wanda said, wistfully. "Almost no wind. Light flurries."

I touched my glass to my cheek and closed my eyes, recalling the sensation of snowflakes melting on my cheeks like tiny cold kisses. When I opened my eyes again, Jessie had gone to refresh our drinks and Wanda's gaze was upon me.

"Are you okay? You drifted off there for a second," she asked, her hand lightly pressing my knee. The gesture alerted me that we'd shifted past friendly conversation. I knew Wanda awaited an in-kind reply.

"I'm a little warm, I guess." I smiled, hooking Wanda's index finger with my pinkie. Her hand settled in, her thumb massaging small circles on the inside of my knee. When Jessie returned with fresh drinks, a slow smile spread across her face when she saw our linked hands.

"Why don't we take these drinks back to our room?" Wanda suggested.

"Yeah! Come back to our place. We've got a huge deck that faces the sea," Jessie said.

"You two have a terrace suite? There are only a half-dozen of those at Atlantis. Are you on a honeymoon or something?" I had seen one during my orientation tour. Oceana advertised them to couples that booked destination weddings.

"Sort of. We had a commitment ceremony last fall, but didn't have time to go away. We're not really into the church-and state-sanctioned marriage thing," Jessie said.

"But we support same-sex marriage, for people who want that," Wanda added quickly, sweeping her curly hair out of her eyes.

"It's because we're polyamorous. Although we're committed to each other, we don't believe in monogamy, and, well, same-sex marriage still privileges that, right?" Jessie pulled her shirt sleeves down her arms awkwardly.

"Right," I said uncertainly. I'd read about polyamorous people and how they differentiated themselves from swingers, but didn't understand the argument against marriage. "Well, congratulations on your commitment ceremony." I clinked my glass against each of theirs.

"Are you poly, too?" Wanda asked.

"No, but I date a lot of couples. So I guess I'd be … non-monogamous?" I didn't like how this came out like a question.

"Cool," Jessie said with a nod.

They were mostly quiet on the walk across the resort. When we passed the shore, Jessie pointed to iguanas hiding in the rocks. We watched them emerge in search of food. The ubiquitous reptiles had been fascinating my first year on the job, but after that, I'd almost stopped noticing them.

I wondered how the night would proceed. Technically, I wouldn't be a unicorn with these two women, a role I more or less understood by then. However, as the new person in a triad, I usually received the most attention, and had to balance this with whoever appeared to be the more sensitive or jealous partner. If I ignored such dynamics, situations like the one with Doug and Suzanne could erupt.

And then my anxieties unravelled like a scratchy ball of yarn:

Suzanne and Todd

Anita

the probation

Oscar

three more years in this job without a promotion

As though sensing my shift in mood, Wanda broke her stride and sandwiched me between the two of them. She grabbed my hand, swung it playfully, and I relaxed again. We walked along the quiet, dark path, wordlessly unclasping our linked hands when we heard strangers' voices and footsteps, and then reattaching when it was safe again.

At their suite, Wanda slid her key card into the lock and Jessie gently pushed me up against the doorjamb, pressing warm lips onto mine. She tasted like rum and pineapples. Warm breath against my ear delivered her hoarse question: "Is this okay?"

"Yeah," I murmured, aware this wasn't a question I'd ever been asked after a first kiss. I closed my eyes and felt sharp teeth scraping my earlobe. Wanda's insistent hand pulled us both into the room, and the door squeaked closed behind us. Jessie opened the sliding doors leading to the terrace, and swept her arm wide in a *See?* gesture, but no one stepped outside to look.

Wanda, half a head shorter than me, sidled close, and looked up, her long lashes batting in a pantomime of flirtation. Her lips were plump and warm, and I remembered just how much I loved kissing. Then Jessie was behind Wanda, her arms reaching for me.

"We don't do this enough, eh, Wan?" Then, looking to me, she clarified. "We play separately with other lovers most of the time."

Soon, we were on the couch, with me in the middle. I couldn't keep track of it all. Whose lips were those? Whose hands were sliding up my inner thigh? I melted into their touches. After a few minutes, as though considering their manners, the women leaned around me, bypassed my mouth, and reached for the other. I had a moment to breathe.

Wanda pulled away, leered at my cleavage, and asked, "Do you have any limits we should know about?"

"Limits?"

Wanda's lipstick was mostly rubbed off, and this made me self-conscious about my own. With my thumb, I wiped at the edges of my bottom lip, then the top, just in case.

"Yeah. Our main limit is safer sex. We use condoms on toys and dams with new people," Jessie said casually, "And oh yeah, neither of us are into pee play, and all the other really messy stuff."

"And we have a safe phrase to let each other know if we're uncomfortable with something," added Wanda.

"Yeah, It's 'red rover.'" Jessie smiled.

"As in 'red rover, red rover, I call Jessie over,'" Wanda sing-songed, and then blushed. "So, any limits for you, Ameera?"

I thought about the bodybuilders from Winnipeg and how I'd made the best of the situation, feigning fatigue after I'd lost interest in them. When Doug had wanted to spank me after Suzanne left the room, I'd gone along with it, even though it wasn't really my thing. Serena kissed with too much tongue, and I'd tried not to be too obvious about turning toward Sebastiano to avoid her wet mouth. I'd been so Canadian about it all; I hadn't wanted to offend anyone.

"Well, safer sex is good. I'm not into 'messy stuff,' either." I had only a vague idea of what the latter meant and didn't want to think about it.

"Cool. Well, we brought toys!" Wanda scampered away and returned with a canvas tote bag inscribed with BEAVER CREEK SKI AND SNOWBOARD SCHOOL. She dumped its contents onto the king-sized bed. "Let us know what you like. I'm mostly a bottom, but I switch sometimes. Jessie's a top. But maybe you figured that out already."

"How about you? Any preferences?" Jessie asked. My face flushed hot under their waiting gazes.

"I think I'm sort of flexible." I knew that sounded vague, but I wasn't all that familiar with their lingo. I scanned their collection. There were two dildos, one in leopard print and another that had two cocks connected together. I imagined a customs officer inspecting them with latex-gloved hands, Wanda patiently explaining their purposes in her friendly, straightforward manner, and Jessie staring at her shoes in embarrassment.

Also in the bag were two black leather things that I guessed were harnesses, a pair of red leather handcuffs, a many-tailed whip-like thing, and a pair of instruments that looked like purple binder clips.

"What are those?"

"Ah, the Nipplettes. They're vibrating nipple clamps," said Jessie. "I can't stand them, myself, but Wanda thinks they're hot."

"Want to try them on?" Wanda asked, sliding the straps of my sundress off my shoulders. I nodded and Jessie guided the dress down to my waist and rested her hands on my hips. Wanda pinched the lavender clamps on, and pushed a button to make them vibrate. The clamps tightened.

"Youch!" I cried out in shock.

"Want 'em off?" Wanda reached to remove them.

"No, leave them for a bit," I said, relaxing into their pinch. Jessie's hands roved under my dress, searching the elastic of my underwear. A finger probed, finding heat and wetness. Wanda's lips reached for mine, soft yet demanding. The Nipplettes squeezed, their buzzing becoming pleasant background noise while Jessie's finger pushed inside me. I opened one eye and caught Jessie's smile in my peripheral vision. She repositioned us so that I was flat on my back, she between my thighs. Wanda stripped off her dress and lowered herself over my mouth. The bed shifted and I felt Jessie move away, only to return a moment later. I couldn't see, but I'm pretty sure she was wearing the leopard-patterned cock.

Δ

A couple of hours later, we drank soda from the bar fridge and munched potato chips. Wanda's head rested sleepily on Jessie's shoulder. I rose from the bed, wrapped a beach towel around my shoulders, and sat in an easy chair facing them. It was still early — just ten-thirty — but I considered dressing and heading back to my room.

Those were uneasy moments for me, right after the sexual play slowed, the energy shifted, and the disinhibitive effects of alcohol wore off. Sheets got pulled high, a bedside lamp might switch on, and the two who knew each other best would reach for familiar arms.

It was like at a school dance, when "All My Life" ended and the principal turned on the lights. The scuffed floors and basket-ball nets were once again visible and the disco ball and special dresses were revealed to be temporary, illusory. The pong of teenage sweat and rubber, cast away for a few hours, returned.

Wanda and Jessie snuggled, looks of contentment stretching across their tanned faces. Would there be a second round after the snack break? I wanted neither to overstay nor to prematurely end things. There was still half a tote bag full of toys to try. I had my eye on a harness and the double dildo, wanted to know what it might feel like to wear them.

Jessie reached forward to pass me the chip bag, jostling Wanda from her shoulder.

"Wanda's a nutritionist, you know. The only time I ever see her eating crap is when we're on vacation," Jessie said, feeding Wanda a chip. I perked up; I was curious about the more mundane aspects of my lovers' worlds. I liked to collect details about daily commutes, nine-to-five work lives, the pets and kids.

"Gotta let go sometimes," I said. "And what kind of work do you do?"

"I'm an archivist. Its pretty dull government data collection and preservation work. But I also do some private stuff on the side," she said. "Family trees."

"Jessie's working on mine right now. She found out my great-grandmother was Ojibwe. I thought I was only Scottish-Irish until recently. It's sort of cool to find out more about who you are," said Wanda.

"That's interesting." I leaned into the chair and my mind travelled faraway for a few brief moments. *Ask. Ask for her help.* I blinked and came back to Wanda and Jessie.

"Yeah. It's amazing what she can dig up," Wanda said, rising from the bed and heading to the bathroom. "Be back in a sec."

"This might be a weird question," I said and then paused to take a deep breath. "How hard would it be to find a phone number for someone in another country with just a few details? I have a first name, where he went to school, and the year of his graduation." Of course I'd pondered this before, but saying the words aloud made them vibrate in and around me, causing a slight tremor in my leg. The words forced me to stand, look for my sundress, not wait for the answer.

"No surname?"

"No. I guess that makes it pretty impossible, right?"

"Not impossible. Everything is computerized these days, right? You can search a university database by first name and graduation year. Alumni associations try to keep track of everyone to bring in donations. They're a goldmine for archivists." Jessie watched me unwedge my dress from between the couch cushions.

"Really?" I shook my dress out roughly, then pulled it over, getting my head stuck in an armhole. I took it off, righted it.

"Who're you trying to find?"

"Just someone my mother knew," I said. Where was my underwear?

"The trick is finding someone at the university willing to help. Sometimes they have strict rules about privacy," Jessie said gently. She crossed her arms over her chest, probably unsure of what to make of my vexation.

"That's good to know." I stepped into my panties, turned away her.

"You don't have to leave just yet, unless you want to," Jessie said. She walked around the side of the bed, and reached for my hand. My arms hung limply at my sides.

"You're heading out already?" Wanda asked, emerging from the bathroom. "I'm getting my second wind!"

The terrace doors were ajar, but the air in the ocean-front suite had gone stale. I struggled to breathe. Both women now looked at me carefully, as though I'd put my dress on backwards. I snuck a look down my front, confirmed that fabric met skin in appropriate places. I glanced up at them again, knew there was no way I could turn the music back on, rotate the disco ball, and be within their magic again.

"I really should get going. I have an early start tomorrow. Fridays are hectic." I looked toward the door.

"Well, thanks for the lovely evening," Wanda said, stepping close and wrapping me in a smothering hug. Jessie joined us for a brief moment, the three of us swaying under the weight of my discomfort.

"If you have any more questions about that search, contact me. I've got a website, Jessie Huang. Dot com. I'd be happy to help." Wanda looked at Jessie quizzically.

"Thanks." I backed toward the door and let myself out.

After I left Jessie and Wanda, I took the long way to my room. I paused near the pool, my mind ticking away at database searches. I gazed into the dark water, envisioning a large steel computer into which I could insert three seemingly unrelated words: *India, McMaster University, Azeez.* And also a number: *1985.* After I pressed enter, what might emerge? A syntax error? A father?

Δ

Mom went to the registrar's office in an attempt to find him. She told me the story when I was twelve, perhaps believing I was old enough to hear it.

She began with a straightforward request: "I need to pass on some news to an international student who graduated earlier this summer. Can you give me his phone number?"

The secretary shook her head. "Sorry, we can't release that sort of information."

"But it's really important."

"Sorry. Against the rules."

Flustered but persistent, Mom explained her knocked-up situation. Chances are her eyes might have welled up, and her skin flushed pink. The secretary stared at Mom's flat stomach, sighed, and relented. She flipped through the file cabinet of recent PhD science defences and asked, "Do you know his last name?" Mom said she didn't. The secretary rolled her eyes.

"Well, there's only one Azeez here. Listen, I can send a letter with your contact information to him."

Once again, my mother pleaded and began to weep. The secretary picked up the phone, perhaps because Mom looked so terrible when she cried. Or maybe she was late for a meeting, or needed a smoke break.

"Looks like a long-distance number."

"He's already gone?" My mother had hoped he might still be in town. She'd confirmed her pregnancy the previous week, but she'd suspected it a month earlier. Standing there in the office, she regretted waiting so long.

It was already afternoon and neither realized that it was almost midnight in India. The phone rang — Nora could hear the loud sonic beeping leaking from the receiver. When the secretary asked for Azeez, she was told he wasn't there and then the line abruptly disconnected.

The secretary passed her the slip of paper with the illicit phone number, along with a surly warning to never divulge its source. Mom scurried out of the office. She forgot to ask for Azeez's surname.

Mom said she attempted the number three more times, and, on her last try, a woman picked up and said something in a language she didn't understand. Perhaps Hindi. When she pressed on, the woman yelled in an angry tone, "Gone! Not here anymore!" Mom didn't try again.

"I realized then that I'd been harbouring a silly hope that he'd come back," she'd said. "He was a one-night stand, a stranger passing through my life. I knew nothing about him. I vowed right then and there to get on with things, to raise you, to find a good job and maybe one day, if it happened, I'd have another relationship." Even though she emphasized the first two wishes, I knew the last one was important to her.

She met Tom two weeks later. He didn't mind that she was pregnant, and that alone made him a good catch. They stayed together until I was two. She ended things after he slapped her face. He'd yelled and broken things before that, but the assault was her limit. I have no real memory of him and Mom destroyed all his photos. I have a vague sense — or perhaps it's imagined — of Tom rolling me in a stroller to the park. I can envision his bearded face and a canopy of green above. He was the second father I didn't know.

Shortly after Mom told me about her visit to the registrar's office, I began my hesitant Internet searches for Azeez. That was 1998 and my middle school had just opened a new computer lab. I'd type: *Azeez. Professor. India.*

Of course, nothing came up. And that was okay, in a way. What would I have done if I had found him?

Whenever the mood struck, I'd enter those three words. When I was peeved at Mom. When I felt lonely. When my skin browned in the summertime. Always with the same results.

When I was sixteen, I asked Mom if she still had the slip of paper with Azeez's phone number.

"Why would I hold on to that?" she scoffed. And then more quietly, she said, "I could have tried calling him again. But then I met Tom. I threw it away."

"Did you remember any of the numbers? Like, if there was an area code?"

"Sorry, honey. I don't. It was so long ago." She frowned and I could tell she was trying to formulate a question. She pressed her lips together, sealing the query within.

I also wanted to know if she still had the napkin, the one on which he'd spelled out his name, his sister's, and brother's. But I knew better than to ask for that.

Δ

A familiar voice called from the bar. Enrique's face was excited, his slender hands waving. I pointed to my watch, protesting that it was late and I was tired and I didn't have time to stop, but his velvet voice drew me in. "*¡Venga!* Come and taste this, Ameera! Just come for a minute. *One minute!*" He held out a red concoction, his latest version of the Atlantis Mantis. I complied, agreeing to a single sip.

"Much better. The right mix of sweet and tangy this time, Enrique." I nodded my approval.

"Yes," he said confidently. He reached out and stroked my arm from shoulder to elbow. Small hairs rose up and undulated in his direction before settling themselves down again.

"Oh, Enrique, you're such a flirt," I sighed.

"Only because you're so beautiful," he cooed. Then, frowning, as though entertaining the question for the first time, he asked, "Does it bother you?"

"No. I know you're only joking with me." My stomach fluttered with the tiny hope that he'd contradict me.

"So how was your night?" He raised his right eyebrow and gave me a knowing look.

"My night?" I leaned in closer to hear him better.

"Yes, with Wanda and Jessie. I saw you talking with them earlier. They asked me about you, wanted to know if you were … you know … gay. I told them to ask you and find out for themselves." He casually wiped the bar top.

"They asked you that? Why?" They hadn't mentioned it to me.

"Gaydar. They figured I'd know the other gay people here. You're bi, right?" He spoke in a half-whisper.

Tongue-tied, I nodded and shrugged at the same time. How had I not known *he* was gay? How had I not even considered the possibility? Now, as I looked back at our interactions over the previous couple of years, I felt foolish.

"How did you know? About … the bi thing?"

"Don't worry, it's our secret. I know you're not too obvious about it. Neither am I, except with people who are close."

"I see." What else had he noticed? Did he assume I'd had a social evening with Wanda and Jessie or a sexual one? I hoped that he couldn't smell traces of them on me. He turned to serve a guest and I gulped back the Atlantis Mantis.

Azeez

∞

Dammit. Enrique and his Atlantis Mantises! I couldn't speak to her for a couple of hours. At least she left the bar after only one and went straight to bed.

Once her body had metabolized the ethanol, I began my droning:

Talk to Jessie.

Talk to Jessie.

Ask her to find me.

Oops.

Ask her to find Azeez.

She was alone inside a falling elevator, all the buttons lit. She gripped a handrail, plummeted twenty floors, and landed at Atlantis where Mr. Doige witnessed her stripping for Jessie and Wanda.

Another trip in the elevator, free falling. She crouched on the floor to reduce the impact of the inevitable. But, somehow, her mind made the machine stop — very gently to not be jarring — and she alighted on the ground floor. I took her hand and we walked barefoot on dewy grass to the foreign workers' wing. I tucked her into bed, and pulled the crisp sheet around her shoulders. I *shhhh shhhh shhhhed* her until she relaxed into a deep slumber.

In the morning, I was her alarm clock. I bellowed:

Ameera! Ameera! Ameera!

Go talk to Jessie!

I repeated the mantra seventeen times before she relinquished a dream in which she was in Gavin's bed, nestled in his arms. He was the big spoon. I felt a little guilty for pulling her away from comfort, but time was running out.

While she dried her body from the shower and yanked a comb through her wet hair, I repeatedly trumpeted my instructions. She pulled on her clothes and rushed out the door.

I nudged her across her tropical amusement park. Pushed her. Prodded her. But I needn't have. Her thoughts had aligned with my own. Finally.

Ameera

Δ

"Is everything alright? You left pretty quickly last night ..." Wanda answered the door wrapped in a towel. Her wet apple-scented hair slapped my shoulder when she embraced me.

Jessie emerged from the bathroom fully dressed, carrying a bottle of sunscreen. She stuffed it into a freezer bag and dropped it into an open suitcase. The Beaver Creek sex-toy tote was nestled amongst Wanda's high heels.

"I had a great time with you both. I really did." I stared at the floor, gathering courage.

"We're glad. So did we," Jessie said.

"I couldn't stop thinking about what we talked about last night. There's someone I need to find. A family member."

"All right." Jessie sat on the bed and patted a spot on their crumpled sheets. I sat stiffly beside her. She opened her laptop. "Give me as much information as you have. I'll follow up when I get home."

"His name is Azeez. Spelled with two *e*'s. He might be a professor in India." I breathed deeply, all the way into my diaphragm, closed my eyes, and remembered my familiar dream, the male voice calling out to me. It was like I could hear him again.

I sat up straight and inhaled deeply, repeating his name in my head: *Azeez. Azeez. Azeez.* And then I heard the voice rasp:

Yes. Correct. It sounded like my own voice, only not me. The thought unnerved me, but I pushed it away. I opened my eyes and turned my gaze to Jessie.

"Have you ever tried doing a search based on what you know? Have you Googled him?" Jessie typed, her keystrokes rhythmic and calming.

"Yes. Nothing came up, but my attempts weren't exhaustive." That was an understatement. I hadn't ever looked beyond the second page of results.

"Okay, what else do you know?" Jessie stopped typing. I remembered my mother's feeble attempt to find him so many years ago, and the phone number she'd found and lost.

"He was a visa student, in science, at McMaster University. He'd just finished his PhD."

"That's where you'll mine the most data, eh, honey?" Wanda asked Jessie, who nodded and continued typing.

I tried to recall what else I knew about Azeez. And then an intensely strong thought came to me: *No. Not that.*

"Try that, but I have a hunch that won't work. I don't know why." Wanda and Jessie waited for me to continue. I concentrated. What else did I know? *Our ages. Our ages.* Yes, perhaps there was something useful there? I didn't know what to make of these new and fast-moving ideas, but I didn't want them to stop. "I think he was twenty-nine years old when he left, if Mom's memory is right. Oh, also, she said I was conceived on summer solstice, June 21, 1985 and he left sometime later that summer." I caught my breath and felt suddenly nauseous. "That's all I know. She never saw him again."

"So we're looking for your father," Jessie said, looking up from the screen.

"Wow. Just wow. That's big." Wanda massaged my shoulders. Heat and pain pooled through them and I eased myself out of her hold.

"Thanks. Look, I'd better go. I really appreciate this." I hurriedly gave Jessie my contact information and hugged them goodbye. *It will be all right*, I repeated to myself, as I rushed across Atlantis.

I caught my breath at the tour desk. I told myself that I didn't have to think about what I'd done, what I'd started, at least for a few days. I'd parked the problem with Jessie and I could deal with the consequences later. While my colleagues sorted departure and arrival information, I held my clipboard to my chest, trying to keep still.

"Do you think that guy will be at the airport?" Roberto had reminded me that the Doiges were scheduled to leave on Oceana's charter that day.

"We'll have to keep an eye out for them." I frowned, remembering Mr. Doige's enraged face. We discussed our strategy to deal with him. Despite the dread he inspired, it was a relief to have a concrete problem, a real man, on which to focus. I recalled the positive thinking that had helped me before: *You can do this. You're stronger than him. Than all of them.*

Later, at the airport, I tensed each time I thought I saw a balding, medium-sized white guy. For a good half hour, things were calm in the terminal. And then, while I was giving a guest directions to the bathroom, Mr. Doige charged at me, yelling about injustice and lawsuits.

"You're a company of incompetent fools!" He barked, while Mrs. Doige ushered the girls away. "I'm going to sue you all!"

Quicker than I could react, Mr. Doige's face was looming over mine, his index finger poking my shoulder. His spittle dotted my cheek. I froze, shut my eyes, turned my face away. His hot breath wafted across my neck.

Oscar, a foot shorter than Mr. Doige, forced himself in front of me, forming his body into a shield. He puffed out his chest and said, "Stop disrespecting my colleague." Within moments, Roberto and a security guard arrived and Mr. Doige backed off.

I met Oscar's eyes and saw respect in his. He patted my arm, and asked, *"¿Estás bien?"*

"Yeah." My pulse thudded in my ears.

Δ

In the bathroom, I splashed water over my face and dried my cheeks with a paper towel. Eventually, I stopped shaking and regained my composure. I stared into the mirror and it dawned on me that Oscar had been protective and kind. Was that genuine? *It wasn't him.*

"Have I been wrong about him all along?" I asked out loud, to nobody. Luckily, the bathroom was empty.

I joined my colleagues and we guided tourists through their lineups. Ten minutes later, Jessie and Wanda cleared check-in. Wanda planted a warm kiss on my face. They enfolded me in their enthusiastic arms and when they finally released me, I noticed Oscar watching with an amused expression.

"I told Anita that you are good with people," he said, nodding.

"Thanks." I flashed him a grateful smile. The grudge I'd held for days fell away like a crumbling brick wall. But on the other side stood the question: if Oscar hadn't been the one to betray me, who had?

Δ

That evening, alone in my room, I puzzled over that question. I glugged back a travel mug full of rum and cola and considered that perhaps it was none of my colleagues who'd double-crossed me. Maybe Anita had spoken to other workers on the resort, but who? My paranoid mind created an anonymous judging audience of Atlantis employees: cleaning staff, security guards, Maria, the Cardio Pump lady. Woozy from booze, I waited for clarity, hoping my internal voice would offer me something useful. It remained silent.

I scanned the *Chatelaine* Mom had sent earlier in the week. Over the past few evenings, I'd reviewed it thoroughly, checking the quizzes and the few kinked pages. I'd expected to encounter more of her in them, perhaps insights into her love life, the aspects of self she'd inventoried and required changing.

When we'd last spoken, I avoided sharing anything about the complaint or the probation, and, self-conscious about my omissions, couldn't find other topics on which to report. "Not much" was the best answer I could manage in reply to "what's new?" To my surprise, she filled the silence with her thoughts on Victor. He seemed considerate, smart, and fun. A good match. But then she anxiously listed his faults: he wasn't intellectual enough; he wasn't interested in cultural events; he didn't like to travel. I wasn't sure what to think. It wasn't like Mom was all that involved in intellectual or cultural pursuits. And she rarely travelled.

"Mom, you have to stop being so picky. You're not going to be perfectly happy with anyone."

"Oh, Ameera. I don't need a man to be happy," she'd scoffed.

Impulsively, I asked, "What do you need to be happy?"

"I *am* happy, Ameera. Everything is fine. Really ... are you okay?"

"Yeah, everything's fine," I'd answered.

I flipped through *Chatelaine*, stopping at a bent page. It was an advice column about strategies to save money to return to school. I laughed out loud at Mom's skilful, indirect prodding.

Azeez

∞

I travelled north in coach, stalking Jessie and Wanda. Certainly Jessie was smart enough to learn the truth about me, but in case she required a little guidance, I wanted to follow her home. I had to ensure I'd be able to locate her quickly if necessary.

It was my first time on an airplane since the crash and while I knew I was safe (What could happen to me? I was already dead.), a vague sense of unease accompanied me on the flight. From the way the middle-aged guy in the seat next to mine crossed and uncrossed his ankles, I could tell he was having a similar phobic response. Had he had a bad aviation experience in a previous life, too?

I put my lips to his and exhaled: *sleep sleep sleep sleep sleep*

Two minutes of this and he was dozing.

I slipped out of the empty seat I was occupying and wandered to the back of the plane, where I found the Doiges. I had no use for the adults after the trouble they'd caused my girl, but I was interested in communing with the children. The younger girl was unaware of her parents' shenanigans and exhaled simple contentment as she rubbed her yellow crayon over an outline of a lion. However, the elder, Marianna, was clearly stressed by the dishonesty she'd witnessed. Only nine years old, she carried the burden in her sore shoulders' fascia. Just like my Ameera's tight muscles. I spoke into her shallow breaths:

Let them drop. Let your shoulders drop. Your parents are not your problem. Let them drop.

She hardened her jaw against my words. I continued for five minutes, then let her be.

Still nervous to be in flight, I occupied myself with other travellers. I read over shoulders and watched television shows on small screens. Finally, we landed and I hopped into a cab with Wanda and Jessie. I memorized their west-end Toronto condo's address.

After I'd returned to Huatulco, I considered what else I could do to help my daughter. I'd neglected her all her life. Surely there was something I owed her besides information about my death?

She was clearly stuck in a muddle that she couldn't resolve. And I sensed a negative force in her midst. I sought my spirit guides' advice and as usual, their help required significant decoding.

Remove yourself from the helping. Be unselfish.

I'm being selfish?

Help her to find help. Help others to help her.

Ameera

Δ

Manuela, Roberto, and Oscar were huddled by the side of the orientation hall on Saturday morning. When I drew closer, they didn't make eye contact with me. Fretfulness skittered across my mind: were they talking about me?

Manuela flashed Oscar an anxious look, then glanced furtively in my direction. I considered going to them, but chose not to interrupt. They hadn't yet handed out the excursion sheets, despite the hall being already a quarter full, so I travelled through the rows of seated guests to distribute them. When I looked back a few minutes later, Roberto and Manuela were at Oscar's sides, patting his arms as though in consolation. I realized that whatever was going on wasn't about me.

"Blythe, any idea what's happening with Oscar?" The room buzzed with chatting and chairs scraping the floor.

"What do you mean?" Blythe looked to where Roberto and Oscar were now greeting new arrivals. Any previous difficulty was now camouflaged by their clipped-on smiles and helpful stances.

"Oh, nothing. I just wondered why no one had handed out the sheets yet."

"Oscar isn't feeling well this morning," Manuela called to us as she approached the stage.

"Is he okay?" I hoped she'd reveal the mystery.

"He's fine. A headache." Manuela's nostrils flared. "He asked me to cover him for the presentation. He's going to take my spot at the tour desk instead."

"Right-o. Do you know the routine?" Blythe asked Manuela.

"Of course," Manuela snapped, "I've been working here almost three years. I've been doing a mini-version at Waves for weeks now."

"Time to start the show," Blythe said, seemingly impervious to Manuela's crisp tone. She climbed the stairs on the left side of the stage. Manuela followed, earlier than Oscar usually would have. She smiled slyly at me. Blythe bellowed a "hallooo" into the microphone, and the hall awoke. Manuela took the second microphone and sauntered forward with the charisma of a pop singer.

"*¡Hola amigos!*"

Before Blythe could begin her usual spiel, Manuela introduced herself and nodded to Blythe, as though conferring permission to speak. Blythe mechanically continued with the presentation, while Manuela nodded from the sidelines, interjecting encouragement, like a supervisor with a new recruit. Her presence enlivened the audience, who stood and sat on cue like enthusiastic congregants at a prayer meeting.

Roberto and I watched from the back of the room, transfixed; the orientation session was being altered for the first time in almost three years.

"Manuela is a natural," I whispered to Roberto.

"*Claro que sí.*" We watched for a few more minutes before exiting the hall. A hot salty breeze licked us as we veered onto the path that led to the main building and the Oceana desk.

"Maybe she should take over the role," Roberto said, earnestly. "Maybe we should *all* rotate roles once in a while."

"Blythe won't want to give it up." She'd claimed the task our first week. I didn't mind; she did a fine job and I wasn't interested in being on stage.

"Everyone should have a chance to be seen as leaders. Otherwise we won't get promoted."

"I suppose it's only fair." I cast a sideways glance at him. Is that what the three of them had been discussing? The promotion? Had they heard something?

Roberto touched my shoulder to slow my stride when we were twenty feet from the tour desk. I watched as two women nodded and smiled while Oscar pointed to posters of various excursions. Easy sales.

"Oscar received a bad memo from head office today," Roberto said, his voice barely audible. "Anita says his numbers have to go up over the next two months. He is on probation."

"What?" I stopped in the middle of the hallway, and Roberto nudged me down to the path, out of Oscar's sightline.

"He's only been down fifty dollars here and there. It's not fair. Oscar has been working in the industry his whole life. His family used to live in this area before the resorts were built here. Their house used to be there, over that hill!"

I followed his pointing finger to where Atlantis's D Block now stood. Manuela had told me about the historic evictions. The official story was that the relocation process was an amicable, negotiated solution among local residents, the resort owners, and the government. That story was repeated on all the tourist brochures until fiction sounded like fact. The truth wouldn't make for good marketing copy.

"It seems like 'probation' is the company's new strategy for dealing with us."

"What do you mean?"

"I'm on probation, too. For those complaints. Apparently, they were 'confirmed,'" I said, forming air quotes with my fingers, "by someone here." My morning coffee crept up my throat.

"This is bullshit," Roberto blurted, his face hardening.

"Anita made the probation bureaucratic. Maybe it's like that for Oscar, too — just a warning." I wanted to sound optimistic, but I didn't really believe my words. Perhaps Anita was going to fire us both.

"Why would they do this to two of their best employees?" Roberto began pacing. Sweat beaded his forehead.

"I don't get it either ... by the way, did you get your new contract yet?" I asked, frowning.

"No. You?"

"No." Was Blythe the only one who'd received hers?

I looked toward the tour desk. One of the women passed Oscar her credit card and he positioned it in the manual imprinter. How many times had I repeated that action?

1. Press down sales slip to make sure it's inside metal tabs. Huatulco's humidity will have curled its edges.
2. Hold the imprinter firmly and slide the handle fast across to the other side and then back again. It might hurt your wrist.
3. Ensure all information transfers across the carbons. Chances are it won't have.
4. Write in the transaction amount, give it to the customer to sign, then laugh at their joke about how they haven't seen a set-up like this since the '90s.
5. Give the customer the "Customer Copy."
6. If you're not fired, repeat over and over for another three years.

"Well, maybe you could put in a good word for Oscar with Anita. You could tell her that Oscar usually does the presentation, and loses out on sales time on our busiest morning. That's why Manuela changed places with him," Roberto reasoned.

I knew what Anita's reply would be: Blythe had less desk time on Saturdays. Roberto had fewer hours the rest of the week because he preferred to lead tours rather than staffing the desk. Both reliably met the quota.

"She won't listen to me." I glumly considered the favouritism I'd once enjoyed. I used be her go-to person whenever she needed to ask about local issues. Had Blythe replaced me as Anita's pet?

"Try. Tell Anita that Oscar is sort of the team leader, especially on arrivals day." On Fridays Oscar was first to arrive at the desk. He downloaded the team's reports and distributed them, like a boss handing out daily assignments. Not inclined to arrive early and take on the extra work, we all tolerated the quirk.

"All right," I agreed, half-heartedly.

"And pretend you know nothing. Oscar wouldn't like us talking about it."

I nodded, recognizing Roberto's trust. We rerouted back to the tour desk, took our seats beside Oscar, and fell into an awkward silence. A couple with twin preschool-aged boys approached Roberto's station.

"Welcome, friends! My colleague over here can help you," Roberto said to the family, his arm sweeping toward Oscar, "I'm still setting up my cash box." He pretended to fiddle with his drawer. The family settled in front of Oscar, who smiled warily at Roberto. I couldn't tell whether his expression belied his gratitude or chagrin.

Tourists flocked to the desk over the next two hours. We moved in a familiar rhythm, our voices rising and falling in a manipulative hum. Our pens scratched out chits, and scribbled numbers on master sheets. Our fingers pointed at photos on glossy brochures and reached for cash. For the first time, I found myself eavesdropping on Oscar's conversations. I wished he could be more suave, more irresistible. I coached him telepathically: *look, he's losing interest! Watch — she's nodding, focus on her, she's the ticket! Don't forget the bug spray!*

Later, when the numbers slowed to a trickle, Manuela placed a cool hand over mine and whispered, "Let's go for an early lunch. I'll ask Blythe, too. The men can handle the last few sales." I nodded. Roberto winked at me when I turned to lock my cash drawer. I smiled back, enjoying the rare experience of being in cahoots with them.

"How'd the orientation go with your brand-new sidekick?" I asked Blythe, as we neared the staff cafeteria.

"At first I didn't know what you were up to," she said to Manuela. "But then you really whipped up the group. You got almost everyone on their feet at one point."

I was pleasantly surprised by her generosity; it sounded to me that she'd been upstaged and yet she didn't feel threatened.

"I made them imitate crocodiles. Ha! I was hoping it would translate into tour sales," Manuela said, waving away the compliment. We travelled the length of the buffet. Manuela selected a green salad, and slices of cold roast beef, having recently eschewed carbohydrates, while Blythe served herself fried chicken, steamed vegetables, and fries. I wandered the hot tray section, settling on rice and beans and lasagna.

"It was a very good decision to switch with Oscar. I'll make sure to mention it to Anita," Blythe said, picking up the conversation's thread when we were seated.

"No, I don't want Oscar to look bad. It was just fun for me to do something different." Manuela stuffed a forkful of lettuce into her mouth.

"Not everyone is a performer. I have to admit that I always thought Oscar was a wet blanket at the microphone." Blythe gnawed on a chicken bone and bits of meat caught between her upper front teeth.

"Oh, come on, Blythe. That's unfair," I protested. Manuela remained quiet. She sliced a straight line into her roast beef, and then made horizontal cuts until she had several bite-sized rectangles on her plate.

"But he is always so bloody serious about it all." Blythe paused, looked up at the ceiling, as though searching for her words. I followed her gaze; a ceiling fan turned slowly, providing little relief from the warm, still air. "Tourists are here to have fun. You have to keep things light."

I stabbed the cheese crust of my lasagna irritably. Yet, I couldn't disagree with her.

"We all have different strengths. Oscar is a good team leader. He's good at organizing all the paperwork, and he knows more about the area than anyone else," said Manuela. I supposed that she and Roberto had agreed on this script.

"We don't have a team leader," Blythe scoffed. "Not yet, anyway."

I swallowed down a bite of lasagna, but had lost my appetite.

"I hope the head office will be fair with the contracts and promotion. And salaries ..." Manuela countered. It was common knowledge that the Mexicans were paid less than foreigners, an uncomfortable reality we rarely acknowledged.

"Well, I'm sure it will be based on performance. They have our sales stats, right? We've been working hard; I'm sure that will be rewarded," Blythe stated. Manuela's jaw squared, and she pushed her unfinished plate aside.

"Our Word of the Week: *Optimismo*. No this is better. *Falso optimismo*." She looked straight at me, eyebrows raised.

"Yeah, Blythe. I don't think things happen as fairly as you imagine," I said.

Then I spilled about my probation.

"Probation! Ay! That's terrible. And unfair. Why is Anita being so crazy about everything?" Manuela fumed.

"Oh! I'm so sorry!" Blythe frowned. "I've heard the new director is a real stickler about enforcing HR performance policies. I get the impression that Anita can't stand her." I nodded, a twinge of jealousy knotting my stomach. Anita had been confiding in Blythe about her boss!

"It's okay. I'll finish up the probation and then hopefully things will go back to normal," I said. Yes, *falso optimismo*.

"So how are things going with Rhion?" Manuela changed the subject. I looked to Blythe, whose face fell. Manuela's expression was guileful.

"Well, you know, we've always been casual. We'll see. So far things are fine," she said, flipping her bangs off her face and standing to clear her tray.

Δ

The week passed slowly and I gradually sank into a dark mood, each day a little greyer than the previous. I worried incessantly about my job, Oscar's job, whether I wanted to stay on at Atlantis as a tour rep. Maybe my friend Malika was correct about Saturn returning to ruin my life.

And then there was Jessie's search. She'd sleuthed a potential surname. A friend of a friend at the university had retrieved a record of an Azeez Dholkawala graduating in 1985. She couldn't access further personal information and they'd reached a dead end. Jessie reassured me that she could begin searching in India, but that would take more time.

As I'd done dozens of times in the past, I entered his name into an Internet search, this time including this new name. Dholkawala. Nothing on the first page of results. Nothing on the second. Or the third. I stopped there.

Dholkawala. I tried it on. Did it fit me? Dholkawala. Ameera Dholkawala.

The progress should have lifted my spirits, but I didn't want to raise my hopes. A possible surname was not a definite surname. And I had a bad feeling about the search, a dread that it some-how wouldn't yield what I wanted.

I dampened my fears in the best way I knew how; I spent Sunday and Monday and Tuesday and Wednesday nights growing tipsy, then drunk. I awoke to dull hangovers and night sweats and didn't care that my sheets held the fruity scent of sugar.

Δ

The online Oceana Human Resources course, part of my punishment, was scheduled for Thursday evening. I sat alone at the kiosk's computer, sipping rum and coke and clicking through a test of Oceana policies about professional conduct. One of them was about alcohol consumption:

True or False: Oceana Representatives may not consume alcohol while in uniform or on shift.

I clicked "true" and pulled my polyester skirt over my knees. I answered five more questions, then clicked "finish" and toasted my score of seventeen out of twenty. Like a pouting teenager, I sent the result to Anita without an introductory message or subject header.

An hour later, lipstick and a red sundress elbowed me out of my funk. I went to see Enrique, hoping he might have time to listen to my rant about the stupid Oceana test. I waited on a stool, but he managed only a cursory hello, occupied instead with a male tourist who smiled and laughed at everything he said. The tourist whispered something in his ear and Enrique grinned and stroked the man's arm.

A wisp of cigarette smoke floated over from the lady on the stool next to mine.

"I used to like menthols. They're like smoky lozenges," I quipped. We introduced ourselves and I pretended I wasn't an Oceana employee. Poppy tipped her pack toward me. We chatted about her mosquito bites, which had left a line of spots up her calves. I inhaled the nicotine and exhaled lightness. I remembered how much I loved that feeling. Gavin and I used to smoke together, cigarettes helping us remain aloft on a cloud of foolish love.

I accepted a second menthol and Poppy and I talked about the hopelessness of relationships. She was on a "cheer up" trip with her three girlfriends after a bitter divorce.

"How do you go from being in love one day and indifferent the next?" She philosophized. I had no answer for her. Where was a helpful *O* magazine grey-shade advice box when you needed one?

I butted out and slid off the stool. I noticed Gina and Ned Cameron, from Buffalo, at the back of the bar. They'd been friendly with me earlier in the week, and I sensed a mutual attraction. I headed in their direction. Why not? I deserved a little entertainment.

I stopped short when I spied another couple, Oceana customers, sitting across from them. Their body language indicated that they were already intimates; Gina played with the other woman's hair while the other man's palm rested on Gina's thigh. A foursome? I turned to go.

"Ameera," Ned called out. He introduced me to Lana and Len. I suspected his new friends were using fake names.

"Come! Sit. We were just talking about you," Lana said with a smile. Len rose to get a round of drinks.

After a few minutes of small talk, Gina, who'd already had a few drinks, said, "So we were having a little bet amongst ourselves, Ameera. The four of us have been having a lot of fun together these last couple of nights and we were wagering whether you'd want to join us."

"I think you have to be clearer, my dear," Len said in a hushed tone. "Ameera, don't think we're perverts or anything. But we're inviting you to have sexy times with us, if you know what I mean."

"You mean … are you … swingers?" I asked, wanting to appear naive, in case they weren't, or were involving me in an elaborate joke.

"I have a feeling I'm gonna win this bet!" Gina chuckled.

"In a word, yes," said Ned. "Although Gina and I prefer to think of ourselves as non-monogamists. Swinger has a unclassy ring to it."

"Oh come on, that's just a stereotype," Len countered. Relieved, I settled into the couch beside the women, taking care to maintain a chasteness in my body language. I kept an eye out for potential onlookers. Certainly no one would imagine that I was considering joining an orgy?

Δ

An hour later, we were in Lana and Len's suite, all of us in a state of undress. Gina and Lana made out on the couch, their legs entwined. Someone had pulled the front of my dress down and hiked it up around my waist. Len and Ned bookended me on the bed. The men were necking, their hands groping my waist and breasts. Ned, in front of me, broke the kiss, and unbuckled his belt. He guided me onto my hands and knees and drew my head closer to him. The smell of leather filled my nostrils. He unzipped his pants. Len, behind me, dragged my wet underwear down to my thighs.

"Spit roast!" Lana yelled from the couch. I recognized the sexual slang, but had never imagined I'd ever be in such a position. I felt like a porn star.

"Nah, that's called something else. The boys are kissing. There's a strict rule against that in a spit roast," Gina giggled.

"Gay spit roast! Aren't they hot when they kiss?" Lana asked. I craned my head to watch the men again, and a bolt of heat rushed up my chest.

"You two, mind your own business," Len joked.

"Mmm-hmmm," Gina said, pulling Lana closer.

Moments later, I heard a slap and Gina's yelp. Then another slap and a yelp. Len and Ned pushed into me to the rhythm of Lana's hand-thwacking.

Azeez

∞

Ameera was making me very angry. I'd come so close and I could no longer talk to her. How was I to help? Evil alcohol!

Like a fish, she drank. Every day. And just like me, she had a low tolerance. And then she had to add tobacco to the mix? If alcohol closed the door to communication, the combination encased her in cement.

She was weak, irresponsible, indolent. Yes, I was growing judgmental. Perhaps the rose-coloured glasses, the honeymoon of our first contact, was wearing off.

My guides urged compassion; that I not bring impatience into my interactions with her.

What interactions? I demanded. *She can't hear me when she's drunk!*

Family forms the frame of one's house. Without you, hers hasn't been solid.

Oh, come on. Her mother was quite capable. There's no excuse for this behaviour.

Yes, she has a foundation, and quite a strong roof. But she has open windows where she needs walls.

I see. She only knew half her ancestry.

I quelled my frustration and returned to the task at hand: I had to help her find others who could help her.

Like her mother, Ameera kept her feelings mostly to herself, hardly confided in anyone about anything. I wondered what had caused my girl to be so inward and private about her problems. So wary. I hoped I'd be able to get through to her in time.

I scanned the resort and was drawn to a lonely man eating dinner in the staff dining room. A dark cloud of sadness shadowed him. He would do.

Ameera

Δ

I realized that orgies were like buffets; one should only gorge at them every so often.

I extricated myself from Lana and Len's suite at midnight. Wired and exhausted, I walked back to my building, smiling to myself at the various combinations I'd taken part in over the previous three hours: Ned, Len, and I. Gina, Ned and I. Lana and I. And then all five of us snuggled in a puppy pile. A month's worth of dates.

I passed the bar, keeping my eyes down, but Enrique spotted me.

"Hey Ameera!" I hoped he hadn't seen me flirting with the two couples. I wasn't in the mood for more of his gaydar.

"I'm off to bed." I waved, but kept walking.

"Wait, your friend is here. Roberto. I think he's had too much to drink."

"Roberto?" Just then, Roberto embraced me from behind, and planted a sloppy kiss on my cheek.

"I'm thinking Atlantis should make this the new welcome drink." Roberto's smile was wide and crooked. He grabbed my wrist and pulled me into the bar. He wore his usual dress shirt, but it gaped open, exposing his bare chest.

"I can't stay, Roberto." I wiped my cheek with the back of my hand.

"The ingredients are cheap — no real juice, cheap rum, and it's got a catchy name. The guests will love it. They'll tell their friends about it, put it on Facebook, you know, Tweeter it." Then he laughed and slapped my arm, his touch turning into a sting.

"What are you doing here so late? It's past midnight." I pulled my arm away. Most Thursdays, Roberto left the resort by five or six. If he ever stayed for a drink, his preference was for a cup of coffee to fuel his commute home. He slid off his barstool, and I reached out to steady him.

"My wife is away, so I ate dinner here. Then Enrique wanted me to try his new drink. Why not, I said? I've had three," he said, holding up three fingers. "I love this guy," he exclaimed, reaching across the bar to grab Enrique's neck and pull him into an awkward hug. Enrique flashed me an open palm, correcting Roberto's estimate.

"You need to sober up." I appraised my co-worker and wondered who'd seen him inebriated.

True or false: This Oceana representative is a slap-happy drunk while in uniform.

"You're so serious, Ameera! I've asked a waiter to bring me coffee. It's only a forty-five-minute ride home. Thirty-five if there's no traffic and thirty if I drive very, very fast!" He clasped a pair of imaginary handlebars and revved his motorcycle's engine.

"You're in no condition to drive." My hands landed on my hips. I looked him in the eye so he'd know I was serious.

"It's no problem." He detailed his route home, as though reading a Google map. Then he sang a coffee jingle, as evidence of his theory that caffeine would deliver him safely.

"C'mon, Roberto, can we call someone to come and get you?"

"You're lucky you live here," he interrupted. "But I still have to go all the way to my empty house and what's the point of that?" I knew he was referring to his wife being away, but I imagined all the furniture, plants, and decor stolen away. A house ransacked. I suddenly felt sorry for him.

He wrapped a heavy arm around my shoulders and drew me close. His damp shirt rubbed against my bare back, transferring a mixture of his faint cologne and musky sweat. His scent was familiar from many days working together in the sun, but I'd never been that close to him. I pulled away and looked to Enrique, who mouthed the words, "Are you okay?" I nodded and he turned to serve his guests. Roberto's coffee arrived. Maybe he'd be easier to reason with after he drank it.

"So, Elena's visiting her family?"

"You ever been married, Ameera?" He slurped his coffee, the cup rattling the saucer upon its descent.

"No. But you know that."

"I hardly know anything about you, Ameera," he whined.

"Uh-huh. Drink your coffee." I was being reminded of how tiresome drunk people could be. Of how tired I was from a week of drinking and worrying.

"You are a woman of many secrets. But I know some of them." He winked and smiled.

I bristled and considered asking him what he meant, but his knowing look had turned to confusion. He anxiously inspected his ankles as though his thoughts had leaked out of his brain and pooled at his feet.

"What was I saying?" He asked, regaining his focus, "Oh yeah. Marriage. Elena. You know she's related to Oscar?"

He didn't wait for my reply. "They're third cousins. That's how I got this job. But Oscar doesn't like to mention that, so keep this between you and me. He doesn't want it to look like *nepotismo*. What's that in English?"

"Nepotism." I looked Enrique's way, but he was busy serving drinks.

"Right! So many words are like that! English is the ugly version of *español*, am I right? Huh! Nepotism," he spat out the word with a grimace.

"Almost finished your coffee?"

He ignored me. "I'd better go before other people see me like this and do *los chismorreos*. That's gossip, in *español*, by the way. There you go: your Word of the Week." He downed the rest of his coffee, hopped off the stool, and stumbled away from the bar. For a drunk guy, he moved quickly.

"Roberto, I'm calling you a taxi. Do you have cab fare?" I asked when I'd caught up to him. He reached into his front pockets, pulled out their linings, and left them sticking out like droopy ears.

"I wonder where I put my wallet?" He looked mystified. He patted his back pockets, and then pulled out his motorcycle keys triumphantly. "Hey, I still have my keys!" I lunged for them, but he weaved from me, giggling. He stopped, bent over, hysteria spilling out of him.

"Fine, walk me home first, then." I thought that I could appeal to his sense of chivalry to buy some time. I probably had enough cash in my dresser drawer for a taxi.

"At your service!" He clowned, bowing.

"Roberto, why did you drink so much tonight?" Now it was me who was whining.

"Elena and I had a fight. A small fight. She left, but she'll be back." His mirthful face turned doleful. His bottom lip quivered.

"What did you fight about?" I softened my tone.

"Nothing," he said. Then he broke away from me, slumped down on a nearby bench, and wept.

Δ

I awoke to the hoarse voice in my head. *Ameera, listen to him.* Listen to whom? What had I been dreaming about?

I turned my face to the shaft of weak sunshine coming through the split in the drapes, the place where the panels refused to meet. I calculated the date and the fact that it was morning. A slow sigh breezed from across the room.

I rolled over and clicked on the bedside lamp. Roberto was across the room, tying his left shoelace. The task appeared to require all his concentration.

"How are you feeling?" I whispered.

"My head hurts," he said quietly. Having attained success with his left shoelace, he leaned down for his right.

"Do you remember last night? How you got here?" I sat up, pulling my knees to my chest. My pajama bottoms were rolled around my thighs. I focused on straightening them.

"It's fuzzy." He frowned and blinked three times. "I walked you home, right? I think I told you about Elena? That's all I remember. But … nothing happened, right? Between us?"

"I brought you back here to get taxi fare. Then you passed out." We'd slept beside one another the way I imagined siblings might, close, but not touching.

He looked at me intently, as though laboriously translating from English to Spanish. He grunted "thanks" as he felt for his top two buttons and made plastic circles fit through fabric holes.

"You're welcome."

"You were talking in your sleep a minute ago. Was it a nightmare?"

"Oh. What did I say?" I grabbed a pillow and hugged it to my chest and once again heard the hoarse male voice calling my name, telling me to listen.

"You said something that sounded like 'A zee,' I think. Something like that. You repeated that a few times."

I sifted his words, a heaviness settling over my forehead, spreading across my temples, my cheeks, my jaw, and then landing on my chest. A zee. Azeez. I'd been saying his name? I breathed deeply, tried to make my chest move, and held my knees tightly.

"Azeez?" And then I heard: *Yes.* I blinked and shook my head. When I looked at Roberto again, his eyes were upon me. "That's my father's name."

"Azeez. Yes, that sounds like what you were saying."

"I didn't know I talked in my sleep. No one's ever told me that." But who would have told me? I hadn't shared a bed for a full night in years. I pulled the sheet up to my chest, studied its frayed edging.

"Last night is a blank. Tell me what I did and said?" Roberto stood, faced the mirror, and tucked in his shirt. I pushed the dream voice to the back of my mind and concentrated on the sparse details of the previous night's conversation; Elena was having an affair and had threatened to leave him.

"What am I gonna do?" he said, too loudly, his words sputtering.

"Shhh. Blythe will hear," I whispered. "Maybe she already has. These walls are thin. You'd better explain things when you see her later. A long time ago, I brought someone back here and she was on top of it like a detective." I looked over at the bathroom door.

"I know, I heard," he said, shrugging.

"Yeah?" I'd always wanted to know what exactly she'd said. "C'mon, tell me. I wanna know."

"Silly stuff about you and the guests, like how late you got in, how you must have been having a good time. But I think who you sleep with is your own business," he said, pointedly.

"I don't like rumours. Look what's happened to me with these complaints …" I laid back in my bed.

"Ameera, there are many eyes around here that like to watch and judge." He moved in front of the window and the shaft of sunshine bisected his chest.

"I still can't figure out who would have confirmed the complaints. I thought Anita was only doing reference checks with Oceana staff." I pulled the sheet to my chin.

"Maybe it was her," he whispered, pointing at the wall.

I turned my head, followed his finger. I shuddered. "No. She wouldn't!" Not Blythe. It couldn't be.

Blythe.

"Yeah. I don't know why I said that." He looked as though he might say more, but didn't. I struggled to integrate the new information. What if it was true?

I gave him a towel and a toothbrush still in my mother's dentist's wrapper. Then I climbed into bed and stretched flat on my back, my limbs heavy. Some time later, Roberto was sitting by my side, smelling of toothpaste, his hand on my shoulder, rousing me awake. My face was hot and wet.

"You were dreaming again. Moaning and dreaming. Was it the same dream?"

"I don't know. I can't remember," I lied, and wiped my face dry with the back of my hand. What was wrong with me?

"I have to go," he said, his palm resting on my shoulder. I reached for his hand, but he stood and took a step toward the door. Panic stirred in my belly. I didn't want him to leave, to disappear. Not yet.

"Listen, you want to get breakfast together? I can be ready in half an hour and can meet you at the cafeteria."

"Okay. I'll take a walk until then. Also, I think I left my backpack at the bar. I think my phone's in it and maybe my wallet. I hope I haven't lost my wallet." He shook his head.

"Roberto, I'm sure Elena will come home," I said. He nodded, and closed the door behind him.

Δ

I toasted two slices of white bread and poured a cup of coffee. Roberto was in a back corner of the nearly deserted cafeteria. He'd found his backpack and except for his crumpled clothing, he looked almost normal. Perhaps I did, too.

"You know, I've never even thought about cheating. Not on Elena, anyway." His eyes were watery and wondering. My eyebrows raised reflexively, but I forced them into a sympathetic frown. Didn't everyone think about cheating sometimes?

"Here, eat this." I passed him a piece of toast. "It will make you feel better. I know, I've nursed tons of hangovers." He took the bread, studied it a moment, crunched a cautious bite.

"So, your father. You think about him a lot?"

"I don't know anything about him, so there isn't much to think about."

"Yeah, Manuela told us." I grimaced. *Los chismorreos.*

"I've asked someone to do a search for him." I pushed this admission down my esophagus with a mouthful of dry bread.

He nodded and gave me a thumbs-up gesture, as though finding a mystery father were a simple endeavour. "So where were you coming from before you found me at the bar last night? Out with friends?"

"Yes, just drinks with some tourists. Nice people." I sipped my coffee, suspecting that he wasn't making small talk.

"I think I saw you walking with them to C Block before I got to the bar. That fun bunch who are always kidding around by the pool." Roberto looked directly at me.

I searched his eyes. I hadn't before noticed how dark his eyelashes were. His gaze seemed to go straight through me. "You know, don't you?"

"Know what?" He looked away, waved at an employee who'd just walked in the door.

"You know that I like dating couples. Men and women." I looked away, my heart beating hard. I placed my hand over it, to slow it's rhythm. What was I saying?

"Yes, well, I wasn't sure but ..." His jaw tightened.

"Suzanne, the woman who made a scene at the airport was one of them. She and her husband."

"Okay."

"It was all agreed on, but she got upset." I couldn't stop the flow of my words now that they were pouring out.

"Listen, it's okay. I'm an open-minded person. I mean, people should do what they want, right? As long as no one gets hurt," he said, pursing his lips.

"Who else knows? Manuela? Oscar? Blythe?"

"Maybe. We've never talked about it," he said.

"No way. You talk about everything else." I pushed my plate away.

"It hasn't come up. Not since the argument between you and Oscar. But that was just Blythe's gossip about you dating guys. You know, normal dating."

"It hasn't come up?" I repeated, disbelieving.

"We like you, Ameera. We don't talk badly about you. We're a team. Like a family," he said, fidgeting in his seat. "But like I said before, you just have to be discreet. Not everyone is going to understand, especially if they don't know you how we know you."

I took a moment to allow his words to sink in. *We like you, Ameera.* I smiled uncomfortably, both grateful and unsure. "Do you really think that Blythe might have stabbed me in the back?"

"It's possible. I don't trust her. You are her main competition for the promotion, right?"

"Yeah, if you look at sales." And yet I did trust Blythe, or had trusted her. For the previous hour, I'd been sorting through memories for evidence of Roberto's theory. Yes, Blythe could be petty, irritating, insecure. But she was familiar like a room-mate, or a relative one has to tolerate. And, of all my co-workers, she knew the most about my comings and goings.

"I'm gonna go. I have to call Elena before things get busy." He slung his backpack across his shoulder.

I focused on the acrylic seaside sunset painting on the wall. The secrets I'd thought I'd been guarding weren't secrets after all. How could I have imagined that my sex life was invisible to Atlantis's tiny village?

And perhaps Blythe had been using it against me.

I felt like an idiot. My eyes welled with tears and I pressed my lids tight to contain them. My intuition told me: *This is not the time to be vulnerable. Breathe.*

I inhaled sharply.

You can find out the truth. You can protect yourself.

I rubbed my temples, and repeated the words to myself, like a mantra.

Azeez

∞

Jessie was on the third mat from the front, at the hot yoga studio. I'd followed her there from the condo she shared with Wanda.

The room was already steaming. She laid on her back, legs spread, chest open, arms at her side. She closed her eyes and her breathing slowed. Funny how they call that corpse pose.

I listened in.

I hope Dholkawala is his last name. I don't want this to be a wild goose chase. Especially if I'm doing this for free ... I'm already behind with my work from being away last week ... but that was worth it ... Wanda and I are good again ... but I wonder why she was so quiet today? The teacher entered the room and the students rose to their feet. They inhaled the room. I waited until they paused in downward dog.

Jessie made a perfect *V* with her body. Her thoughts quieted.

Dholkawala is correct. 100 percent, I yelled.

Easy-peasy.

It has to be right. Azeez Dholkawala, she affirmed.

I allowed that thought to take root in her mind's fertile soil before I offered another idea. Sweat dripped off her chin, causing her to wobble in her triangle pose. *Summer solstice 1985*, I screeched at her five times. She switched to the other side. *The Air India bombing*, I squawked eight times.

Her soft gaze turned hard. She knew about the disaster, had heard about it in the news. *When was that? Was that the same year?* she asked herself.

Again, I waited, not wanting to flood her with too much too fast. I stayed close, listening to the random thoughts that accompanied her exhalations. *I have to phone Mama tonight ... Wanda's birthday is in a month — should I plan a party? Maybe a surprise party? Wanda loves surprises ... oh yeah, pick up onions on the way home.*

During the last *shivasana*, she drifted into a brief but deep sleep. I yelled: *Azeez Dholkawala. The Air India bombing. Azeez Dholkawala. The Air India bombing. Azeez Dholkawala. The Air India bombing. Azeez Dholkawala. The Air India bombing. Azeez Dholkawala. The Air India bombing.*

The instructor mispronounced *namaste*, and Jessie stirred awake, believing my words to be her own. She rushed home to her computer, forgetting to buy onions. She barely acknowledged her partner. She didn't phone her mother that night.

Ameera

Δ

First to the tour desk, I prepared it for the day and then logged into my e-mail. There was an Oceana bulletin with the subject header, "Ottawa Victoria Day Closure" and a message from Anita titled, "Contract Extension."

Dear Ameera,

Thanks for completing the HR procedures on-line course.

I'm pleased to be able to offer you a three-month contract extension, beginning June 1, 2015 and ending August 31, 2015. Normally, we'd renew for a three-year period, but, given the recent complaints and probation, I'm unable to offer more at this time. However, my intention is to review your employee record in mid-August, and pending no further problems, to extend your contract for the rest of the term.

I want you to know that we are impressed by your sales record and your recent handling of the fraud situation.

Attached is the two-page contract. Please print, sign, and scan it back by May 7, 2015.

Best,
Anita

So I was being paroled for good behaviour. That was reassuring. But what if another complaint materialized before mid-August? And what if I was offered a full extension? Did I want it? A part of me wished I could shut down the computer, fold back the tour desk's ledges, close its cupboards, and never unpack it again.

Roberto arrived, and, unable to form a sentence, I pointed to the screen. He looked over my shoulder, murmuring as he read.

"Well, she's showing some faith. That's good," he reasoned. "Let me log on. I want to see if I got mine." I moved out of the way and a few minutes later, he was nodding at the screen.

"Good news?"

"Yes. Three-year extension." He glanced at me guiltily.

"Congratulations … should we do the printouts?" I itched to do something.

"Leave it to Oscar. He's had a difficult week, a real blow to his ego." Even with our scheming the previous Saturday to give Oscar more desk time, his numbers remained low.

"Do you think he's going to be renewed?"

Roberto's long sigh was like a tire deflating." I don't know. Look at the way they are treating you, and you make them lots of money."

He checked his phone. I could tell he still hadn't heard from his wife. I wanted to reach out, pat his back, take his hand. Instead, I watched him shift the brochure rack, which leaned to the left. He steadied it, stepped back, readjusted it, then sat again.

Oscar frowned at us when he arrived. "Why are you here early?" Could he tell that Roberto was hungover and wore yesterday's clothes? Roberto made an excuse about not being able to sleep and coming in early. He and Oscar spoke in Spanish about traffic, the quiet of the early hour, the new security guard stationed at the front gates. They spoke lethargically and humourlessly enough that I could understand.

I moved to my regular stool to allow Oscar to take over the computer. Roberto and I formed a plodding assembly line, stapling duplicate lists and fastening them to clipboards. Guests passed in bathing suits, on their way to the beach for one last dip.

"And how's everyone this lovely morning?" Blythe called out her arrival. She waggled her eyebrows at Roberto and me.

"Just fine." I went back to stapling. *Remain alert.* I shot Roberto a look.

"Blythe, let's go get coffee. We're almost done with the lists." Roberto ushered Blythe away and whispered into her eager ear. I slammed down the stapler, trying to picture Blythe as the sort of person who would deliberately harm me. I didn't want to believe it was possible.

"What's going on?" Oscar stacked the clipboards one atop the other, their metal clips striking. "I hope he's not talking about me. I know you were all talking about me last week."

"It's not like that," I began, then faltered.

He held his hand up to stop me. "I know your intentions are good. You were all trying to protect me." He returned to the computer, working the mouse in jerky movements.

"It's unfair, this quota thing," I said.

"And our probations." He glanced at me over his bifocals. I guessed he'd heard the news from Manuela.

"Yeah."

"Maybe it's time I made a change. Left this place." He jutted out his chin.

"What kind of change?" He'd worked in the tourist industry and nowhere else. What else would he do? But perhaps we weren't that different. I travelled the length of my own career trajectory: door-to-door fundraiser, sandal salesperson, travel agent, tour representative. What next? What else would I do? I came up blank. And then I thought: *it might be time for a change.*

"I don't know yet. I have a few ideas. Don't say anything to anyone. I want to wait until I have something definite." It was a rare thing for him to share anything private, let alone with me, so I didn't ask any questions. He stared into the computer monitor, his eyes glazing over.

"I got a three-month contract renewal. It should convert to a full renewal, pending no more complaints," I blurted. "But I don't know if I want to renew."

"I thought this was a good job for you foreign reps. Good pay and working conditions, your food and room covered." He continued to stare at the screen.

"It is," I admitted. "Maybe I'm just having a weird morning."

"*Buenos días.*" Manuela approached from behind, then seeing our serious faces asked, "What happened? What's wrong?"

"Nothing, she's having a weird morning." Oscar gave me a conspiratorial look.

Δ

The outbound tourists were through the security gates, and we'd been notified of a two-hour delay caused by inclement weather in Toronto. The buses turned off their engines, and the refreshment sellers packed up their wares. We deliberated outside our kiosk.

"Maybe we can close the kiosk until the plane lands," Roberto said, wanly. Now many hours into his hangover, his face was pale, his skin clammy-looking.

"Yes, there's no need for us to stand around in the heat," Blythe agreed. Manuela grabbed sodas from the buses, and together we went inside the air-conditioned arrivals hall to watch the deserted runaway. The luggage conveyor shut off with a gravelly cough. Through a glass wall at the far end of the hallway, we glimpsed the crowded departure lounge. A woman paced near the window, agitatedly tapping words into a cellphone.

"They're probably saying, 'Why didn't you tell us? We could have had two more hours at the beach!'" Oscar scoffed.

"At the bar!" Blythe smirked at Roberto, who glared at her and then slumped low in his seat.

"Yes, someone will send a complaint letter. Probably that lady," Manuela muttered, gesturing to a woman near the glass wall.

I looked at each of my colleagues. *We like you, Ameera.*

"Imagine. Next year we might be doing this routine twice a week, if Oceana expands," Blythe said. I regarded her short blond hair, freckles, big blue eyes.

"We'll need more staff," Roberto said.

"I've heard that they'll reassign duties for now. Less desk time. Restructuring. Outsource the excursions. More efficient scheduling," Blythe replied. I tried to interpret her smug expression.

"I'm beginning to think that maybe I won't stay here much longer," I said impulsively. I told them about my three-month contract offer. And then, looking at each of my colleagues, I asked, "Has anyone been offered the promotion yet?" Oscar stared at the floor. Manuela and Roberto shook their heads. Blythe bit her lip.

"Blythe?" I demanded.

"I wasn't supposed to say anything yet. This is uncomfortable ... I'll be the Huatulco team leader starting at the end of June. Anita wanted to confirm all the placements before she announced it." I turned away so no one would see me tearing up.

"*No me soprende,*" Oscar said, crossing his arms over his chest.

"It doesn't surprise me, either. I was only offered a renewal of my contract. The same job. No raise," Manuela said.

Roberto nodded. "*Yo tambien.*" He, Oscar, and Manuela continued the conversation in Spanish, speaking quickly, tensely. I understood only every second word, but it was clear they felt that Oceana had overlooked them.

"Ameera, I hope you will stay," Manuela said, picking up my news, and perhaps responding to Blythe's in a backhanded way. "The company should be recognizing your talents more."

"We don't have much control over what a multinational company based in Canada thinks of us, do we?" Oscar asked.

"Listen everyone," Blythe broke in, "Oceana will continue to expand. Anita gave me the sense that any one of us, being part of the original crew in Huatulco, could be promoted at some point in the next few years." Roberto and Manuela looked at her, doubtfully. I again studied Blythe's expression for duplicity and found only what appeared to be innocent concern. Perhaps it was self-centred concern, the desire to be liked by her colleagues, but nonetheless, she seemed genuine. Maybe, like the rest of us, Blythe had been caught up in Oceana's tides.

And now that she was going to be our supervisor, I'd never know if she was the one who'd confirmed Suzanne's complaints that I was a swinger. I sank into the vinyl airport terminal chair, exhausted.

Don't give up yet, my internal voice said.

"I hope that's true, Blythe," Manuela muttered. Roberto shrugged, leaned back, and rested his head against the wall. An uneasy silence took over our group.

Ninety minutes later, the plane landed, and its first passengers crossed the tarmac. It would be another hour before they'd clear customs and collect their bags, but we headed outdoors, just for something to do.

"Did you hear the semi-annual inspection has been cancelled indefinitely? There was an e-mail today," Blythe announced.

"I didn't get that e-mail," Oscar said. The others mumbled their agreement. It seemed Blythe was already being treated as the boss.

"At least we won't have to wear our ties and scarves ever again." Manuela's face was drawn, her lids heavy. I helped her to turn down the counter and unlock the doors of our kiosk.

"Hey, what are these?" I asked, looking at five matching daisy-and-bluebird-printed lawn chairs stored inside the kiosk.

"I brought them over a few days ago," Oscar said with a smirk. He unfolded them and passed them out one by one. We each took a chair and stood in front of it, as though confused about its function. He settled into his and gestured for us to do the same. "Sit. Please. Join me."

My butt and thighs relaxed into the canvas. I laughed out loud, wondering why none of us had thought to break the rule years earlier.

Azeez

∞

Jessie typed "names of victims" and "Air India bombing" into the search engine.

Yes, correct. 100 percent! I cheered.

She tapped and clicked, tapped and clicked. And then an interminable list tumbled open, three hundred and twenty-nine of us intoning our names.

I wanted to cover my eyes, plug my ears. Getting to this point had been like rooting for my team. I'd prodded, encouraged, guided. But now, the reality of our goal made my spirit fall like a stone. Like an aircraft plummeting from the sky.

There I was: Azeez Dholkawala, twenty-nine. Two words and a number. Evidence that I'd existed. Evidence that I'd perished.

"There he is," Jessie said to Wanda, who at 10:00 p.m. had come to coax her partner to bed.

Together, they silently scrolled through the names.

Meena and her mother were on the list. What had happened to them? Had they reincarnated yet? So many of us had died too young, long before our parents and spouses and siblings. Perhaps I wasn't the only one who'd lingered in the ether.

"Click on that photo," Wanda said. They scrolled through an article about a memorial that had been erected on Toronto's waterfront in 2007. It was for the victims, for us. I memorized the address.

I travelled south from their home and around the curve of
Lake Ontario. It was a windy night and the lake tested the shore.
I found the structure, a small plaza with low granite walls and
a stone sundial surrounded by water and gardens. Etched into
stone was the inscription:

> *Time Flies, Suns Rise and Shadows Fall, Let it
> Pass by, Love Reigns Forever Over All.*

Yes, that seemed right.

Also carved into the wall were our names, all of them. I rested
in that gentle space, reading and rereading each and every one
through the night, my voice fluttering up to the stars.

While the sundial's shadow moved around its circle, and the
sun rose and the moon tucked itself away, people came and went.
Dog walkers and joggers and a tour group. When the gnomon
marked solar noon at the crash site, a rollerblader stopped and
recited the Al-Fatihah, the first verse of the Koran.

Bismillāhi r-raḥmāni r-raḥīm, I sang along with her.

And the wind, too, whispered God's name. And the grass rustled its approval. And the lake splashed its praise.

Ameera

Δ

The hall hummed with conversation and laughter. Vacationers milled about calling, "My name starts with a *W*! Anyone else start with a *W*?" or "Any of you *D*'s? My husband is an *L*." Blythe and Manuela had introduced a new interactive activity, one that ought to have evacuated the hall like a toxic gas leak. But the tourists were not only taking it in stride, they were enjoying themselves. Two men approached Roberto and me.

"I'm Rahul and this is Alain. Do either of you have the same first initials?"

We smiled at the men and pointed to our name tags. After handshakes and small talk, Rahul and Alain wandered off to continue their search and Roberto and I left for the tour desk.

"So, how are things? Did Elena call you back?" I asked. Roberto's eyes were reddish, the wells beneath them dark.

"She's agreed to come home, to end the affair. She wants to see a marriage counsellor," he said, scowling.

"But that's good, right?"

"No way. I'm not going to tell a stranger all my problems. I don't know if I can ever trust her again. Once a cheater, always a cheater, right?"

"Sometimes sex is just sex. Cheating doesn't have to end a relationship." I told him about an *O* magazine article that counselled reflection and re-commitment after infidelity.

"You're kidding me, right? I think you Northerners are different about these things," he said, his tone shirty. We neared the tour desk, and he snapped, "Same plan as last week regarding sales — let's direct more people his way. Oscar's got no chance of a promotion now, but maybe he can hold on to his job."

"Fine," I assented, irked by his shift in mood. "But you know, he knows about that. He appreciated us trying, but didn't like us going behind his back."

"He found out?" Roberto asked, incredulously. "You told him?"

"No! I wouldn't! He figured it out himself," I said defensively. We neared the desk in silence. Oscar was explaining the waterfall tour to a young couple.

"Sounds very beautiful," the young woman said.

"My ancestors consider it a spiritual place. Magical," Roberto piped up.

"Really?" The young man asked excitedly.

"You're such a joker, Roberto!" Oscar admonished, then looked back at the couple. "Don't believe this guy. The truth is that it's a very scenic location, worth seeing. You'll like it." The couple conferred. Roberto shook his head at Oscar.

"Maybe we'll pass on it," the man said.

My lineup was busy most of the morning. Halfway through, I moved to the computer to allow Oscar more customers. I re-read Oceana's offer. I still had a few days to decide. I clicked Anita's e-mail closed.

There was a note from Mom in the short stack of messages. Her big news was that she now had wireless Internet at home. Victor had introduced her to online television and she'd cancelled her cable. Her message made me smile. She must really like the guy, to make a huge commitment like that.

Just as I was about to turn off the computer, Jessie's e-mail loaded. The subject header was, "Can we chat soon?" She gave me her Skype moniker. I inhaled deeply and thought, *Okay. Let's do this*. I opened Skype and added her. Within moments, she popped up on my screen and waved at me. I suggested that we chat since I didn't have headphones or privacy. She frowned and typed:

Should we wait until later? I have big news and you might want privacy for this.

My hands tingled as I wrote:

No. It's ok. Tell me.

She looked uncertain.

I had a weird intuition. I don't usually work this way ...

OK ...

U said he left 4 India after June 21, 1985.

OK ...

She inhaled sharply and looked to the left of the screen. She typed something, deleted it, paused, and then continued typing.

Did u ever hear about the Air India bombing?

I wasn't sure exactly. Perhaps I'd read something in the news? My throat went dry.

Maybe?

It was a huge disaster.

I waited, held my breath, and watched her type:

I found a list of names. Azeez Dholkawala was on the plane. He was 29 yrs old. There were no survivors.

She looked me in the eye, and mouthed the words, "I'm sorry."

You sure? It's him??

I allowed myself to breathe again. *Yes*, I heard in the back of my mind.

Pretty sure. There are further steps I can take 2 verify. I also found a news item about him. In the Mac student paper. Sending u links.

Two links chimed into the chat.

Thanks

R u ok? Her watery eyes radiated sympathy through the screen.

Yeah. Gotta digest this. But ok.

I'll check in with you later?

Thanks

We disconnected, but I kept the chat open, scrolling up and down to absorb her words.

There were no survivors.

My colleagues and the short queue of tourists fell away, disappearing, when I clicked on Jessie's first link. It was a *Vancouver Sun* article with a full description of the bombing and the list of victims and their ages. Most on the list were South Asians, in groupings of two, three, five — entire families. I got to the *D*'s and found him. Just one Dholkawala. He was alone.

I calculated the date. He left Canada the day after he met my mother. He died fewer than two days after I'd been conceived. He didn't even know about me.

My hands navigated the keyboard as though detached from the rest of my body. I wanted to stop, but my fingers wouldn't allow it. The cursor moved to the side of the article, and clicked on an arrow button. A trailer for a documentary began to play. I watched as an airplane's wispy fuel trail crossed the screen, and then disappeared. The plane just disappeared.

I clicked open Jessie's second link, an article from the McMaster campus newspaper, *The Silhouette*, written two weeks after the bombing. It was a short remembrance, two paragraphs. Gifted student and researcher. Attentive teaching assistant. Considerate roommate. Lost potential.

He was dead. Dead before I was born. I'd hooked a fragile hope on the possibility of finding him, meeting him, letting him know I existed. I imagined his dumbfounded expression as I explained who my mother was, and how she'd named me after his sister. He'd get a faraway look, and I'd know that he'd remembered her, had never really forgotten her. And then he'd stare into my eyes, and recognize something in me that was his own. He'd know then that I was telling him the truth. That I was a part of him.

I know now.

No! He couldn't be dead. But he was dead.

My heart raced, its thud growing louder until the vibration in my chest was all I could hear.

I stepped away from the Oceana desk, disoriented. I looked right and left, chose right, walked. Manuela called, "We're going to lunch, do you want to come?" I couldn't speak. I listened to my heartbeat, and its insistence that I needed to get away. From Atlantis. From my colleagues. From my life.

I strode across the resort, passing swimming pools with novels saving chairs for people who weren't coming back, bars full of guests drinking the first of too many watered-down cocktails, restaurants filling with diners loading plates with more than they could eat. I passed maids pushing trolleys stacked with plush towels and hundreds of tiny shampoo bottles.

I darted across pathways, reaching the less crowded places within Atlantis. The manicured lawns and gardens succumbed to desert shrubbery, cacti, and grasses. A butterfly flew before me, guiding me as I scrambled down a rocky cliff. The uneven earth against impractical shoes made me stumble, and my ankles and shins scratched against dry earth.

I reached Wild Beach, the place tourists hardly ever went, where the tide was too strong for even experienced surfers. I waded into the push-pull of the water, forgetting to slip off my pumps, the spray first dampening then drenching me, up my thighs, past my waist, and then all the way to my shoulders. I wondered what it would be like if I went deeper, so deep that I could no longer touch the sandy bottom. If I allowed my body to sink like a stone.

I know now.

"I don't want to know!" I screamed at the sky. I plunged my head underwater. I released all my air, and it bubbled to the surface while I sunk deeper.

Stop this.

"No!" I screeched like a toddler. Water rushed into my mouth.

Stop this!

I propelled myself to the surface, gagging on salty, sandy water. I scrambled halfway up to the shore, coughing the water out of my windpipe. I clung to a submerged rock and it steadied me in the tide. And then the tears came. First in trickles that coated my already damp cheeks, then in streams as my chest heaved and spasmed. The roar of the surf met my sobs. My grief, the grief of losing something I'd never had, overtook me. I held on to the rock, my whole body aching with despair until I was too tired to cry anymore. Numb with exhaustion, I washed the tears off my face with the spray of the Pacific.

An hour later, with my shoes and clothing drenched, I walked barefoot across the resort, ignoring the glances of curious staff and guests. Once inside my room, I stripped off my clothes, letting them puddle on the linoleum. I stood in the shower a long time, the bathroom disappearing into steam. When the water went warm, then tepid, then cool, I got out and put on my bathrobe, glad for the scaffolding of rough terry cloth.

A minute later, there was a knock at my door. Manuela held an orange cafeteria tray in her hands, a large wedge of chocolate cake upon it. I wiped the wet from my eyes and let her pass. She placed the tray on the bedside table and embraced me. She squeezed me three times before releasing me. I couldn't meet her eyes.

Blythe knocked on our shared bathroom door. "Mind if I come in? Are you all right?" Blythe's voice was quiet, caution and the wooden door muffling it. I unlocked and opened her door. Humidity pushed past me, warming the already muggy room.

"Yeah, I'm fine." My wet clothes had created a tendril of water that was slowly snaking across the floor. Blythe stepped over it.

"We're all worried, you know. Roberto said he followed you for a bit, but that you ignored him," Blythe said.

I shrugged. "I didn't see him."

"What happened?" Manuela asked. When I didn't answer her, she continued, "Is it regarding your contract? Did something happen?"

"That's the least of my problems."

"Is it your mother?" Manuela asked. The mattress shifted as she sat beside me. Blythe nodded earnestly. They looked like children waiting for a bedtime story.

I shook my head. I studied my fingers. My skin had puckered first from the ocean and then from the shower. I stroked my long middle finger, rubbed the birthmark in the middle of my palm, the only parts of me that resembled Mom. For so long it was just us.

Where could I begin? My feelings didn't make any sense. I couldn't yet form words to talk about my father. Instead I said, "There's been a death in the family. I don't really want to talk about it."

"It might make you feel better," Blythe said, matter-of-factly. Although she and I had spent brief moments in one another's rooms before, her presence felt wrong. I stood, adjusted my robe, tightened the sash.

"No, I really can't. But there is something else on my mind ... why do you think Anita took those online complaints about me so seriously? I can't figure it out — there was no proof of me doing anything wrong. I have a strong sales record. She liked how I dealt with the fraud."

"Well, Oceana is a conservative organization. They want to be known as a family-friendly operation, not a swingers' club. Don't take it personally, Ameera," Blythe said. Manuela remained silent.

"I guess." I flopped down onto my bed. "Look, I'm really tired."

"Well, we should let you rest. Feel better, okay?" Blythe rose, and the door to our shared bathroom clicked closed.

"You want me to go, too?"

"No, please stay," I whispered.

Manuela arranged plates and forks. "So, what's really happening?"

I smiled wanly at her, glad for her friendship. I related Jessie's news in spurts while Manuela listened, wide-eyed, not interrupting. I told her about the bombing, about the finality of the search for my father.

"¡*Dios mío!*" she said. "This is horrible!"

"Yeah, I had a fantasy of meeting him one day, you know? Going to India, and seeing if I had half-brothers or sisters ..."

"You could. Maybe there are aunts and uncles? Cousins? Grandparents?" Manuela said hopefully.

I nodded. "I have to tell Mom. But I sort of feel guilty for doing a search without telling her first."

"Why would she mind? Wouldn't she want you to find him?" Unspoken, the questions were like childhood garments stored carefully for decades within a satin-lined trunk. Now, as I unhinged the latches and looked inside, they were only clothes, ordinary and out of fashion.

We tucked into the cake. I barely registered the chocolate; I stared at the linoleum's faded pattern, the pock-marked walls, the room that had been my home for three years. After a half hour, Manuela gave up trying to talk and left me alone, exhausted and full of cake.

I didn't sleep much that night. I drifted from one dream to the next, each one related to Azeez. I drowned, salt water burning down my throat, kelp and tiny fish expanding my stomach. Then I was in an airplane that exploded in mid-air, sunshine bursting through its hull. When I awoke at 3:00 a.m., I imagined I saw him bent over me, murmuring. I pulled the sheets over my head and turned onto my belly. When I peeked out again, the apparition was gone.

Azeez

∞

There was so much my daughter needed to know, to understand. I stayed with her all night, speaking into her inhalations, letting her breathe my story.

I gave her my memories of flight and falling. I feared it might be too much for her to bear. But just as Nafees did with my insertions, Ameera's imagination took control and offered her simpler fictions. When she sank into the sea with me, she grew water wings, and then suddenly she was in her childhood swimming lessons again, and later in a muddy lake with teenage friends.

I inserted the notion that I was still with her. At one point she roused from sleep and I could tell that the clarity of my presence reached her for a millisecond. I feared I startled her.

And then she curled back into sleep while I sang her made-up lullabies about ancestors whose spirits live on to care for those still on earth. I repeated over and over: *Yes, I am gone. But I am here. I am with you.*

I knew that mere fragments would reach her consciousness, and even less would be consciously remembered.

My poor girl's head was swimming.

Ameera

Δ

I piled eggs, sausage, and beans onto my plate, and drank two cups of milky, sweet coffee. I was famished; cake was all I'd consumed since the previous day's breakfast. I gorged as though my life hadn't been turned upside down.

But I knew I was a changed person, almost as though my DNA had been altered. I'd found and lost my father in the same day. And yet, what had really changed? I carried on. As on any other Sunday morning, I helped Roberto organize the excursion lists.

"Are you still going to leave?" He pulled off his floppy hat and scratched his head.

"I don't know yet. I'd miss the endless supply of chocolate cake," I said with a forced smile. I considered telling him about my father, but didn't have the energy for it. "How are things with Elena?"

"Not good." We climbed the stairs to the lobby. I touched Roberto's shoulder, my hand sliding down to his elbow, where it rested until we reached the landing. He opened his mouth, hesitated, and then said, "She doesn't think she loves me anymore."

"Oh, Roberto! I'm so sorry." Roberto's chest caved in and he turned away from me. A tourist approached us and we snapped into work mode. More vacationers milled about and Roberto grinned and joked with them, pretending that he wasn't having the saddest day of his life.

After the bus loaded and Roberto left with the turtle seekers, I traversed the resort, passing the stone path in progress. Over the previous week it had inched forward and now almost reached its endpoint. The newly laid rocks resembled puzzle pieces, carefully chosen and fit together. A pickaxe, shovel, and bag of sand lay unattended beside a pile of stone slabs. I had an urge to lift a rock, speed up the process. A worker approached and nodded to me. He wiped his brow, picked up the bag of sand, and emptied it on the side of the path. I was due at the tour desk and so I pushed on, routine carrying me forward.

"What are you doing here, Manuela? It's Sunday." Cardio Pump's music thundered and women danced frenetically across the parquet floor.

"Blythe asked me to switch. How are you?" She had gone light on her makeup that morning.

"I'm sort of numb. It's a lot to take in."

"Yes. I think maybe I had a dream about him last night."

"My father?"

Manuela nodded. "He introduced himself to me. Said I should help you. That's all I remember. Maybe I'm taking it all in, too." She frowned.

"Weird." I recalled splashes of my own dreams. I didn't believe in ghosts, but I'd awoken in the middle of the night imagining that he was with me.

"Did you see Anita's memo yet? She sent it yesterday." I shook my head and Manuela tapped the keyboard with furious fingers and then moved aside so I could read the message. Its subject header read: "Supervisory Changes."

We are pleased to announce that Blythe Hall will
be appointed Team Leader for our three Huatulco

resorts, beginning June 1st. She will oversee new
staff training as we continue to expand our services in the area in 2015 and 2016.

Blah blah blah about her skills and experience.
Blah blah blah about congratulating Blythe.

> *Best,*
> *Anita*

The job was even better than Blythe had described on Friday,
with more responsibilities. I dabbed my eyes with my shirt collar and clicked the message closed. Manuela pouted and shook
her head in reply. I realized that she was just as disappointed
to be passed over.

"It doesn't seem fair, does it?" I sniffed.

"I thought you had a better chance than her, at least before
those complaints. And we all knew none of *us* would get it,"
Manuela said. I nodded at her reference to her compatriots.

"Yeah." I said, but I was only half-listening. My mind was
sifting through other details that, like sand in my hands, were
difficult to hold. Something critical. Something Blythe had said
the night before. What was it?

"Well, nothing we can do about it now. Anita made Blythe
the boss. Like she said, it's a conservative organization." Manuela
shook her head.

And then it came to me. *Not a swingers' club.* Had I misheard
her? *Not a swingers' club.* No, I was sure. Anita had promised me
that she wouldn't reveal the specifics of the complaints. Had she?
I closed my eyes, breathed deeply.

No. And then I thought: *Those were Blythe's words.*

"Do you think —" my voice shifted to a whisper as I considered
that Suzanne might not have been the one to write the complaints

"— do you think that Blythe wrote those complaints against me?"

Manuela's look was blank, uncomprehending. "What do you mean?"

"You know, as a way to eliminate me from the competition?"

"Her? No!" But then she frowned. "Maybe."

"Anyone can send in online complaints. They're anonymous. And she certainly has enough ammunition against me to concoct something. And then to confirm them when Anita called for a reference."

"Maybe." Manuela repeated. She stared off in the distance, considering the idea. Then her eyes widened and she asked excitedly, "But how can we prove it?"

"There must be a way, right? If we could find a computer expert?"

We pondered the question. We made a list of all the people we knew who worked in IT: Manuela's sister's boyfriend, one of my old high school buddies, Manuela's neighbour. But none of them had any access to Oceana's system. I closed my eyes again, concentrated.

And then the Cardio Pump music stopped and Lykke Li's lyrics took their place in my mind:

Oh, oh, Jerome

Jerome Lewis. I remembered the odd conversation I'd had with him when I was dealing with the Doiges. Maybe. I added him to the brainstorm. Manuela nodded, mulling it over.

"Do I call him directly, or go through Anita? What if she doesn't take me seriously enough to check out my hunch?" I asked.

"But Anita might think you're being sneaky if you don't tell her first ..." Manuela warned.

"If I called him at home, made this less of an official request? I have to find his number." I didn't wait for her reply. I rushed off to my room. Did I still have his home phone number?

I fumbled through my stack of magazines, and, when I found the lavender message slip Manuela had written weeks ago, I held it up in victory. For the first time in weeks I felt as though I was in charge of something. But what if Jerome denied the request or if I was wrong about Blythe?

When I returned to the tour desk, Manuela asked, "You sure this is the best way?"

I nodded. But I wasn't sure. We reviewed what I'd say to Jerome, and Manuela took notes for me. I extracted the telephone memo slip, already damp from perspiration, from my pocket.

"I'm glad you're standing up for yourself. This is all so crazy," Manuela said.

I strode to the lobby to use the small, private office, the same one in which I'd received Anita's disciplinary calls three weeks earlier. Just as on that day, my body thrummed with fear, but this time, I possessed a sense of purpose. I looked at the scrap of paper, punched the dial pad eleven times, and then waited as the phone rang in its minor key. When Jerome answered, his voice once again reminded me of Gavin's and I flushed warm and a flurry of emotions flooded in.

"Hello?" Jerome asked a second time.

I corralled my brain and hurriedly introduced myself. "I hope it's okay that I'm calling you on a Sunday on your private line. You left the number for me a while ago."

"Oh yes, Ameera. I remember you. You dealt with the fraud." He sounded nervous.

"I'm actually phoning about the complaints that were lodged against me on the online customer feedback form." I swallowed hard, my mouth dry, my tongue heavy.

"Oh, right, the swinger complaints. I saw those when they came in. I'm surprised the company took them so seriously. Anonymity breeds a kind of insanity," he opined. Encouraged, I looked down at Manuela's notes, and pressed on.

"What if they didn't come from a customer?" I blurted. "What if they came from a staff account? Would you be able to track that?" I explained my hunch that a jealous co-worker could be responsible for discrediting me.

"Interesting. That would take a little detective work, but it wouldn't be impossible. There would be a regional identifier and unique IP address associated with the staff account. We have all that on record and I could cross-reference."

"So it's possible?" I asked hopefully.

"I think so. We should have programmed the form to exclude Oceana IP addresses, and I don't think we did." His voice grew excited as he rambled on, using technical terms I didn't comprehend. "Have you spoken to Anita about this yet?"

"No. I wanted to find out if you'd be willing to check it out for me. I didn't want to stir up trouble if it turns out my suspicions are incorrect." When he didn't reply right away, I added, "I'm on probation. I'm not exactly the most credible person in her eyes right now."

"I see. I'm not her favourite person, either. I found a pretty obvious security problem that allowed the Doiges hacker access. Essentially, it was my fault and I worked day and night to fix it. Which is why I phoned you back then, to see if you had further information. Luckily, it all blew over."

"That's good," I said with a neutrality I didn't feel. His mistake had cost the company money and resulted in a lot of stress for me. On the other hand, the online complaints hadn't had any real impact on Oceana and I'd been put on probation! I inhaled deeply and told myself to stay focused.

"Listen, give me your colleague's name and I'll compare that e-mail with the complaint IP addresses tomorrow. If there isn't a match, I'll cross-reference with other staff addresses. I'll have to tell Anita if I find a match."

"Of course. And if you don't, could you not mention that I called?"

"Let me think on that," Jerome said. My heart sank.

Δ

Artificial lights from Atlantis's buildings and neighbouring resorts blinked to life, forming haphazard constellations across the horizon. Without any work to do, I ruminated about Jerome. Had I behaved impulsively by calling him? I knew I'd gone through an Oceana side entrance instead of knocking on the front door, the way I probably should have. I hoped I wasn't making things worse.

I slipped a sundress over my head, one I knew Enrique liked, and sauntered to the bar. He glanced my way, smiled, but only for an instant; he was busy chatting with a guest. I stifled my longing. I couldn't take the ache of disappointment that would trail behind it.

Eventually, Enrique poured me a drink, and then another. Twice, he asked me, *"Ameera, ¿que pasó?"* Each time I shook my head, and stared down into my Atlantis Mantis, watching the red of the cranberry blend with the ginger ale's gold. The bar's jolly din mingled with Passenger's "Let Her Go."

When I called out for a third drink, Enrique carried it around to my side of the counter, and with a gentle hand against my lower back, guided me out of the bar. My spine tingled with his touch, even after he dropped his hand. We walked silently down a deserted path, sat on a bench, and stared up at the almost full moon. Tears dripped down my cheeks, but I refused to tell him what was causing them. I couldn't — it was all too much. How could I say that I'd just found my dead father who had died in a terrorist plot? Or that I believed my co-worker was actively sabotaging me but I had no proof?

I rubbed my face with closed fists and he pulled me into a sideways hug. He rested his ear against the top of my head, as though listening for stray thoughts.

"I heard that you were upset about something. That you're thinking about leaving." Then, in response to my raised eyebrows, he said, "Roberto told me. So? *Háblame.*"

"I don't want to talk. And you should get back to work." I squirmed out of his embrace.

"Okay." He looked at me for a moment, his eyes holding mine. His breath was warm against my forehead and his lips parted slightly. I reached up, pulled his face down, and pressed my mouth against his. I felt resistance in his jaw, unwillingness in his lips. I mumbled an apology and turned away from him.

"I will walk you home." He squeezed my shoulder too hard.

"I can get there myself." He ignored me and took my arm. At my building's door, he held me in a tight hug. Lightheaded, I steadied myself within his embrace.

After he left, I wandered to the beach. The night breeze carried the day's leftover heat and the ocean's brine. The air lapped at the wet under my armpits. Crests shimmered white before crashing foamy against the sand. I stood where the surf approached and retreated, teasing it to wash over my feet.

"Hey, it's Ameera, right?" I turned toward a voice that was warm but unwelcome. It was Rahul, from Saturday's orientation session game. The R who matched Roberto. I supposed that his friend, the A who matched me, was in tow.

"I almost didn't recognize you without your uniform. And your hair's down. Much better, girl," he said, appraising me from head to toe. Alain joined us a moment later, carrying two cocktails with tiny yellow umbrellas.

"How are you enjoying yourselves?" I asked mechanically.

"Oh, it's nice here, just what the doctor ordered," Alain said.

"Good." I was already tired of the conversation. I crossed my arms and held my shoulders even though it wasn't cold.

"We're thinking about going to the disco. It doesn't open until nine-thirty, right?" Alain asked.

"It's open already." I held a finger to my lips and pointed my chin to a building from where "Buffalo Soldier" played softly. "There it is. The DJ loves to start with a string of Bob Marley.

Michael Jackson comes next. Then he goes back and forth. ABBA after that if he's in the mood."

"Really?" Alain asked. "The same music every day?"

"Every day. He'll mix it up a little if you make a request," I said, blandly.

"Well, we might need to find other entertainment tomorrow." Rahul raised his eyebrows at Alain.

"You wouldn't happen to know if there were any gay bars in town, would you?" Alain asked. "Or gay-positive ones?"

"No. You'd have to go to some of the larger centres. Puerto Vallarta, Acapulco ..." I contemplated another drink; my tipsiness had faded.

"We did Puerto Vallarta last year," said Alain. "We sort of wanted a more authentic Mexican experience this year."

"Authentic? You came to an all-inclusive for authentic?" A giggle escaped, then a guffaw. Alain regarded me carefully, perhaps gauging whether to be offended. His smiled widened, turned into a chuckle. I snorted. We batted giddiness like a shuttlecock across a badminton net, our laughter growing as our game progressed. I bent over, shaking, holding my aching stomach. Soon, Alain was mirroring my posture. Rahul watched us with a bemused expression.

"Ameera, come with us! We'll make this two-bit disco fun." Rahul took my arm.

"No, no," I said, my protest interrupted by bursts of laughter, "I've had a really tough day ... I meant to have a quiet walk on the beach." Then I sniggered, causing Alain to chuckle again.

"Come on, we're going to need a female chaperone to dance at the disco," Rahul said, and then covering his mouth as though to tell me a secret, "it's kind of heteroville here, no offence."

"Well, it's not quite that bad. I saw a lesbian couple over by the pool," Alain countered.

"He's an expert at turning lemons into lemonade," Rahul said, rolling his eyes.

"And then there's that hunky bartender. What's his name?" Alain asked.

"Enrique." I shuddered with embarrassment, remembering that stupid kiss. I'd have to apologize properly the next day.

Rahul tugged my arm, and together we walked to the disco. The strain of the day slipped away and I forgot myself for an hour. We made fun of the DJ's limited musical choices and the men invented dance steps I couldn't follow. When "Don't Stop Til You Get Enough" played, strong hands grabbed my waist and lifted me in the air. I squealed in delight and shock, and the other patrons watched while Alain twirled me round and round. It was like I was flying, safe and free. A moment later, he set me down, and my limbs were light, still levitating.

Later, the DJ played "No Woman No Cry" and they guided me into a slow-dance triangle. I rested a hand on Rahul's steady shoulder, and another on Alain's slim waist. We crooned along with Bob Marley, mostly out of tune. The men rearranged, and then I was in the middle, their arms encircling me. Through his linen shirt, Rahul's heart beat against my collarbone. I closed my eyes, felt his warm breath in my hair. My chest tightened, and a sob threatened my throat.

I craned my neck to look at Alain, who gazed into the distance, blissed out. Rahul met my wet eyes, and held me more tightly. He sang the song's comforting chorus. Just then, another man's face swept into view, imagined, but imagined so often he'd been rendered real. Azeez. His dark hair, brown skin, and perfect smile beckoned to me in the darkness. For a minute or two I believed everything was going to be all right.

When the song ended, I excused myself, citing fatigue I didn't need to feign.

"Stay another few songs, one more set, come on, Ameera, the night's still young," Rahul protested.

Alain cajoled, "ABBA hasn't even started!"

Although tempted, I let go of the hands that held on snug and warm. At the disco's door, I turned to wave goodbye. Rahul and Alain slow-danced, swaying within one another's embrace.

Azeez

∞

Oceana's Ottawa headquarters was just like the pictures Ameera sometimes dreamed at night. Jerome's corner cubicle was on the same floor as Anita's, but with a smaller desk and an inferior view of the city. I nosed through three filing cabinets and two drawers before I found his home address.

He lived in a square box eleven stories off the ground. From his concrete balcony, I could see the Canadian Parliament buildings in the distance.

He'd just returned from the gym when I caught up with him that Sunday evening. While he showered and changed into clean sweatpants and a singlet, I slunk about his one-bedroom condominium to learn his interests. What would motivate him to help my girl with her problem?

Atop his coffee table were computer magazines. I flipped through them, surmising that he'd view Ameera's quandary as a technical glitch, an enjoyable coding problem to solve. Perhaps I wouldn't need to meddle at all.

He put some pasta on to boil, added orange powered cheese, and ate the concoction from the pot while watching three episodes of *The Big Bang Theory*. I settled on the couch next to him. I'd watched many comedies while at Nora's home, but had never viewed that show. I found it quite hilarious, but despaired that, as usual, there were no substantial roles for Indians on American television.

It grew dark and he carried his laptop to bed. He typed "amateur" and "chubby" and pulled the covers around him. While I'd had little sexual experience in my previous life, I was well acquainted with the activity in which Jerome was engaging.

I broke my usual rule about witnessing human sexual practices and lingered in his bedroom. I know it was questionable, but sometimes our interventions have to be risky.

As he watched his lewd program, his heart rate and blood pressure elevated. His movements under the blanket quickened. Too warm, he threw off the covers, revealing his nakedness. His respiration increased and deepened. Finally, in the sudden stillness of climax, I blew my daughter's name into his open mouth.

Ameera

Δ

I spent Monday, my day off, huddled in a corner of the staff cafeteria, learning about my father's death. The Internet was full of Air India bombing references. One video clip led to a hyperlink, which took me to a blog entry followed by a book excerpt and two online documentaries. It was like stumbling into a forest, the tree canopy growing thicker, the light dimmer with each step.

One of the films recreated the hour-by-hour details of June 22, 1985. I pressed pause whenever a personal home movie or victim's snapshot was included in the footage. I scoured these images for young men who looked like Azeez.

He would have passed through those doors at Pearson.

He would have laid his luggage on that conveyer belt.

He would have stood in that security line.

He would have buckled up in one of those seats.

He would have fallen from that sky.

He would have drowned in those waters.

I couldn't get over the multiple, preventable mistakes surrounding the bombing. The bumbling CSIS investigation that couldn't thwart the most amateur terrorist operation. The hapless, overworked airline clerk in Vancouver who allowed the suitcase with the bomb to be checked through all the way to India. The baggage scanners that broke down at Pearson International

Airport. The overwhelmed handler who let the bag go, even though his hand-held device shrilled a warning. How could so many mistakes have happened? The terrorists could have been stopped if just one of those errors had been caught.

And then my father would still be alive. And maybe he would have reached out to Mom. Or she would have found him. I might have grown up knowing him. I would have had a father. If only one of those errors had been caught.

When I finally emerged from the darkness, five hours had passed and I was parched and starving. I forced myself to turn off the computer, eat something, and return to my room. I listened for Blythe next door, but all was quiet across the bathroom wall.

I didn't have the energy to think about her. Not that day.

I picked up Mom's *O* magazine and flipped open an article by Deepak Chopra on detachment. The page was slightly crinkled — had Mom stopped there, too? Deepak advised that removing the ego from aspiration helps to reduce anxiety. I rolled my eyes at the facile advice, but then something made me pause. Frankly, I needed all the guidance I could get.

Remove ego from aspiration. I puzzled over how to take away the *I* from my father's death. From the complaint problem. It was hopeless. I moved on.

Deepak urged the reader to consider that no one can be robbed of their truest, deepest self. I frowned and concentrated.

A memory of a recent dream flashed in my mind. I was walking under a full moon and the night air smelled of salt water, gasoline, and roses. My dreaming mind told me I was in a Mumbai suburb. Despite being completely alone, I wasn't afraid, and my gait was purposeful and confident. I was like a powerful animal, or something or someone bigger than myself. Or maybe I was myself then, my truest, deepest self.

Azeez

∞

My girl rolled herself into her bed sheets. I could tell I had reached her, if only for a few precious moments. I blended my words into a hymn that lulled her to sleep:

I am here
My perfect, beautiful daughter
You are mine
And I am yours
You are mine
And I am yours
Now that we have found one another
I'll be yours forever.

The only thing was, I didn't know if the last part was completely accurate.

Ameera

Δ

A pipe rattled somewhere within my wing, plumbing waking up. Early-morning sunshine streamed across my face. The shower stall was dry when I stepped in, a rarity.

I was oddly calm and expectant. I somehow knew the call would come that morning. I sat with Oscar at the tour desk and waited. At 11:00 a.m. the phone rang.

"I'm glad to have reached you, Ameera. I'm following up on something important that Jerome, our Online Services Supervisor reported to me," Anita's tone was formal.

"Okay." My heart threatened to break through my ribs.

"He informed me of it yesterday morning." She inhaled sharply and released her words in one long, jittery sentence: "Jerome has been revamping the online feedback form and decided to do some kind of testing on how to track complaints and he used the complaints against you as an example and found out that the person who sent them was not a tourist, but someone internal to the organization."

"Really?" My mind scuttled over Anita's words, looking for a place to land.

"Blythe. I'm sorry to tell you that it was your colleague Blythe."

"Oh. Wow." It *was* her. And Jerome had covered for me.

"I'm very sorry. For all the stress. I don't know anything about computers and I wish I'd thought to ask Jerome to try to track things before, but it didn't dawn on me that a staff person would do something like this." She sighed long and loudly at the end of her sentence.

Too many thoughts swarmed in and I couldn't speak. I let her continue.

"You know, when I spoke with her after the first complaint, she hinted that she knew more about the situation, but she came across as your loyal friend. Protective. I thought she was hiding something. Then after the second complaint, she changed her tune, and apologized to me for not being open. Then she gave me this crazy story about you being a compulsive sort of sex addict. She played me. I still can't believe it. I trusted Blythe." She sounded as though she might cry.

"I trusted her, too." I silently continued the sentence: *but what's wrong with me? With us? How did she fool us all?* Aloud, I asked, "But why? Why'd she do it? Did she say anything?"

"She denied it at first. When she realized we had proof, she said she was protecting the company, Oceana's reputation. I figured out from her rant that she'd been building a campaign to make you look bad and gain my trust for some time. So that she'd have a better chance at being promoted."

"It worked. You bought it," I said tersely. I didn't care if I sounded angry.

"I'm sorry about that. I should have trusted you more."

"I still can't believe it," I said, ignoring her apology. "She's been my co-worker for three years. *I* thought she was my friend. "

"Yes, it's really unbelievable. Listen, going forward ... for now, I'm going to ask you to keep this matter confidential, at least for a day or two," Anita said. I heard the request, but resisted, mentally drafting a list of people I'd need to speak with next: Manuela, Roberto, Oscar, Blythe. No. Blythe first.

"There are a number of bureaucratic issues I have to wrap up. Of course, this will mean you are no longer on probation. We'll expunge the complaint record from your file and we'll be looking at other contract changes as well."

"Thanks for telling me," I said numbly. Anita apologized again. She mumbled truisms about rumours and gossip and putting her trust in the wrong place. I rushed her off the phone.

And then, like a beast preparing for a fight, I bolted to the staff wing, my eyes and mind trained on my target. My legs and arms pumped to their own rhythm. I didn't notice anyone in my path.

I knocked on Blythe's door. Then I banged on it. When there was no answer, I unlocked my own door and stamped into our shared bathroom. All of Blythe's things had been cleared off the counter. My skin flushed cold. It was quiet on the other side of the door. I rifled through a drawer, found a bobby pin, and rattled the lock until it yielded. The door swung wide.

She'd stripped the bed. A faint stain, the shape of a large fish without its fins, covered the centre of the mattress. Blythe's bed sagged like mine, only I hadn't noticed it before, because it had been covered with a luxe duvet and half-dozen pillows. We'd always joked that my room and hers were like the before and after photos in an Ikea catalogue.

Her drapes, too, had been removed and sunshine glared through streaky windows. Empty hooks dotted the walls, revealing cracks and pock marks that framed photos and paintings had hidden. The dresser and side tables were wiped clean of their knick-knacks. I pulled open a drawer and saw that it had been emptied. Her closet, too, was bare. The only possessions remaining were a small rolled-up rug, and a wicker chair. Without its decoration, Blythe's room was once again a mirror image of my plain bedroom.

High heels clacked against the hallway's linoleum. I waited, spread my feet on the tile, my stance more confident than I felt.

"What are you doing in my room?" Blythe demanded.

"Tell me why you did it," I said quietly.

"Did what?" Blythe asked.

"I know. I just spoke with Anita." My voice was calm and steady. It was like my head had momentarily detached itself from my pulsing-with-adrenaline body.

"I've been bloody fired because of you!" Blythe said indignantly. She snatched up the rug.

"Why'd you make the bogus complaints?" I planted myself in Blythe's chair as much to anchor myself as to communicate that I wasn't going away.

"Bogus! We both know they were true. You're a nympho. Everyone knows that. Even Rhion. You know he once suggested we have a threesome with you? The asshole," she spat.

"What?" For a moment I was confused. I traced the tiny freckles that crept up Blythe's neck, past her pink lips and small nose. Her features were familiar to me, and yet her face was now unrecognizable. I'd never before seen her so angry, so spiteful.

"It doesn't matter. I broke up with him. Weeks ago."

"That has nothing to do with me, Blythe."

"Whatever. You can't control yourself. You're as bad as Nancy the pedophile."

"No … no, that wasn't the problem for you." I could feel my head clearing. "It wasn't about sex, was it? It was about the job." And then, I thought: *a meaningless job*.

"I wanted Anita to notice the other candidates," she said, pointing at her own chest.

"You went too far." I shook my head. I couldn't make sense of her fury. It all seemed so unnecessary, so petty.

"I suppose you're back to being Anita's favourite again, aren't you? You never deserved that. I would have been a way better supervisor than you." Blythe blinked back tears.

"Blythe, weren't we friends?" I attempted. I knew I ought to have been meaner, angrier. My chest felt heavy. My heart ached.

"Get up! I'm taking that chair. I've got a golf cart waiting." She scowled. I stood and she piled the rug onto the chair. She carried both, her spine bent backwards with the weight of them. I realized that Blythe wouldn't be able to offer an explanation or apology.

"Where are you going?" I wasn't sure why I cared. Yet I did.

"It's none of your business but I've applied to Sunshine Tours. They agree that I was wrongfully dismissed. They appreciate whistle blowers over there. I'll likely get a post in Acapulco." Blythe continued down the hallway. She pushed at the door with the edge of the chair, but it wouldn't move.

"Whistle blower? That's what you think you are?" I asked incredulously.

She grunted, put the chair down, turned the knob. She hefted her load and pushed again. The chair was wider than the door, so she had to turn it and wedge it and turn it and wedge it until it was through. Then the door slammed behind her.

I lay on my bed, Blythe's departure like a strange dream. She probably would convince her new employer that she was a victim and somehow land on her feet. And what about me? Where would I land? I'd expected to feel triumphant after revealing the truth, getting my redemption, and confronting Blythe. But there was no victory, only betrayal and loneliness wafting across our shared bathroom.

I needed my mom. I Skyped from the cafeteria to her kitchen table and told her about Blythe and the complaints and the plan I'd hatched with Manuela to contact Jerome. I omitted the swinger part of the story, of course.

"My goodness. What a lot of stress you've been under. How long has this been going on?" She applied a coat of lip balm to her lower lip and then her upper lip.

"The last couple of months," I acknowledged, knowing that she didn't like it when I summarized my problems after I'd already dealt with them. "But it's okay, it's all resolved now."

"That woman nearly ruined your career opportunities. Do you think you'll be offered the supervisor job now?'

"I might. But listen, there's something bigger I need to tell you." The confession about Azeez was harder. It wasn't a final report, but a story still unfolding. I took my time, uncrinkling the edges, flattening the creases. I explained about Jessie and her research.

"Mom, he died the day after you met him. In the Air India bombing." It was weird to say aloud. Images from the documentaries pushed forward: the smashed airplane awash in the Atlantic, the bodies recovered, the grieving family members interviewed years later. The family members. It dawned on me that I was one of them now.

Her gaze turned glassy as she took it all in. After a moment she spoke, "I remember the news, but I always assumed he was leaving weeks later ..." she went quiet again. I knew she'd believed that Azeez was just another guy who'd taken advantage of her.

"I bet he would have called you if he had left later," I said with conviction. "I bet you made an impression on him. I bet you were hard to forget." She gave me a brave smile.

"Maybe. Well ... this is a shock. It makes sense now, that time I called India. I wish I'd known ... what really happened. I don't know what to say." She sighed, air rushing from her microphone, across the continent, and through my headphones.

"Yeah, me too." I nodded, watching her face compose itself. She was rallying, as I expected she would. I gave her time. I needed her to rally.

"How are you dealing with all of this, Ameera?"

"It's surreal. He was always a figment of my imagination. Now that I know who he was and what happened to him, he seems ... more real," I fixed my gaze at the camera, just above her head, so that she'd feel like I was looking into her eyes. "I feel close to him, somehow now, even though he's dead."

"Huh," she murmured. "Well I suppose that's good."

"And there's more, Mom. Jessie, the archivist, is now looking for his family. My namesake aunt. His brother, his parents. I think that maybe I'd like to meet them. You know, one day." I watched her face carefully. She was still composed, almost stock still.

"I understand." She bit her lip and I knew she was reining in errant feelings, ones that she deemed inappropriate or self-centred or too big to say to me. She applied more lip balm. "Of course. You need to know more about them."

Azeez

∞

Jessie reached Nadeem at his office. Family reunifications were the best part of her work, but she approached him neutrally, knowing she should appear to have little stake in the concern.

"You're certain of this information," he asked, in his lawyerly manner, after she'd delivered the news. His voice was steady, but I heard a storm building in his exhalations. Disbelief crackled forward. Was this a joke? What kind of a person ...? Then, he softened and gratitude breezed out. A niece. Could it be? Some essence of his brother returning to him.

Yes. It's true, I told him. *A niece.*

"I'm fairly sure. Azeez told Ameera's mother that he had a brother named Nadeem and a sister named Ameera."

Nadeem held his breath, but I nudged him to inhale my words: *Yes, I talked about you.*

"He also told Nora he had just completed his PhD at McMaster. We matched his surname to the university's records."

Nora. What a curious name, Nadeem thought. *My brother once had a lover named Nora.* It reassured him to know that I'd known the love of a woman.

"I see," was all he said to Jessie.

"They didn't know one another long, or well. You see, it was just a single meeting. Nora didn't know he'd left the next day, or that he'd died."

He frowned and thought: the girl was a product of a single meeting? *Yes, it's true.*

"How old is the girl, then?" He looked at his desk calendar, forgetting for a second that it was 2015, and not 1985.

"Ameera is twenty-nine."

"Twenty-nine," he whispered. He pulled out his calculator just to be sure. His mind was sluggish and he laboured through the simple arithmetic: 2015 minus 1985 minus nine months.

"Ameera would like to make contact with you, with the family. If you are agreeable," Jessie said gently.

"Yes. That's fine." He pressed the "equals" button on his calculator. Twenty-nine. *It's true*, I reassured him. *This is no joke.*

"Can I pass on your contact information? I think she might want to begin with an e-mail first. I recommend that, actually. It can be less awkward."

"All right." Nadeem spelled his e-mail address. He repeated it to make sure she'd heard it correctly. And then he hung up, feeling as uncertain as the young man who'd gone to Cork to retrieve his older brother's body. He wanted to cry, but held back his tears.

Ameera

Δ

None of my colleagues were shocked when I told them about Blythe. Manuela hugged me and called me brave for executing our plan. Oscar shook his head and wondered aloud about Blythe's psychological health, muttering "*Loca.* There's your Word of the Week." Roberto said he was relieved that he wouldn't have to report to her for the next three years.

They carried on with their routines, nonplussed by Blythe's departure, easily picking up her slack and filling the shift gaps, while I, on the other hand, was still processing her duplicity, but even more, her absence. I heard the quiet across the wall. Having the bathroom to myself still felt odd. I'd visited Blythe's empty suite many times over the previous days. I'd needed to see the blank room to believe that she was really gone.

"This means you'll stay on, then, right?" Roberto asked with a smile.

"Maybe?" I replied.

I really didn't know and wasn't ready to make any decisions. What I didn't tell my colleagues was that Anita had offered me the supervisory role and I'd requested a few days to consider it. It ought to have been a no-brainer, right? It's what I'd wanted before Blythe tried to cut me down. But so much had happened since then.

Blythe's false complaints had shone a spotlight on an un-expected yearning. I realized that I no longer wanted to continue my twilight existence at Atlantis. I wanted to live in a way that allowed me to do as I wished. I mean, despite the risk, I hadn't stopped seeing swingers. Being a swinger. Being myself.

And yet, unemployment was no better. No, I wasn't ready to decide about the job.

And there was my father. Jessie told me that she'd found Azeez's brother and would phone him that week if I wanted.

I'd said yes.

All of that seemed so much bigger than my tiny walled-in life at Atlantis.

Δ

I eyed the airplane waiting on the runway. The last of the arriving passengers were walking across the tarmac.

"Looks like we're in for a minimum sixty-minute wait before they come through," I grumbled.

"Well, then, we should get comfortable, should we not?" Oscar said, carrying out the canvas chairs. He unfolded them one by one, their metal legs landing with a decisive clack against the white pavement.

This time, none of us hesitated; we gratefully accepted our chairs and rested our feet. We sat in a semi-circle and I glanced furtively at the spot of pavement that Blythe's chair would have occupied.

"I have an announcement to make." Oscar looked at the cloudy sky. Then he loosened his tie, pulled it over his head, and stuffed it into his pants pocket.

"¿Qué pasa? " Manuela asked.

"I'm resigning. Me and my cousin are opening a café beside the crocodile sanctuary. We'll have drinks and snacks. Clean bathrooms," he explained in slow Spanish.

Roberto questioned Oscar about his venture dispassionately, as though discussing which route to take for their commute home. Manuela crossed her arms over her chest, her expression difficult to read. I realized that I was the only one unsurprised by Oscar's announcement.

"I'm sure it's going to be a success, Oscar," I said. "That's a prime location."

The sun parted the clouds and its rays beat down on us. There was a lull in our conversation as we took in Oscar's news.

"I also have something to say," I announced. "Anita offered me the supervisor job."

"Congratulations." Manuela smiled weakly. Had she expected the news, even prepared herself for it?

"What? Do they only promote foreigners or something?" Oscar asked. Manuela flashed him a look.

"Yes, that's good news," Roberto agreed.

"I think you'll do a good job, by the way." Oscar said.

"I haven't decided yet. I'm not sure if it's the best thing. I've got to give Anita an answer by Monday." I looked at my hands self-consciously. "I'll probably say 'no.' It might be time for me to go home."

The first guests came through the doors, ending our conversation. I stood and folded my chair.

Δ

"So what's the problem?" Manuela asked when we finished our shift that evening. "I thought you wanted the job."

"I did. But now I think I want to take time off to travel. I was thinking India. I might have some family to visit." I filled her in on Jessie's narrowing search. Earlier in the day, she'd sent a three-paragraph summary of her conversation with Nadeem Dholkawala and instructions on how to contact him.

"Wow." Manuela's eyes widened and she grabbed my arm. "Family for you to meet! They are going to be excited!"

But I wasn't so certain. What would it mean, thirty years after Azeez's death, to know that he'd fathered a child? Would I unearth sad memories? What if they didn't want me?

"Yeah, I hope so," I said, pushing away the fears.

Azeez

∞

"What I can't get over is why now?" Ameera frowned. It was the same expression she'd worn as a young girl, whenever she was upset. I used to mimic her, scrunching up my forehead to make her laugh.

"I don't know. Perhaps she only just found us?" Nadeem had wondered the same thing, but he hadn't given much attention to the question. "It must have been difficult. She didn't know our surname until recently."

"I just … I find it … suspicious. And she has the same name as me!" What I could hear in her breath was: *I'm afraid.*

"He talked to her mother about us, told her our names. The day before he left."

I remembered that moment vividly, and offered it up to Nadeem: the awkward coffee shop banter. The rush of excitement when I realized she was flirting back. The saccharine sweetness of the donut and double-double. I showed him how I wrote our three names on a paper napkin:

AZEEZ
NADEEM AMEERA

I recreated the formation, standing behind the couch between my siblings. Nadeem only took in pieces of my description, but it made him sigh and smile.

"But how do we *really* know that Azeez is the father? Yes, he might have known this Nora person. But it could all be a scam." Her voice still faltered when she said my name. I moved closer to reassure her, but her breath was shallow, a shield against me.

"A scam?" Nadeem's smile disappeared. "But she hasn't asked for anything. She only sent an introduction."

Ameera crossed her arms over her chest. "She must assume that we are well-off? Perhaps she's found out that you are a lawyer? That we have property?" She was referring to the five-storey apartment building they'd inherited from our parents. Each of their families resided on a floor and they rented the other three flats for a tidy income.

Ameera is an independent young woman. She has her savings. She doesn't want yours, I said to both of them. Neither paid any attention.

"So what do you want? I was going to invite her to come visit us. It seemed like ... like the right thing to do. Perhaps I was too hasty." Apprehensive thoughts replaced the softer *uncleji* ones he'd entertained earlier.

"Visit us? Without verifying who she is first? We don't know the first thing about this girl, Nadeem." She shot him a stern look and shook her head.

Ameera

Δ

Anita received my resignation on Saturday and offered Manuela the supervisor job on Monday afternoon. The Oceana hamster wheel rolled on.

Although she'd been third in line for it, Manuela was obviously thrilled, her eyes bright and her grin wide. Soon, she'd be training three new Oceana staff in preparation for the upcoming season. I listened as she giggled into the phone to Anita. Then they chatted about Ottawa's rainy spring. Finally, she passed the phone to me.

"Ameera, I filed all your termination paperwork." Anita explained that my last workday would be the following Saturday, May 16. I heard her flipping through papers and pictured her sitting in her cramped Ottawa high-rise office, from where I'd once admired her framed Huatulco honeymoon photo.

"Sounds fine. When do I fly out?" I glanced Manuela's way. She was listening closely.

"The following Friday. I hope that's all right. We have a lot of space on the May 22 charter. So that means you'll have five days of free time to enjoy before coming home." She babbled on about how I should take advantage of the beach and sun.

"Okay." Ten more days in Huatulco was both not enough time and an eternity.

"But listen, Ameera, I'm sorry you resigned. You explained your change of heart, but I'm very surprised."

"Yeah, me, too." I was still catching up with myself.

"We have an opening here in sales in case you're interested. Better pay than what you've got now. But worse weather, of course. Deadline's coming soon," she said, typing on her computer. "I've just forwarded it you."

After we hung up, relief hit me like cool air on a muggy day. It had finally happened; I was leaving Atlantis's glass bowl. I was moving on. A necessary ending; one of my own choosing.

"So?" Manuela asked.

"Next Friday." I blinked back tears.

"*Estoy triste. Triste.* Your Word of the Week."

"I'm sad, too, Manuela."

Δ

On Wednesday night, I broke my rule about single male tourists. It no longer applied, right? And Craig, a Jamaican-Canadian social worker from Toronto, was too cute to pass up. He earnestly confessed that he'd never before had casual sex, embarrassment sliding across his brown face. I lied to him, telling him I hadn't, either, enjoying the idea of sharing a first with a stranger.

There was a moment when, panting on our backs, I revelled in the spaciousness of the bed while also sensing that something, or someone, was missing. A worrisome thought uncoiled before me: had I ruined myself for regular sex? What was that even called? Twosome sex? I supposed I might need to adjust when back in Hamilton. Or maybe I wouldn't; perhaps being home would give me an opportunity to explore my sexuality even more than I had in Huatulco. I could create a profile on an online swingers' dating site or check out a club. A Toronto couple had told me about an Etobicoke bar that had rooms full of mattresses, dim lighting, disco music, and condom bowls. Unicorns would be just as much in demand there as in Huatulco, possibly more so. Or maybe I wouldn't be a unicorn anymore and would instead look for a partner who was into the same things as me.

Noticing my distraction, my date rubbed his thumb across my bottom lip and then kissed me hard. I wrapped my legs around him, the softness of my inner thighs meeting his slim waist. My worries rolled themselves into a tight ball and trundled away.

Δ

I received Nadeem Dholkawala's reply the next morning. I'd sent him a message earlier in the week, four shy paragraphs introducing myself and telling him that I was interested in making contact with the family in Mumbai.

I stood barefoot on the prickly lawn between my building and the lobby, trying to catch a signal. I crouched on the grass and read:

> Dear Ameera,
>
> Thank you for your e-mail.
>
> We are still quite shocked at the news that we might have a niece in Canada. We weren't aware that our brother had a girlfriend there.
>
> You seem like a very nice girl and if you are indeed my brother's biological daughter, I am sorry you never got to know him. He was very kind, ethical, and intelligent.
>
> All the best,
> Nadeem Dholkawala

The sun shifted, its rays slipping past the branches of the tree above, the glare rendering the screen unreadable. Nadeem hadn't responded to my request to meet. The family wasn't interested in opening their doors to me. Tears blurred my vision and I raised myself up, stamped feeling into my feet, and closed the laptop.

And then I stopped and thought: *No. Persist. Send him a photo.*
I composed:

> Dear Nadeem,
>   I very much appreciate your reply. I understand
> that you are shocked. I almost can't believe it my-
> self, but my friend Jessie, who did the search for
> me, and my mother, Nora, are sure that your broth-
> er Azeez is my biological father.
>   I thought about searching for him for many
> years, but didn't have the courage. I didn't know
> that he'd died and always hoped to meet him one
> day.
>   I'm attaching a photo of myself. I was wonder-
> ing — would you have a photo of Azeez that you
> could scan and send to me? My mother described
> him to me many times, but I've never seen a pic-
> ture. It would mean a lot to me.
>
> Warmly,
> Ameera

The photo I attached, one that Manuela had taken on my
birthday, was a close-up of my head and shoulders. The sunlight
is golden on my cheeks and I'm smiling a toothy grin.

Azeez

∞

Nadeem blinked at the unopened e-mail from Ameera. He was a man who could be decisive in matters related to work and finances, but personal issues were another thing. He stared at his screen, overwhelmed to be in charge of this significant correspondence. I slipped downstairs and prodded Nafees to go to his uncle.

"Hi, *Mamaji*," he said, looking over his shoulder. "What are you doing?"

"I've received another e-mail from the girl in Canada."

"What does it say?" Nafees saw that it hadn't been opened, but played dumb.

"Your mother thinks we should ask for a DNA test. Proof that she's related." His finger wavered over the mouse.

"I know, she told me. But I think that's going to make her feel bad. Imagine how scared she must be. She doesn't know us, and has never even met her own father." *Yes, that's exactly right. One hundred percent*, I cheered on my Nafu.

Nadeem bobbed his head left and right, considering Nafees's words. He clicked open the message. Nafees read along with him.

"Let's see what she looks like!" Nafees clasped his uncle's shoulder.

Nadeem moused over the attachment. Her image filled the screen.

"She's pretty. And she looks like she could be related, no?"

"Maybe," Nadeem said, averting his eyes from the screen.

"Are you going to send her a photo of *Mamaji* Azeez? How about this one?" Nafees took down a frame from the study's wall. Max had taken the close-up of me in front of the house the spring before I'd died. I'd mailed it to my mother, knowing how much she missed me. The air had been chilly and I'd worn a green scarf around my neck. But the sun had been bright, shining warmly down on my face.

Nafees held the frame beside the computer screen, my daughter's photo and mine side by side. It was the first time I'd seen our faces together and I was stunned at how her features matched my own. Her skin was lighter, but the shape of our faces, our jaw lines, our eyes, our smiles were almost identical.

"There's your DNA test, *Mamaji*," Nafees whispered.

Ameera

Δ

In the space between departures and arrivals, we lounged in our semi-circle of chairs. Oscar had unfolded them all without thinking, and one sat conspicuously empty. None of us felt compelled to remove it.

"Ask for a suite with its own bathroom," I suggested to Manuela, who was talking about moving into staff housing at Atlantis. "But hey, you're not turned off by living in an all-inclusive resort anymore?"

"My sister will be back from college soon. It will get too crowded again. But I'll go home on days off. I'll need 'real' life." She gave me a look of recognition, and I smiled, remembering our conversation from years ago, when she'd resisted my pressure to move to Atlantis.

"I may ask for Ameera's old room," Roberto mumbled, causing all of us to turn and stare at him.

"Oh no! Things aren't going well?" I asked.

"It's temporary. We need some space while we are figuring things out." Oscar whispered something in Spanish to Roberto. Manuela pursed her lips in disapproval.

Moments later, the first arrivals approached the glass doors, and we hid away our chairs and stood in formation.

Manuela beamed. "Welcome to Huatulco."

Δ

I filled my five final unstructured days with errands and activities, but each diversion became an exercise in nostalgia.

I joined Manuela's family dinner on Sunday evening. I teared up when Sara served me her signature dish. *This will be the last time she cooks for me*, I thought.

"Have you bought your tickets yet?" Manuela asked.

I nodded. "I'll stay with my mother for a couple of weeks and then go to Mumbai in mid-June. I bought an open ticket."

They lobbed a flurry of questions at me about my biological family: *What are they like? How do you feel meeting them?* I really didn't want to think too much about all that. I'd purchased the ticket impulsively, hopeful it would turn out all right.

At the door, José patted my back and the four Méndez women made a joke of lining up from tallest to shortest, like nesting dolls, for hugs. I laughed, but my nose and eyes dripped from the farewell. Was this going to be like all the other jobs where I'd made promises to stay in touch, but never had? No, not this time, not with Manuela.

Δ

On Monday, I hiked to Wild Beach. *This will be the last time I stand on this shore*, I told myself. I took sixty-two photos of water crashing against rocks and shoreline. Indeed, that whole week I attempted to view all of my surroundings like a tourist, toting my camera and notebook wherever I went. I scribbled everyday Spanish vocabulary I was sure I'd forget when I returned to Hamilton. I recorded as many Words of the Week as I could recall, enlisting my co-workers' assistance. We could only remember a few dozen.

On Tuesday morning, I awoke early and wandered the resort. It had rained overnight and the earth smelled of petrichor. I passed the large hall, its empty chairs arranged for the evening's show. A hand-painted sign advertised: MEXICAN FOLKLORIC DANCE PERFORMANCE TONIGHT! There was an illustration of four twirling women with wide flying skirts. I usually avoided the shows, but considered attending one last time. I'd linger near the exit so the exuberant and handsome dancers wouldn't pull me up onto the stage during the show's audience participation segment. Or maybe I'd climb onto the stage for the first time ever.

The Oceana desk was still shuttered. I picked up a crinkled brochure from the floor and knew the memorized excursion details — prices and bus schedules and activities — would needle my dreams for months, just as my mind had tripped through scripts about Birkenstock soles and miraculous sick children's recoveries long after I'd left those jobs. The thought reassured me.

At the swimming pool, I stretched out on a lounger. The pool's bottom was robin's-egg blue, the paint chipping at its deepest point. The water's surface was still, untroubled. The morning sun shone down on me, warming my forehead, nose, cheeks, and chin. I knew I'd be weathering the other three seasons once again. I'd have to grow accustomed to grey skies.

But it would be springtime at home. In my mind's eye, I stepped through Toronto airport's sliding doors, cool air blowing through my sundress. I'd wait at the taxi stand. Perhaps I'd tell the driver I'd been away for three years. Or maybe I wouldn't say anything, letting him believe I was just another Canadian back from a vacation. *Nice tan*, he might comment.

Before we'd drive away, I'd gaze back at the terminal, noting the last place on earth Azeez had stood before his death. Just prior to entering the building, he might have searched the sky and uttered a silent prayer for his journey home.

A prepubescent girl cannonballed into the pool, a few cool, chlorinated drops landing on my bare feet. A man in his forties followed, his body striking the water with a splash that sprayed all the way up my thighs. I closed my eyes again and breathed in warm air, and thought: *you'll be breathing in Mumbai air soon.*

That evening, a large padded envelope from Mom was waiting in my mailbox; she'd posted the magazines right before I'd made my decision to quit. I rushed to unseal it, perfume and ink tickling my nose. May's issues focused on the fertility of the season: gardening and sex. I flipped open *Chatelaine*, landing on an article about expressing fantasies to a partner. The page had a slightly bent corner and I hoped Mom had read it. She and Victor were still seeing one another, and from her subdued enthusiasm about us all having dinner together, I guessed their relationship was feeling secure to her. I hoped so, anyway. I wondered what it would be like to stay in my old bedroom, now her guest room, while she had a beau. Perhaps I'd spend one of my weekends in Toronto with Jessie and Wanda to give them some space.

Δ

On Wednesday, my second-last day, I went to La Crucecita for the last time. I perched on a bench in the *zócalo* and watched as children played and their parents gabbed. A pair of young lovers sat three feet to my left and necked, oblivious to the activity around them. They clung to one another, their lips and tongues insistent and aggressive. I left them to hunt for souvenirs for Mom and my friends. I couldn't figure out what objects would symbolize my time away. Straw hats and T-shirts with crocodiles wouldn't work. In the end, I bought five small black clay jars, each slightly irregularly shaped and large enough to store spare change, stray buttons, and safety pins. I packed them between layers of underwear and sundresses, hoping they wouldn't shatter in my luggage.

That night, I ambled into the bar, seeking a couple I'd noticed days earlier on the beach. When I'd overheard them speaking, I was surprised at their German accents; I'd assumed they were Indo-Canadians. Monica and Jay introduced themselves and spoke in a manner I recognized as easy, direct flirtation. They knew four languages and laughed at my clumsy French. Off for a year, they'd been travelling across North America for the previous ten months and planned to go to Guatemala next.

"But, you know, I miss Berlin," Jay confessed.

"Not me. Not yet. I wish we had even more time off," Monica said.

"How about you, Ameera? Just two days before you go home. How does it feel?" Jay asked.

"I dunno. I know it's time to go. But beyond that, it's hard to picture what's coming next." I told them about my travel plans and uncertain return date. The truth was that I still hadn't heard back from Nadeem Dholkawala. After his unfriendly e-mail, I'd decided to focus on the itinerary I'd been mapping out in my head for years: Mumbai, Delhi, Agra, Jaipur, Kolkata, Goa. I'd go regardless.

"It will be monsoon season!" Monica protested.

"I know. But I have to go this summer. My savings will run out by the fall." I really didn't care about the weather.

We finished our drinks and went back to their suite. I wasn't bothered about who might see us, and behaved like the carefree tourist I was. My skin, warmed by three years of almost constant sunshine, resembled theirs. Jay remarked that my nipples matched his wife's and Monica held hers up against mine to compare them, our soft skin pushing together. When I licked and sniffed throats and armpits and elbows, their scents were familiar despite having just met them.

At 2:00 a.m., we drowsed. I curled up snug against Monica's hip. I stayed the night, sleeping soundly with strangers.

Δ

Out of habit, I helped Oscar collate Oceana's departure and arrival documents on Friday. He'd given his notice a week after I did, and was still finalizing his plans for his café venture with his cousin.

"Will you miss Atlantis?" I asked him.

"The café will be better." I studied his expression, but he gave nothing away as he methodically stapled and affixed lists to clipboards. He looked half-naked without his tie.

"I'm glad to go, but I'll miss this place," I said. "I'll miss you. And the others. I don't think I'll ever be back here again. That's a strange feeling." Our eyes met and he nodded.

The others arrived and congregated around the tour desk, busying themselves with administrative tasks. As always, we operated as a team, even though one of us had left a couple of weeks earlier and two others would soon depart. Together we folded the desk's flaps, shut cupboards, and closed Oceana's desk until it once again became a tidy rectangular box.

At the top of the staircase, tourists circled us like gulls flocking around a man with breadcrumbs. I could hear fragments of their cawing, their almost frantic queries about food at the airport, and securing a last piña colada after their plastic wristbands had been cut off. My colleagues took a collective deep breath and spoke calmly and softly. I weaved through the throng to deposit my keys and say brief farewells to the front desk staff.

Δ

I'd said a more difficult goodbye the night before. Enrique had been expecting me when I arrived at his bar Thursday night. He gestured for me to follow him out and we strolled across the resort, our arms linked, like spouses on holiday. We chatted about unimportant things like my departure time, the flight's length, if anyone would be meeting me at the airport. We walked past the shore, and I stopped to watch an iguana on the beach. I tried to commit its spiny back and leathery skin to memory.

"Look, they finally finished it! They've been working on it the past couple of months." I pointed at the stone walkway.

"Was it not always here?" He looked puzzled.

"No, it's brand-new. I watched them lay it down."

"But I've come this way before. When I worked at the swim-up bar, it was a short-cut from the lobby."

"These stones are new," I said, insistent. He pushed out his bottom lip and shrugged, and for a moment, I doubted myself.

We looped back to the bar, and his eyes swept over me flirtatiously. He complimented me on my red sundress, the one I'd specifically chosen for him that evening. Then he stepped behind the bar and a long line formed before him.

"Ameera," he yelled, as I walked away, "stay in touch, okay?" He passed me a napkin with his e-mail and mailing addresses, and I realized I hadn't known where he lived. But he'd been my friend. We'd had regular, if incidental contact. For the time we'd met, we'd stayed firmly within each other's sight lines.

Halfway back to my room, my eyes welled with tears. I wiped them away with his napkin. I told myself that unrequited crushes were fun, but hurt a little, too.

Δ

When the buses arrived, I took my usual spot in Bus Number Three's jumper seat, even though I was wearing civilian clothes and there was plenty of room farther back. I made small talk with the driver, inquiring about his family. I didn't want to think about how I wouldn't be on his bus for the return trip. I didn't want to imagine myself passing through the security gates, and entering the glass-walled lounge that separated the arriving from the departing, and the staff from the tourists.

I waited at the back of the line, allowing everyone else to be processed by security before me. When I could loiter no longer, I stood before my colleagues. There was a handshake from Oscar, and hugs from Manuela and Roberto. Manuela and I cried for the group while the guys pretended not to notice. I approached the security gate, handed over my passport for inspection, and the doors closed behind me.

That day, my very last in Huatulco, there were no delays. I walked onto the tarmac, looking back at the aquamarine wooden kiosk. When the plane took off, I looked down and thought I could see four tiny figures sitting in bluebird-and-daisy-adorned folding chairs, waving in my direction.

Azeez

∞

On June 13, my girl waited in the British Airways queue. There were large groups of Indian families, some in Indian garb, most dressed semi-formally as though about to attend a fancy party. She wore jeans and a T-shirt, and had packed a hoodie for the flight. Nora stood with her, keeping her company in the lineup.

Ameera's breath was shallow, but I heard her expectation and nervousness for the journey ahead. She checked the time, calculating if she would be late despite getting to Pearson three hours early. She fiddled with her tickets and passport and felt for a folder of papers tucked into her purse, printouts of her hotel reservations and prepaid train tickets. She pressed the papers between her index finger and thumb, and their crispness slowed her heart rate.

The folder also contained our address in Mumbai, Ameera's destination for three days hence. I'd wanted my family to squeeze into their car and greet her at the airport as a delegation. I'd hoped they'd have insisted she stay with them rather than book a hotel. Never mind, I knew it would only be a matter of time before their cautious hearts opened.

Nora hugged Ameera goodbye and I inhaled maternal worry: *Be safe. Come back to me.*

I boarded with Ameera and took the vacant middle spot beside her window seat. For the first few hours of the flight, an ancient unease caused us both to fidget in our faux-leather seats. I whispered peaceful thoughts while she dozed, but I knew I was really calming my own fear of flight, a phobia that would follow me for the next two lifetimes.

As we neared Ireland, I drifted out over the Atlantic. I remembered rumpled wing tips, twisted scraps of fuselage, fragments of charred passenger seats. Hundreds of falling bodies. I dove under the bitterly cold water and swam until I came to it: my body's final resting place. And I was not alone. While our physical remains were long gone, I sensed an undersea city of sorts, an impromptu gathering of Kanishka's souls. I knew I'd drawn them to me through sheer will, for I required one last look. Amongst the assembly were Meena and her mother, the attractive stewardess, and the older lady who'd sat beside me on Flight 182. There were too many of us to count, children and adults, those whose bodies had been recovered and those who were never found. We were together again, just for a few moments, a haunting reunion. And then, as though we never existed, we dispersed across the ocean.

I drifted up, broke through the water's surface, and continued to float higher. I caught up with my girl's airplane and watched it form a white trail across the sky.

And then, without thinking about it, without consulting anything or anyone, I soared higher and higher, up and away from the earthly lives I'd been overseeing for nearly thirty years. I was unsure of my path, but certain that I needed to keep going.

Acknowledgements

This book has been a journey like no other. I am grateful to everyone who guided me and offered encouragement along the way:

Those who read early versions and excerpts: Silvana Bazet, Esther Vise, Elizabeth Ruth, John Miller, Sally Cooper, Karleen Pendleton Jimenez, Alex Flores, Hershel Russell, Carrianne Leung, Brian Francis, Cory Silverberg, Sarah Schulman, Jeff Round, Angie Abdou, and Vivek Shraya (who also took my author photo).

My lovely psychotherapy peer supervision group who permitted me to bring Ameera to them as a case study.

The generous strangers who helped me figure out details about employment at all inclusive resorts and universities: Craig Norton, Dave Nicholson, and John Rick. There were countless others who answered my questions on Facebook about Brownie sashes and Tim Hortons locations.

Shannon Whibbs, Jim Hatch, and the rest at Dundurn who are so dedicated to publishing. Someone please give them raises.

My agent Bev Slopen and the Writers Union of Canada, for having my back.

Thanks to the Ontario Arts Council for a month of writing time.

All those who keep the souls of Air India 182 in public memory.

And to Reyan, whose love helped carry me to the finish line.